Second Death

Jeff Kerr

Copyright © 2024 by Jeff Kerr

All rights reserved.

No part of this publication may be reproduced, distributed, or transmitted in any form or by any means, including photocopying, recording, or other electronic or mechanical methods, without the prior written permission of the author, except as permitted by U.S. copyright law. For permission requests, contact the author at **jeffkerr@jeffreykerrauthor.com**

The story, all names, characters, and incidents portrayed in this production are fictitious. No identification with actual persons (living or deceased), places, buildings, and products is intended or should be inferred.

Book Cover by Cheynne Edmonston

"But the cowardly, the unbelieving, the vile, the murderers,
the sexually immoral, those who practice magic arts,
the idolaters and all liars—their
place will be in the fiery lake of burning sulfur.
This is the second death."
—Revelations 21:8

1

Ralph Spencer eased his Chevy Silverado pickup into the gas station and stopped at the pump farthest from the convenience store. He hopped out of the truck cab, pulled his gimme trucker hat low over his eyes, and fished a small key from the pocket of his grease-stained jeans. With practiced movements, he inserted the key into the lock on the pump. After a quick turn, the front panel popped open. He tugged on it to make an opening large enough for a small electronic device to fit through. Reaching a hand inside the pump, he clipped the device's cable to a wire and turned it on. Satisfied, he pulled his hand back and closed the panel.

With the hard part behind him, Spencer breathed a sigh of relief. He swiped a credit card through the reader, removed the truck's gas cap, and began pumping diesel fuel. The credit card was fake. Spencer had made it himself using a number he stole two days earlier with a card skimmer at a station in the next county. The device attached to the pump allowed him to buy three hundred gallons of diesel fuel for pennies on the dollar, but why not use someone else's pennies to do so?

After two minutes, Ralph had pumped twenty-five gallons of fuel, but the gauge on the pump registered only a gallon. By the time he finished, it would read sixteen gallons for a bill of around seventy bucks. All charged to the poor sap he got the card number from. Ralph's visit would appear routine to the clerk inside the store. But thanks to a battery-operated pump in his truck that moved fuel from the gas tank to a three-hundred-gallon storage tank concealed in the truck bed, Ralph would steal enough diesel to keep him from needing to find a real job for at least another month. Especially once Dennis Webb agreed to his demand to increase the hush money he was paying.

The operation would take about twenty-five minutes, so Ralph needed to find something to do to make his lengthy stay appear plausible. He made a show of checking the air pressure in each tire and either adding or removing air. That used up five minutes. Popping the hood and checking the oil only took a few seconds, but fishing an empty oil container from his truck bed and pretending to add oil bought more time. The wiper fluid level was low—he had made sure of that before his arrival—so he refilled the reservoir. He washed each window and followed up by wiping the glass with a paper towel, taking special care with the windshield. Satisfied, he made a leisurely stroll into the store for an unhurried trip to the bathroom. On his way out, he browsed the snack aisle, selected a candy bar, and paid for it and a pack of cigarettes at the counter.

Back at the truck, the pump had stopped. Ralph replaced the nozzle and, using his key, opened the pump door and removed the device he had used to fool the flow meter. Taking care to conceal it from the security camera overhead, he tossed it into the truck cab and opened the pack of cigarettes.

Ralph knew he shouldn't smoke. His father had died of emphysema, fighting for every small breath at the last. Lung cancer claimed his grandmother. Cigarettes killed. He believed that. But he liked smoking. He liked the hot feel of the smoke in his mouth, the rush of the nicotine hitting his brain. And so far, he felt no ill effects. He could always quit later, couldn't he?

Ralph took one last look at the plywood panels hiding the tank in the truck bed and smiled. What a foolproof operation. Fuel was untraceable. Once he left the lot, no one could touch him. There was no law against carrying extra gas around. He flipped a cigarette into his mouth, brought his lighter up close, and flicked the wheel, ready for that first satisfying drag. Then his truck exploded.

2

Noble County Deputy Adam Cash surveyed the destruction before him with disbelief. A late-model Chevy Silverado pickup truck, no longer in flames but twisted and charred to a blackened mass of smoldering steel. Surrounding it was a huge circle of blackened concrete. Beside it, crumpled gas pumps, the hoses melted to shapeless rubber lumps, the plastic displays shattered. As a soldier in Afghanistan, Cash had seen what an M1 Abrams tank could do to a truck loaded with Taliban fighters. This looked about the same.

Cash slipped under the police tape perimeter and strolled over to the dead body thrown from the truck. Noble County medical examiner Frida Simmons was already at work, gloved hands probing, turning, twisting what remained of the unfortunate soul that perished in the explosion. "Find anything yet?" Cash said.

Frida didn't look up. "The fire didn't kill him. The body is burned, but not enough to account for such a quick death."

"So, what was it?"

Frida rotated the man's head. He was lying on his back, legs bent at impossible angles, arms splayed out by his side. Cash estimated he was in his mid-thirties. "Look here," said Frida. "See that scalp laceration over his ear? He hit the ground hard to make a gash that deep."

Cash knelt beside her. "And that killed him?"

Ignoring the question, she turned the head to bring the face into view. "And look at his pupils. See how unequal they are? This one on the side of the laceration is a lot bigger than the other one."

"Don't pupils dilate after death?"

"Yes, but they should do so equally. These are asymmetric."

"What causes that?"

Frida rocked back on her heels and turned her gaze toward Cash. "Epidural hematoma. There's a major artery here." She ran a finger over the scalp laceration. "The middle meningeal artery. I'm betting X-rays will show a significant fracture in that same spot. The jagged bone tears the artery, spilling blood into the epidural space."

"You're losing me, Frida."

"The blood gushes from the artery but, because it's inside the skull, it has nowhere to go. A clot forms, keeps getting bigger as more blood leaks, and shoves the brain to one side. That crushes the brain stem."

"And that's bad?"

"Yep. Shut off the brain stem and you stop breathing."

"Did he die right away?"

"Quickly, yes, but not immediately. It takes time for the clot to become large enough to cause herniation. I'm guessing he also suffered a significant enough concussion that he was knocked unconscious."

"So, even if the blast didn't kill him outright, he never had a chance."

Frida stood up. "Not really."

"Mind if I go through his pockets?"

She handed him a fresh pair of gloves from her kit. "Knock yourself out."

Cash donned the gloves and began his search. He found a leather wallet in a rear pocket of the jeans, glanced at the driver's license, and set it aside. A front pocket yielded a set of keys. Another produced a cell phone and a large coin. Cash held it up for Frida to see. "What's this?"

"I have no idea."

He brought it closer. Gold in color, the coin was about an inch and a half in diameter. One side featured a robed woman standing on a rock. In one hand she held a shield, in the other a trident. The letters encircling her read, "One ounce fine Gold Britannia 2014." Inscribed on the rock was the word "Nathan." The other side featured a side view of Queen Elizabeth, her name, and some Latin words Cash couldn't translate. Beneath the image were the words "100 pounds."

"One ounce fine gold," Cash said. "It looks like the real thing."

"I wonder what it's worth."

"It says a hundred pounds, but gold is worth more than that." Cash slipped the coin into a plastic evidence bag. "The question is, what is it doing in this guy's pocket?"

***

Graffiti sprayed on the concrete walk in front of the convenience store halted Cash in his tracks. Red block letters screamed, "Go back to India, you brown bastard." Cash shook his head and pulled the door open. Inside, he approached the distraught station owner. "Who decorated your sidewalk, Avi?"

From behind the counter, Avi Rao blinked as if awakening from a trance. "Probably the same asshole who blew up my station."

"Do you know something I don't?"

"Just a guess."

"Maybe the surveillance footage would show us."

He shook his head. "I've got cameras trained on the pumps and here inside the store but nothing outside the door."

"Are any of the cameras inside pointed toward the door? It's made of glass."

"Yes, but all it shows is some guy wearing a hoodie. He kept his back to the camera the whole time."

"Let's take a look."

"Sure. Let's go in the back."

Cash couldn't blame Avi for looking shell-shocked. He had purchased the station only six months ago and now a significant portion of it lay in ruins. Cash still recalled the excitement on Avi's face the first time he had seen him behind the counter. He had saved for years to buy the place and move his family from Houston to pursue the American dream. Since then, he had become active in the Chamber of Commerce and the local Kiwanis Club. He sponsored a Little League team, donated generously to the high school football team's fundraiser, and decorated his antique Ford Mustang to showcase it in the annual rodeo parade. In short, Avi had made himself a part of the community. He loved Pinyon, and in return the people of Pinyon loved him. Most of them, anyway, the ones who didn't spray graffiti. But in Cash's experience, there were jerks in every community.

As Cash followed Avi into the back office, he said, "Insurance will cover the damage, right"

"Yes, but I'll be out of business for a while. Even when I reopen, I'll be short two pumps."

"People will still need gas. They'll use the pumps that do work."

"I suppose." His voice betrayed disbelief. "But even a small drop in business will hurt. The profit margin of a gas station is thin."

They reached the office. Avi flipped a laptop open and tapped on the keyboard. The screen displayed a grid of images of the outside pumps seen from different overhead angles. When he clicked on one, it enlarged to fill the screen.

"It happened around two-thirty. I was filling the soft drink cooler. Thank goodness no one else was outside."

"Was there anyone else in the store?"

"Yes, a man on his phone. He left pretty quick."

"Did you know him?"

"No."

They each settled into a chair. Avi tapped the keyboard a few more times. "Okay, we should see it soon."

They watched as the Chevy Silverado pulled into the station. The driver, whom Cash recognized as the dead man, got out and knelt beside a pump.

"What's he doing?" said Cash.

"I can't tell."

The driver inserted the nozzle into the gas tank.

Cash said, "He's getting diesel. Took him long enough." They watched some more. "And look how he's checking those tires. He's moving slower than molasses."

As the screen showed the man entering the store, Cash said, "The name on his license is Ralph Spencer. Do you know him?"

"No. I've seen him a few times, but he doesn't talk much. Just buys cigarettes, maybe a lottery ticket, and goes on his way."

"Okay, here we go," said Cash as Spencer returned to the truck. He replaced the nozzle, closed the gas cap, and stuck a cigarette in his mouth. A blinding flash lit up the screen. Cash winced. It reminded him of explosions in Afghanistan.

"It's when he lit his cigarette," Avi said. "That's strange."

"It's strange that gas fumes explode?"

"He was on the other side of the truck. Away from the pumps. Sure, you shouldn't smoke when you're pumping gas, but I see people do it all the time. None of them ever blew up. And this man was getting diesel, which isn't very combustible."

"Show me the guy in the store."

Avi clicked the mouse and an inside view of the store popped onto the screen. "That's him."

The man was large, with short black hair, and dressed in jeans and a denim work shirt. His back was turned to the camera as he held a phone to his ear.

"Is there audio?"

"No."

"Too bad."

The man took the phone from his ear and appeared to look at it. His head swiveled to give him a view outside. Moments later, several items fell from the shelves.

"That's when the truck blew up," Avi said.

"He doesn't look very surprised."

The man turned around so Cash could see his face. He was in his mid-thirties, clean-shaven with the tanned skin of someone who spent a lot of time outdoors.

"And you don't know him?"

"No."

Cash turned to leave.

"Where are you going?" Avi asked.

"I'm gonna go take another look at that truck."

****

Frida was finishing up her examination of the body as Cash returned. "Do you have a tow truck coming?" he asked.

"Why would I need a tow truck?"

"To take it back to the station. Don't you need to examine it more?"

"It looks like an accident to me."

"He was pumping diesel. Avi says that's not very combustible."

"Not combustible and not very combustible are two different things."

"Hang on a second." Cash walked to the rear of the truck. He dropped to his back and pulled himself beneath the vehicle. The chemical stench of burned rubber, metal, and plastic overpowered him, making him momentarily lightheaded. Fighting off the assault on his nostrils in the cramped space, he eyed what remained of the gas tank. A fill pipe coursed down from above to enter the tank, but what was that next to it? Another, thinner pipe dangled from the undercarriage. When Cash shook it, the pipe rattled against the tank's side. He slid a finger toward it and found a hole in the tank the same size as the diameter of the pipe.

Cash extricated himself from beneath the truck and stood up.

"What did you see?" Frida asked.

Without answering, Cash hopped into the truck bed and poked among the rubble. "Look here."

Frida peered into the bed.

"See this melted plastic? I think it was a water storage tank."

"So?"

Peering behind the misshapen plastic mass, Cash saw a pipe poking up through the truck bed. "So, it could have been used to hold something other than water. I think he was stealing gas."

He jumped out of the truck. "You need to take this back to the station and really search it."

"What am I looking for?"

"Some type of electronic device. Probably in the cab, if it wasn't completely destroyed in the fire. Hang on, I'll take a look."

Cash walked to the passenger door and yanked it open. With Frida peering over his shoulder, he spotted an amorphous lump on the floor stuck to a small square of charred plywood, from which four blackened bolts protruded. Pointing at it, he said, "I think that's it."

"Educate me. How did he use that to steal gas?"

"It was capable of disabling the flow meter so it looks like he got, say twenty gallons, when in fact he filled up the auxiliary tank in the truck bed."

"Great idea. Unless it leaks fumes. And he's dumb enough to smoke while pumping the gas."

"Maybe."

"The stupid son of a bitch blew himself sky high."

"I'm still bothered by the fact that Avi says diesel isn't very explosive."

"I think we're looking at evidence that says otherwise."

The pieces weren't adding up for him. "I guess." Another thought came to him. "When I check the credit card number he used to pay, I'll bet I'll find out it was stolen."

"This guy had it all worked out."

"He could have been working with someone else. Maybe that's who killed him."

"Sounds like you've got an investigation on your hands, Deputy."

Cash felt his heart rate kick up a notch. "Indeed, I do."

3

F red Uecker's gut roiled as he stepped into the lobby of the Noble County sheriff's office. He knew he should have skipped the sausage in his morning breakfast taco. Sausage never agreed with him. The problem was it tasted so good.

Weighing more heavily on him was the bad news he had to deliver. He didn't like delivering bad news. Especially when it contradicted something he had told Sheriff Santos earlier. Acting Sheriff Santos, he reminded himself.

He found the office quiet, with only the receptionist, whose name Uecker couldn't recall. She was absorbed in her computer screen. Probably watching TikTok videos. Whatever it was, she remained oblivious to his presence.

Uecker cleared his throat. "Good morning, Valerie."

The woman glanced up from her screen. She looked so young. "It's Vicky."

"Right. Sorry about that."

"That's okay. Can I help you?"

"I'm here to see the sheriff."

She picked up her phone. "I'll let him know you're here."

***

Sheriff Gabe Santos stared open-mouthed at a spreading pool of hot coffee on his desk. What was it, the third time this month he had knocked his cup over while filling out yet another pile of forms? When would he learn to be more careful?

Scalding liquid seeped beneath the keyboard and dripped into Santos' lap. He swore and leapt from his chair, grabbed a roll of paper towels from a nearby windowsill, and began mopping up the mess.

Someone rapped at the door.

Santos wiped faster. "Come in."

The door opened. County Commissioner Fred Uecker stepped into the room. Santos' morning had just gotten worse. "Grab a seat, Fred. I'll be just a second here."

Uecker dropped into a padded leatherette chair. Santos hastily mopped up the coffee in his seat and sat down. He gritted his teeth as warm liquid soaked through his pants. Folding his hands together to appear under control, he said, "What can I do for you?"

"I came by to update you on what happened last night at the county commissioners' meeting."

"Oh?"

Uecker shifted in his chair. He avoided looking at Santos. "We had a long discussion about recent events in Noble County."

"Any recent events in particular?"

"Sheriff Turner's death, for one. And you being named acting sheriff." He paused. "Also, the recent election. We had to make some difficult decisions."

Santos knew Uecker was referring to the murder a month ago of his predecessor Griff Turner. The chief deputy at the time, Clovis Ward, had produced evidence implicating an old army buddy of Santos',

Adam Cash. Cash, who had just lost the sheriff's election to Turner, went into hiding. With Santos' discreet assistance, he was able to prove that Ward and another deputy, Judd Noteboom, had framed him for the murder. He also exposed a human trafficking ring in which Ward and Noteboom were using Pinyon as a way station between San Antonio and Fort Worth. Turner had discovered the conspiracy and moved to shut it down. To prevent that, Ward killed him. Cash's efforts culminated in his exoneration, but not before a violent confrontation in which Santos saved Cash's life by shooting Noteboom. Ward was now awaiting trial.

Santos was left as one of two remaining Noble County deputies, the other being Deke Conrad. The commissioners' choice for acting sheriff was not difficult. While no one disputed Conrad's courage, his only other positive attribute was that he displayed the loyalty of a good dog. Unfortunately, the dog was smarter.

The commissioners elevated Santos to sheriff with the understanding that he would serve out Griff Turner's four-year term. At least that's what Santos remembered Uecker telling him. Now it sounded like he was about to learn otherwise.

Santos set his jaw and said, "Tell me about these difficult decisions."

Uecker's gaze darted to the window and back. "The good news is that we approved funding for you to hire another deputy."

"You already told me I could do that." He had hired Adam Cash.

"Yes, I did. This makes it official, though."

"What's the bad news?"

Uecker glanced out the window again. *Here it comes*, Santos thought.

"The court was concerned about the fairness of an acting sheriff holding the office for almost an entire four-year term. They decided to schedule a special election." When Santos didn't say anything, Uecker added, "If it's any consolation, I voted against it."

Santos leaned back in his chair and scoffed. "Good for you."

"I'm sorry, Gabe. I think it's ridiculous."

"Would this have happened if my last name was Smith?"

Uecker bit his lip. "Probably. I will say, though, that not all the commissioners are colorblind."

Santos said nothing. He didn't have to guess names.

"You'll run, won't you?"

Would he? As his eyes drifted to the coffee-sodden papers on his desk, Santos fought off the urge to tell Uecker to take the job and shove it. But he liked being sheriff. For years, he had taken orders in the army; now he got to give them. And a new sheriff might be as bad as the old one. Turner hadn't deserved to die, but sometimes Santos had wanted to kill him. Santos wanted to keep the job in part so he wouldn't have to work under a knucklehead again. "Yes, I'll run."

"Good. You'll have my vote."

"Is anyone else running?"

When Uecker looked out the window again, Santo wondered what the hell was so interesting about the parking lot. Apparently, Uecker wasn't through delivering bad news. The commissioner said, "That's the thing. I hear Mitch Eaton wants the job. To tell you the truth, I think he put some of the other commissioners up to calling the special election."

Santos swore under his breath. Mitch Eaton's family had been ranching in Noble County since the 1880s. Not that Eaton himself knew anything about cattle. He graduated from Pinyon High School in the eighties, left the state to attend Tulane University in New Orleans, and never looked back. After earning a bachelor's degree in business administration and an MBA in hospital administration, he took a job at Scott and White Hospital in Temple, worked his way up the ladder, and then moved to Waco as CFO of Baylor Scott and White Medical Center. When his father died five years ago he left that job and moved back to the three-thousand-acre family ranch. From what Santos heard, Eaton took a hands-off approach to running the spread, entrusting that task to his ranch manager. Eaton liked to pass himself off as a good old country boy, but Santos thought otherwise. The self-proclaimed rancher owned a new CVO Tri Glide motorcycle, the most expensive bike in Harley's lineup. He had just moved into a custom five-thousand-square-foot house. And he maintained a membership at Waco's Ridgewood Country Club, where he golfed at least once a week with a group that included the president of Baylor University. Not too many good old boys could afford country club dues. With the money at his disposal, Eaton would be able to dwarf any campaign expenditure Santos could afford.

Eaton's one electoral disadvantage was his track record with women. He had just divorced his fourth wife amid accusations of philandering. Similar allegations had swirled around his other three divorces as well. Each wife had been younger than her predecessor, with the most recent barely out of her teens. That marriage lasted only a year and a half.

Uecker commented, "Eaton will be tough to beat. You'll need to run a good campaign. Do you have anyone in mind who can help you?"

Santos was no politician. Nor did he have any political connections. But he did know someone smart enough and tough enough to take on any challenge. "Yes. Edie James."

4

A blast of July heat sucked the wind out of Cash as he climbed out of the squad car. Catching his breath, he slipped his hat on and waited for Santos. When the sheriff did not emerge from the vehicle, he peered in through the passenger window and saw Santos still blindly gripping the steering wheel. Cash rapped on the glass. "Are you coming?"

With an exaggerated sigh, Santos pushed the door open and stepped onto the pavement. "Damn, it's hot." He looked at Cash. "You can tell her, right?"

A sudden panic gripped Cash. He had assumed that Santos would deliver the news of Ralph Spencer's death to his widow. "Me? You're the sheriff."

"That's right," Santos said, putting his hands on his hips. "Which means I'm in charge. I'm delegating the job to my deputy."

"Come on, Gabe, don't make me do this."

Santos' shoulders slumped. "Cash, I just can't do it. Please?"

In Afghanistan, Cash had seen Santos accept dangerous assignments with stoic calm. Now his friend's face bore the panicked expression of a child being asked to jump off the high dive. "All right. But you owe me."

"Hey, I saved your life last month."

"That only paid me back for saving yours in Afghanistan."

Santos emitted a soft groan. "Okay, I'll owe you this one."

The Spencer house was located on an acre of barren land ten miles outside Pinyon. As far as Cash could tell, little effort had been made to maintain the property. The rusty front gate hung precariously on its one remaining hinge. In the yard beyond, cedar saplings sprouted like weeds, threatening the prairie grass with shady oblivion. A dead Spanish oak had fallen onto a barbed-wire fence, crushing one of the posts and jerking two others from the ground. The one-story house was in bad need of repair, with missing shingles, flaking paint, and warped siding pulling away from the frame.

As Cash and Santos marched up the cracked walkway, Cash reflected on the fact that he had never been the bearer of such difficult news. The only experience that came close happened during his first semester at Sam Houston State. He had returned from his final tour of duty only weeks before. A good friend of his named Tony Walker had been killed by a sniper while standing right next to Cash. Walker hailed from Goodrich, less than an hour away from campus, and Cash drove over to pay his grieving parents a call. After an hour marked by tears and awkward silences, Cash made an excuse and departed. To this day he worried he had done more harm than good.

They reached the front door. Cash rang the bell and tried to still the butterflies in his stomach.

Santos said, "Get right to the point, okay?"

Cash shot him a deadly glance. The door was opened by a weary-eyed woman in jeans and a faded T-shirt. Worry lines already etched her youthful face. A girl with suspicious eyes clung to the woman's legs. An older boy watched TV in the den behind her. "What can I do for you?" she said, her frown deepening at the sight of uniforms.

"Mrs. Spencer?" said Cash.

"It's Collins. You can call me Alissa."

"Aren't you Ralph Spencer's wife?"

"We're not married. He just lives here."

"Oh. I'm Deputy Cash and this is Sheriff Santos. May we come in?"

She stepped away from the door and ushered them into the den. When the girl on her leg began whining, she picked up the child and calmed her. "What did Ralph do this time?"

"Maybe we should sit down."

Alissa set the girl down. "You and your brother go play in your room." When the girl protested, she swatted her rear and said, "Now. Get."

The boy clicked off the TV and disappeared down a hall. His sister ran after him. Their mother gestured at a worn sofa. "Have a seat."

Cash and Santos eased stiff-backed onto the edge of threadbare couch cushions. Alissa dropped into a creaking lounge chair.

Cash said, "Miss Collins—"

"Alissa."

"Sorry. Alissa. I'm afraid we have bad news. Ralph was killed in an accident today."

Cash held his breath waiting for a flood of tears. Instead, relief spread across the woman's face. "Saves me the trouble of kicking him out."

Cash didn't respond to that.

"What happened?" she asked.

Cash gave her the details of the explosion at the gas station. He finished by saying, "I'm very sorry."

"Life goes on." Her eyes were dry.

Cash and Santos exchanged puzzled glances. Cash said, "There's something else I need to mention." He waited for her to react. When she didn't, he went on. "It looks like Ralph was stealing diesel fuel from the gas station. I was wondering what you can tell us about that."

Her face darkened. "Why would I know anything about what that man was up to? He never told me a damn thing."

"You didn't know about the diesel?"

"No, but I'll bet he was doing it on account of that bastard Emmett Fuller."

"Who is Emmett Fuller?"

"Friend of Ralph's. He's a real son of a bitch."

Cash thought of the man in the convenience store. "How do you mean?"

"The man is a born liar. He couldn't tell the truth to save his life."

"Can you be more specific?"

She produced a mirthless laugh. "I'll say. He told my kids his friend had a pet alligator. Can you beat that? Where would somebody get an alligator around here?"

This lead was looking better and better. "Do you know where Emmett Fuller lives?"

"Yeah, in a trailer out on FM 3557."

"Have you ever been there?"

"Once. I was with Ralph and he stopped off to pick something up."
A gold coin? "What?"

"He didn't say."

"Do you think Fuller and Ralph were working together?"

She looked at Cash as if he were dense. "If Ralph was up to something, Emmett was in the thick of it too. In fact, if he was stealing gas, it was probably Emmett's idea."

"Did Ralph ever talk about it?"

"No."

Cash decided to switch gears. "Did Ralph have any knowledge of electronics?"

"No way," she scoffed. "The only things he knew much about were gambling, drinking, and fishing. He was a right expert on the drinking."

"One more thing." Cash reached into his pocket for the evidence bag holding the gold coin. "Do you know why Ralph would have this in his pocket?"

She took it from him. "What is it?"

"It's a gold coin."

"That's real gold? Is it worth a lot of money?"

"I believe so."

She stared at it like it was a winning lottery ticket. "Do I get to keep it? We ain't married but we lived together like man and wife."

Cash took the bag from her. "That depends on what's in his will."

"I don't know if he had one."

From the looks of the place, probably not. "Alissa, I'm curious. Do you know where Ralph would have gotten a coin like this?"

She kept staring at the coin, reluctant to let the subject of ownership drop. Finally, she said, "No."

"Has money been tight for the two of you?"

She thought for a long while before replying. "Money's always tight, ain't it? But that's the reason I let him stick around. He moved in with me about a year ago. At first, he was nice but then he turned on me. He never hit me or the kids but he started hollering all the time. Cussed a blue streak too. I told him not to use that language around the kids but he said they was gonna learn it one way or the other. I would have kicked him out a long time ago except for the money he was bringing in." She sighed. "I guess there won't be no more of that."

"How did Ralph make his money?"

"I don't know. He never told me."

"And you never asked?"

"You don't look a gift horse in the mouth, do you?"

Santos spoke up. "How did the two of you meet?"

"I was working at the Dairy Queen. He came in a few times. We'd get to talking and then one day he asked me to go dancing with him over in Sonora. Not long after that, he moved in. He acted real nice at first, but that changed."

"So you said."

For the first time, she rubbed a tear from her eye. "Called me all sorts of names."

"Where was he living before he moved in with you?"

"With Emmet. He said he had just moved to town and Emmett was putting him up until he could find his own place."

Cash said, "Do you know where he moved from?"

"Not exactly. He had Louisiana plates on his truck, but he never said where he came from. I asked him once and he told me to mind my own business."

A long silence followed, reminding Cash of his trip to Goodrich to see Tony Walker's parents. He stood up. "Thank you. We'll be going now."

She followed them to the door. As they started down the sidewalk, she called after them. "Hey, what do I do now?"

5

On the drive back to town, Cash asked what Santos thought about Alissa's reaction to Spencer's death. Santos said, "Sounds like it was something other than love keeping them together."

"Where do you think his money was coming from? From what she said, he didn't have a regular job."

"There are a lot of people like that in this county. Just picking up odd jobs when they can. How they scrape by is a mystery to me."

"But he wasn't scraping. At least not according to Alissa. She said money was coming in regularly."

"What's your point?"

"Maybe he was into something illegal."

"Duh, he was stealing diesel. Anyway, what difference does it make? The man's dead."

Cash fell silent. Santos had a point. Then he remembered what was in his pocket. "What about that coin? I looked up gold prices before we came out here. If it's real it's worth a couple thousand bucks."

Santos was impressed. "In that case, I can see why that woman wanted to keep it."

"Come on, Gabe. You've got to admit—"

Santos held up a hand. "Right now I've got other things to worry about."

"Like what?"

"Like we're late for an interview with another applicant for deputy."

"We?"

"I want you to talk to her too."

Cash raised an eyebrow. "Her? It's a she?"

"You got a problem with that?"

Cash quickly backpedaled. "If I did, Edie would kick my ass from here to Lubbock. What's her name?"

"Keisha Hodge."

"Keisha Hodge. Good. We could use a woman on the force."

Santos commented wryly, "We could use another mammalian life form on the force."

***

Cash downed the last of his chocolate milk and resumed thumbing through Keisha Hodge's file. The applicant looked great on paper. After earning a degree in political science at the University of Texas, she completed police training at the Capital Area Council of Governments, or CAPCOG, the same Austin academy where Cash trained. This was followed by another eight months of instruction at the Austin Police Academy and two years on the Austin police force. She was applying for the job out of a desire for a change of scenery.

So, a change of scenery. Okay, but why Noble County? Cash flipped back to the first page in the file and found the answer. She was born in Junction, the closest town to Pinyon with a hospital. Cash understood the desire to return to small-town living, having made a similar decision after finishing college at Sam Houston State. He made the move over the objection of his parents. Especially his mother, who couldn't let go of the fantasy that he would someday attend law school.

Vicky strutted into the room, interrupting his thoughts. She threw him a glance, plopped down across the table, and opened a sack lunch. Cash said, "Kind of late for lunch, isn't it?"

"I was at Tyler's house over my lunch break." She flashed a malicious grin. "We didn't have time to eat."

Cash said nothing. He had no desire to find out what had kept the two of them from eating.

"I guess you could say we're going together now." She took a bite of her sandwich. "Of course, if things don't work out between you and Edie ..."

He risked a peek at her. She wasn't pretending to eat.

"How are you and Edie doing?" Vicky asked.

"Still madly in love."

"Oh. Well, if something happens, you'll let me know, right?"

Santos saved Cash from having to answer by poking his head into the room. "Hey, I'm finished. Your turn now."

Relieved to dodge Vicky's question, Cash followed Santos into his office. He was introduced to Keisha Hodge, a slender Black woman whose height almost matched Cash's six-foot-two frame. With her slacks and short-sleeved blouse and her hair pulled into a tight bun, she exuded an air of urban professionalism more fitting in a bank executive than a sheriff's deputy.

Santos left. Cash shook Hodge's hand and beckoned her to a seat before slipping into the chair behind the desk. "Your credentials are impressive," he said, settling into the padded leather.

"Thank you."

"I see you attended UT."

"Hook 'em Horns."

"Are you a sports fan?"

"I was on the basketball team."

Cash raised an eyebrow. Playing for a Division I powerhouse like Texas was no small accomplishment. He wondered what it would be like to face her one-on-one. "I played high school basketball here in Pinyon. Football and baseball in college."

"Where?"

"Sam Houston State."

"We played them a few times. Beat them pretty good."

"Right." He flipped open the folder to buy himself time to think. "I have to ask. Why Pinyon?"

"Do you mean why would I leave a cool place like Austin to come live with the hicks?"

That was exactly what he meant. "No."

"My boyfriend got a job in Michigan. I didn't want to go with him. That's why he's now my ex-boyfriend."

"You didn't have to leave Austin just because he left."

"I wanted to come home."

"Do your parents live here?"

"No, they live in Austin. My grandmother is here, though. Out in the country. Growing up I always spent summers with her."

Cash struggled to come up with the proper way to ask his next question. "I can't help noticing that you're—"

"A woman. I know."

"I was going to say, well ..."

"Oh. Black. You can say the word. I'm not offended."

"Right." She was tough. He liked that. "Given that fact, are you sure you'd be happy in Pinyon? There aren't a lot of Blacks in this town."

"Do you think a Black person can only be happy living around other Black people?"

"No, that's not what I meant."

"Oh. Maybe you meant it's best if I stick with my own kind, then."

Uh-oh. This was getting dicey. "Of course not. I just worry about how the rednecks around here might treat you."

"As long as I treat them with kindness and respect, I expect they'll treat me the same. At least that's what my grandmother taught me."

Being six-two would help. "She sounds like a smart woman."

"She is." A pause hung in the air. "Did you know that Black folks were among the original settlers in Noble County?"

Cash shook his head. "No."

"It was right after the Civil War. A group of them in Austin didn't feel welcome so they came here. Their community was known as Hodge Colony."

Cash twitched in surprise. He had heard of Hodge Colony but hadn't made the connection with Keisha.

"So, this really is a homecoming for you."

"If you'll have me."

Cash closed the file. "Maybe we could have a game of one-on-one sometime."

"Sure." She smiled. "As long as you don't mind me kicking your ass."

6

Cash hopped into his new Ram pickup truck and fired up the engine. He smiled as he listened to its soothing hum. It was a far cry from the clattering roar of his old Ford Fiesta. He had sold that piece of junk to a high school student for an amount of money that would buy a steak dinner for him and Edie. When he warned the buyer of the car's unreliability, the kid told him he liked working on engines and planned on having this one purring like a kitten in no time. Cash took the money and ran.

He could have taken a squad car out to see Emmett Fuller, but he hadn't yet had his fill of driving his new truck. As he turned onto the farm-to-market road leading to Fuller's land, he reveled in the lingering new car scent. He had never bought a new vehicle before, much less a dark blue Ram 1500 pickup with over three hundred horsepower. At first, he had balked at the price, not much less than his annual salary. When his parents kicked in five thousand toward the down payment, though, he reconsidered. The clincher had come from Edie, who said, "YOLO." You only live once.

Fuller's property was unfenced. From the road, Cash could see a large motorcycle parked beside a weathered RV and a stock tank beyond that. He guided his truck past a "No Trespassing" sign and followed tire tracks beaten into the caliche to reach it. A thick cedar brake rose to one side of the trailer. On the other side was a fire pit stocked with a neat pile of oak logs. A thin stream of smoke rose from embers in the pit. Upon closer inspection, the motorcycle was a Harley Nightster.

Cash stepped up to the RV and rapped on the door. No one answered. He was standing on his toes to peek through a window when a man's voice sounded from behind. "What are you doing?"

Cash turned to see a tall man with bulging muscles emerge from the cedar. He wore jeans and a T-shirt with the sleeves cut off. In one hand was a chainsaw. He dragged a long, skinny oak branch with the other. Cash recognized him as the man in the store on Avi's surveillance video.

"I'm Adam Cash, deputy with the Noble County sheriff's department. I'm looking for Emmett Fuller."

"You got no right to be on this property, Deputy Cash." He made Cash's name sound like an insult. "Didn't you see the 'no trespassing' sign?"

Cash sensed that the only thing preventing a fistfight was his uniform. "I apologize. I mean no harm. I just wanted to talk to you about Ralph Spencer."

"What about him?"

"Are you Emmett Fuller?"

"Yeah, that's me."

"Could we go inside and sit down?"

Fuller dropped the tree branch and set the chainsaw on a cinder block. He gestured at a cluster of camp chairs surrounding the fire pit. "We can sit over there."

After they were settled in, Cash said, "Did you hear about Ralph's recent death?"

"I did. What about it?"

Picking up on Fuller's defensive tone, Cash held up his hands. "I'm not implying anything. As far as I can tell it was an accident. There are just a couple of odd things that stand out."

"Yeah? Like what?"

"For one thing, it seems he was stealing diesel fuel."

Fuller grunted but said nothing.

"Were you aware of that?"

"No."

"That's what he was doing when he died. The explosion might have been triggered by him lighting a cigarette." He was watching Fuller's reactions. "It's tempting to think the flame caused the diesel fumes to ignite. The funny thing is, diesel fumes don't ignite very easily."

"Is there a question in there somewhere?"

"I'm getting to that. Spencer had a solid gold coin in his pocket. It's worth over two thousand dollars."

"I still don't hear a question."

"I was just wondering where he got it."

"There's no law against a man carrying money in his pocket, is there?"

Cash shrugged. "No. But a gold coin isn't something you see every day."

"Maybe he found it."

"That would be one lucky find." When Fuller said nothing, Cash went on. "You were in the store the day that truck exploded. There's video footage."

Fuller's face flashed with momentary surprise before settling back into a disdainful smirk. "Yeah, I was there."

"Did you see anything suspicious?"

He scoffed. "You mean other than a truck blowing up? Nope."

"How well did you know Ralph Spencer?"

Fuller stood. "I've got no more time for questions, Deputy. It's time for you to go."

Annoyed, Cash rose and pointed at the smoldering embers. "Are you aware of the countywide burn ban?"

Fuller measured Cash for a moment and then unzipped his fly. Startled, Cash didn't move. Fuller stepped up to the fire pit and cut loose with a heavy stream of urine that hissed against the embers. The pungent stench of ammonia forced Cash to step back. Fuller zipped up, turned, and started toward the RV. Without looking back, he said, "Don't let me catch you on my property again."

7

"Are you working hard or hardly working?"

Santos forced a weak chuckle at the lame joke. "It isn't work when you like doing it."

Virgil Hall, president of the Pinyon Rotary Club, slapped Santos on the shoulder and let loose a genuine laugh. "That's the spirit I like to see in a man." He leaned in and lowered his voice. "We're having chicken fried steak today. Mashed potatoes and cream gravy. Although I can do without the gravy. I like ketchup on mine."

Unable to think of a response, Santos nodded and smiled. He wished Hall, a short, stocky man with thinning hair and ruddy cheeks that looked like ripe tomatoes, would stop yakking and start the meeting. Making small talk with the man was taxing his patience. He had already listened to an endless story about a happy customer at Hall's tire store.

Hall leaned in again and Santos braced himself. The club president had a habit of thrusting his head forward with each sentence as if he were about to reveal a juicy secret. "How's your new deputy playing out?"

"Do you mean Cash?"

"Yeah. You know, I knew his daddy. We didn't always see eye to eye but he was all right."

"Cash is doing great. He's a good man."

"I heard you're hiring another deputy too."

Santos blinked in surprise. He hadn't told anyone but Cash and Fred Uecker. Cash would keep the news to himself, so Uecker must have blabbed. He should have known the county commissioner couldn't keep that to himself.

"Yes, her name is Keisha Hodge."

Hall drew back in feigned surprise. "A woman deputy. Well, I'll be dogged. Noble County is going woke."

Santos kept his mouth shut. He had expected such a reaction from at least a few folks in town.

"Keisha, huh?" Hall went on, a puzzled look on his face. "That's an unusual name. Is that Russian?"

"No, sir. She's Black."

Hall leaned in again. "She is, is she? Do you think the people of Noble County are ready for that?"

Heat rose up Santos' neck. Some people had asked that same question about his hiring. "If they're not, they better get ready, because she starts next week."

Hall clicked his tongue and gestured toward a table. "Why don't you take your place, Sheriff? The meeting's about to start."

Santos' anger at Hall had the fortunate effect of pushing his anxiety over today's gathering to the back of his mind. He spotted Edie James at the back of the room chatting with two men. He had asked her only this morning about being his campaign manager and was relieved when she said yes.

The meeting was being held in the private dining room at the Firewheel Café. Although he dined at the Firewheel regularly, Santos recognized few faces in the room. There was Jeanine, manager of the credit union, and Frida Simmons, the county medical examiner. One-time Houston Oiler and current antique shop owner Will Anson was sitting in the front row. Beyond that, Santos drew a blank.

Hall stepped to the lectern and rang a bell to start the meeting. He read through a list of announcements before leading the group in the Pledge of Allegiance. As he started to recite the Rotary Club's Four-Way Test, loud laughter interrupted him from just outside the door. Moments later, three men strode in. Two of them were strangers to Santos, but the third man's face was well-known to him from the campaign posters already showing up around town. Mitch Eaton.

Eaton caught Hall's eye and waved. "Howdy, there, Virgil. I hope we're not too late for the meeting."

Hall spread his hands in a gesture of welcome. "Not at all, gentlemen. We were just getting started."

Eaton took his time finding a seat, stopping along the way to shake hands and greet people. Watching him, Santos' stomach sank. The man was a natural politician. What chance did he have against someone like that?

Once Eaton finished with his glad-handing, Hall got through the rest of the club's business and introduced Santos. "I'm sure y'all know him by now," he said, "so I don't have to say much about him. What you might not know is that he's running for sheriff."

A hand went up. "Isn't he already sheriff?"

"Yeah, but then Mitch pointed out to the commissioners the rule about calling a special election if there's an opening with this much time to go in the term of office." Hall caught Eaton's eye and grinned. "Pretty sneaky, Mitch."

Everyone laughed. Santos swore under his breath. So the election was Eaton's doing.

Hall rapped his gavel. "All right, everybody, let's give a warm Rotary welcome to Acting Sheriff Santos."

As Santos stepped to the podium, he decided to throw out his prepared speech and speak off the cuff. Everybody was fawning over Eaton as if he was predestined to win? So be it. Santos would go down swinging.

He started by reminding everyone of his qualifications and experience, including his time as a soldier in Afghanistan. His story about being wounded in a village ambush caught everyone's ear, but when he described Cash's heroic dash into danger to save his skin the crowd's intensity startled him. A long silence followed the story's conclusion, broken by Will Anson, who said, "Hell, Cash should run for sheriff."

Despite knowing that the old man had meant his comment as a joke, Santos said, "He did. Not enough of you voted for him."

Santos concluded by reminding the crowd that he and Cash functioned as a team. He expressed sorrow over Griff Turner's murder and lauded Deke Conrad for his courage and tenacity. Finally, he explained his decision to hire Keisha Hodge, avoiding any mention of her gender or skin color. He was prepared to pounce if anyone broached either topic, but no one did.

The first few questions from the crowd concerned Santos' military service. Frida Simmons then asked for a rundown of the department's budget along with his ideas about prioritizing departmental goals. When he was finished answering, Santos said, "At any rate, that's my opinion."

One of the men who had come in with Eaton said, "What do you think Mitch?"

All eyes turned toward Eaton, who shrugged and responded with a string of platitudes about his tough stance on crime. When Eaton stopped talking, Santos pointed to a woman with her hand raised.

Before she could ask her question, a man called out, "Mitch, what about drugs? I've got two young girls I'm worried about."

Eaton launched into a long monologue on the evils of drugs and the need for those in leadership positions to "bring morals back into the equation of governance." Several people clapped. One man shouted "Amen."

When yet another question was addressed to Eaton, Virgil Hall stood up. "Folks, I need to remind you that our guest today is Acting Sheriff Santos. Does anyone have any more questions for him?"

When no one did, Hall banged his gavel to close the meeting. Chairs scraped as people rose and clustered around Eaton. Santos stepped away from the lectern and, red-faced, strode toward the exit. Edie cut him off.

"Don't let this get you down, Gabe. You impressed a lot of people today."

"Yeah, that's why they're over there fawning over Mitch Eaton."

"What can I say? People are jerks."

"I have to get back to work."

"You should stick around in case anyone wants to talk to you."

Santos nodded at Eaton holding court. "Like I said, I have to get back to work."

***

After Santos left, Edie stuck around chatting for a few minutes before heading for the door. Before she reached it, she heard a man call her name.

"I thought that might be you," Eaton said, all smiles as he approached. Edie wondered how he recognized her, as they had never met. He shook her hand. "I'm Mitch Eaton."

"I know," said Edie. "You made quite the entrance."

Eaton chuckled. "I didn't mean to. I hope I didn't disrupt the meeting."

"You're running for sheriff too, I understand."

"That's right. That's what I want to talk to you about."

"Oh?"

"I'll get right to the point. I need someone to run my campaign. I'd like for it to be you."

Edie was puzzled by the offer. "Me? You don't even know me."

"I know what I've heard. You're a tough, brave woman. The way you got out of that jam with Clovis Ward was impressive."

"I had help. Deputy Cash was there. So was Sheriff Santos, by the way."

"Yes, they are to be commended as well. But they don't have the experience that you have."

"Experience!" Edie said, laughing. "Where did you get that idea?"

"Didn't you manage Deputy Cash's campaign?"

"If you know that, you know how it turned out."

Eaton flicked his hand. "That was a hopeless cause. You squeezed blood from a turnip and got thirty percent of the vote." When Edie didn't respond, he added, "This time it's not a hopeless cause. You'd have my financial resources at your disposal."

"I don't know." She paused. How to put this? "The fact is, I've already agreed to help Gabe."

"How much is he paying you?"

The question took Edie by surprise. "He's not."

"I can give you five hundred a week. I know it's not much, but as more donations come in we could raise it."

Not much? Edie's mouth fell open. Five hundred a week! She didn't know what to say.

"You'd be backing a winner. Who knows where that could take you.?" He lowered his voice. "From what I can tell, you've got too much going for you to be slinging hash at the Firewheel."

"Five hundred?"

"A week."

She felt her thoughts moving in directions she wasn't proud of. She had already told Gabe yes. But an extra two thousand dollars a month? How could she turn that down?

"Can you give me some time to think about it?"

Eaton flashed a triumphant grin. "Sure. Why don't I give you a call in a day or two?"

"Okay."

"It's settled then. I'll talk to you later."

They exchanged cell numbers and Eaton left. Edie stood rooted to the spot long enough for Virgil Hall to notice. "Edie, is everything all right?"

Snapping out of her trance, she said, "I'm fine."

"I couldn't help but notice you were talking to Mitch Eaton. What were you two gabbing about?"

She fixed Hall with a glare. "Virgil, is that any of your business?"

8

"Enjoy," the young man said as he set two glasses of dark brown beer on the table. "On the house."

Cash looked up in surprise. "Really? Why?"

"Boss's orders."

Cash picked up his beer glass and held it up to the light. Seeing nothing suspicious, he said, "There's only one reason Steve sent two free beers to our table."

"What's that?" said Edie as she studied the black liquid in her glass.

"It's a new concoction. He loves using me as a guinea pig."

"Isn't that what best friends are for?"

Cash took a sip. "Not bad, actually. Tastes like a stout."

She sipped hers and made a face. "Oh, stout indeed." She pushed it away. "Too strong for me."

They sat at a walnut-stained pine table in the Packsaddle, a brewpub housed in a historic building on Pinyon's town square. It was owned by Steve Jenkins, Cash's friend since elementary school. Steve had cemented his status as Cash's best friend a month ago by allowing Cash to hide in the brewpub's basement after he was falsely accused of murder. He also let Cash use his truck while in hiding and gave him the money necessary to conduct the investigation that ultimately proved his innocence.

Cash raised his glass in a toast. "Cheers." They clinked glasses. Cash slipped a hand beneath the table and slid it along Edie's thigh. "You look great tonight."

"Easy, cowboy," she said, nudging his hand away. "This is a family-friendly place. And you say that every night."

"That's only because it's true."

"You're such a charmer," she said, though she was not displeased. She leaned an elbow on the table. "Changing the subject, they're making Gabe run for sheriff."

"Yeah. Against Mitch Eaton too."

"He asked me to run his campaign."

The news didn't surprise Cash. Edie was a smart, hard-driving woman. That's why he had asked her to run his own failed campaign. He didn't blame her for the defeat, since without her help he would have fared far worse. "You told him yes, of course."

"My track record isn't all that great. But yes, I told him yes."

"You're an amazing woman. You'll do fantastic." He took her hand and kissed it.

She pulled it away. "Save it for later."

Before Cash could answer, a firm hand slapped his back. He flinched and sloshed beer on the table.

"Watch it, Romeo. This is a family-friendly restaurant."

Steve, beer in hand, pulled up a chair. "Edie just said the same thing," Cash said.

"If things get too hot and heavy," Steve joked, "you can use the basement."

"No thanks. Too many memories. None of them good."

Steve took a long sip of his beer. Wiping the foam from his lip, he said, "What do you guys think of it?"

"Not bad," said Cash.

Edie said, "If I liked stouts, I'm sure I'd love it."

"I call it 'The Beerth of July.' You know, because it's almost—"

"The Fourth of July," said Cash. "We get it."

"That's terrible," Edie said.

Ignoring her remark, Steve said, "How's the sheriffing business?"

"I'm a deputy, not a sheriff," said Cash.

"Okay, how's the deputying business?"

"Picking up lately." Cash told him about the truck explosion.

"I heard about that. Poor Ralph."

"Did you know him?"

"Enough to say hello. He came here a lot. Sat right over there at the bar. Usually had two beers and left. He was a lousy tipper."

"He was stealing diesel. That's why his truck blew up."

Steve was surprised, and Edie added, "Tell him about the gold coin."

"I found a solid gold coin in his pocket. I have no idea where a guy like that would get a gold coin. As far as I can tell, he was unemployed."

"He always seemed to have enough money in here. Always paid cash. And I do know where he got it."

"Do tell," said Cash doubtfully.

"He won it playing poker." When Cash shot him a look of disbelief, Steve added, "Seriously, over at Terry's."

Terry's Poker Club operated in the back room of a thrift store on the square. A hundred dollars bought an annual membership, granting access to the poker games and pool table. Since Cash didn't play poker, he had never been inside the club. He clicked his tongue in mock disapproval. "Have you been gambling?"

"Private club, dude," said Steve. "Perfectly legal."

"Not exactly. The owner profits from the games."

"He doesn't take a dime of anybody's winnings."

"He profits indirectly from the memberships."

"Now you're splitting hairs. Besides, if it's illegal, why don't you guys shut it down?"

Cash knew the answer to that. Terry Moreno had always operated at the fringes of the law. Years ago he had a massage parlor that employed young women with no training in massage. After that, he ran a store that sold used farm implements along with the finest weed in Noble County. Now Moreno operated the poker club. Cash knew he had never been arrested because most people in the county had been a customer at one time or another. He shrugged. "We've got bigger fish to fry." When Steve didn't respond, Cash said, "Getting back to Ralph Spencer."

"Right. I know who he won that coin from."

"Who?"

"Some woman."

"You do know there's more than one of those in Noble County, don't you?"

"I don't know her name, smartass. I just know she's a regular at the club. So was Ralph. The other night they were the only two players left on a hand with a big pot. Each of them kept raising until the woman ran out of chips. Then she pulls a gold coin out of her purse. It had the queen on one side and a lady with a spear on the other."

"Trident."

"What?"

"It's not a spear. It's a trident."

Steve dismissed the remark with a wave of his hand. "Whatever. So, she lays this coin on the table and says, 'Is this enough?' Everybody's eyes light up. Ralph says, 'Sure, what do you have?' She shows him an ace-high flush. Just as she's reaching for the pot, he plops his cards on the table. Know what he had?"

"Something better than an ace-high flush?"

"Son of a bitch was holding a straight flush. Can you believe it?"

"And you saw this happen?"

"No, I was there the next night. Everybody was still talking about it."

"So, who is this mystery woman?" Edie asked.

"Like I said, I don't know her name. I just know she comes in most Thursday nights."

Cash said, "Was Spencer a regular?"

"Not after that night. He got into a fight with Moreno when he told a racist joke about Mexicans. They were really whaling on each other, from what I heard. Moreno finally threw him out and told him never to come back."

This was a new angle. "Was it bad enough for Moreno to want to kill him?"

"No, I've seen him toss guys before. He never killed any of them."

"That you know of."

"Right."

"I guess Spencer's off the Christmas card list."

"Duh, he's dead." Steve reached for Edie's beer. "If you're not gonna drink that." He turned to Cash. "Are you going to talk to that woman?"

"Tomorrow's Thursday," said Cash. "Guess I'll go play me some poker."

***

The next morning, Cash found Santos at his desk staring at a computer screen. He rapped on the door frame. "Got a minute?"

Without looking up, Santos said, "Sure, come on in."

Cash dropped into a chair. "You sound like your dog just died."

Santos sighed and leaned back in his chair. "When Fred Uecker told me about this job, he didn't mention all the damned forms I'd have to fill out."

"Got you buried in paperwork, do they?"

"Do they ever. Budget reports, time sheets, vacation requests ... it never ends."

"I hope you aired those complaints at your campaign appearance yesterday."

Santos buried his face in his hands. "Don't remind me. I tried to get out of it, but Edie pretty much ordered me to do it. That woman should have been a gym coach."

"Tell me about it," said Cash, chuckling. "How did it go?"

"On a scale of one to ten, I'd give it a negative five."

"Ouch."

"Mitch Eaton showed up. You'd have thought George Strait just walked into the room, the way everyone was fawning over him."

Cash tried to cheer him up. "Yours went about as well as mine."

"What happened to you?"

Cash told him about his appearance at the Rotary Club during his failed campaign for sheriff. A man had asked him if Texas should secede. "I told him that issue was settled by the outcome of the Civil War."

"I'm guessing he didn't like that answer."

"No, he did not. Anyway, forget that. I came by to tell you I went to see Emmett Fuller."

"Who's Emmett Fuller?"

"Ralph Spencer's friend. You remember. His girlfriend told us about him."

Santos wasn't following. "What is it you think you're looking for? The explosion was an accident. Is there a crime here I don't know about?"

"I'm telling you, Gabe, this is just weird. Ralph Spencer hasn't had a steady job since he moved here. Yet his girlfriend only stayed with him because of his money. Not only that, he was flush enough to be a regular at the poker club. That's where he got the gold coin. He won it off a woman in a poker game."

"Damn, that sounds serious. We should alert the authorities." He turned back toward the computer screen.

"We are the authorities."

"I know that. And if I want to remain an authority, I have to win this election."

Cash rose. "You've got my vote."

"Thanks. By the way, I hired Keisha. She starts next week."

"Good move."

"Know what Fred Uecker said when I told him?"

"Was it a question about her gender or her skin color?"

"Neither one. He wanted me to ask her if she'd help his daughter with her jump shot."

***

Cash arrived at Star of Texas Thrift Shop at 6 o'clock. The store occupied a historic rock building on the east side of the square. Next door was what had until recently been Barry's Gelato Palace, closed since its owner Barry Novak was arrested for human trafficking the month before. Novak had been a central player in the plot by deputies Clovis Ward and Judd Noteboom to frame Cash for the murder of Griff

Turner. Now Noteboom was dead, and Ward would soon stand trial for Griff Turner's murder. Novak faced a variety of charges, including kidnapping, human trafficking, and rape.

Six-pack of Packsaddle Kolsch in hand, Cash entered the store and was greeted by its owner, Sadie Billings. They exchanged pleasantries before Sadie pointed toward the back. "Terry's opening up now if you want to go on through." Cash strolled through the aisles marveling at the amount of junk Sadie had for sale. Furniture, dishes, old sports equipment, and more filled every available cranny. Cash stopped at the sight of a jigsaw puzzle featuring a scene from one of his favorite movies, *The Matrix*. Seeing something from his childhood stirred fond memories.

In back was a small room cluttered with rusty tools and hardware. Cash passed through it and pushed through a door to enter Terry's Poker Club. Little more than a large storage space, Terry's featured two cloth-covered tables, metal folding chairs, a refrigerator, and, according to a sign on the wall, "the nicest pool table in town." Given that the only other pool table was a threadbare relic in Grumpy Greg's Barbecue, the claim was hard to dispute.

As Cash stowed his beer in the refrigerator, club owner Terry Moreno entered from the alley. A cheerful man who had once coached Cash's Little League baseball team, Moreno had a son named Hector who was about Cash's age. Hector was now in his final year of a pediatrics residency at UT San Antonio.

Moreno raised his hands. "Uh-oh. It's a raid."

Refusing to take the bait, Cash reached out for a handshake. "How's Hector?"

"He doesn't call his father often enough, but other than that he's okay."

"Will he open a practice here when he finishes his residency?"

"No, but maybe over in Junction. He tells me Pinyon's too small to support a pediatrician."

"I guess he ought to know."

"I didn't know you were a poker player," Moreno said, assessing him. "Or are you here for the pool table?"

Cash retrieved one of his beers from the refrigerator. He popped it open. "Neither one." He offered the can to Moreno.

"No thanks. I don't drink when I'm working."

Cash winced at the thought that, technically, he was working too.

"If you're not here for poker or pool, what does bring you by?"

"I'm looking for information on one of your customers. I don't know her name, but I'm told she recently lost a solid gold coin to Ralph Spencer in a poker game."

"Ah, poor Ralph. What a terrible way to go."

Cash saw through the false sympathy. "Do you know the woman?"

"Why do you want to know about her?"

"I found the coin on Spencer's body when he was killed. I'm curious."

Moreno pressed his lips together. "If my customers find out I'm talking about them to the law they might not be my customers anymore."

"Come on, Mr. Moreno. She's not a suspect or anything."

"Mr. Moreno. You always were a polite kid." He crossed his arms. "You must mean Bonnie Hart. She's been coming in regular for about a year. Plays a mean game. She doesn't lose much. Spencer was lucky as hell to win that hand."

"How well do you know her?"

"Just enough to say hello. She's pretty serious about her poker. Generally just comes in, takes a seat, and says 'Deal 'em up, boys.' She'll talk a mean streak, but only with cards in her hands."

"Is she rich?"

Moreno shrugged. "I wouldn't know. Like I said, I don't know her very well. How come you're asking all these questions? Is there something going on I should know about?"

"No, nothing like that," said Cash, shaking his head. "I'm just gathering information."

Moreno grunted and wandered off to ready the card tables. Cash grabbed a well-used cue stick from a wall rack and practiced his pool shots. The room began filling up. When a man set a dollar bill on the pool table's top rail, Cash yielded the table to him. He grabbed another beer from the refrigerator and found a seat from which to watch the poker action.

By now, poker games had started at both tables. With one exception—a cashier at Dollar General named Rose—the players were men. Cash watched the games with only mild interest, as he had never seen the lure of gambling. By seven o'clock he was bored enough to think about leaving. Then a woman he assumed to be Bonnie Hart arrived.

She slipped into the room unnoticed by the other players. Dressed in knee-length shorts and a loose-fitting T-shirt, she looked as if she had just come in from the river. She had a round face with a trace of wrinkles at the corners of her eyes. Her blonde hair hung down to her shoulders in loose strands. She wore no makeup. An alligator tattoo peeked out from beneath one shirt sleeve. She moved like a cat, graceful and silent.

She bought a stack of chips from the game's banker. A man at one of the tables saw her approach and scootched over to make room. She placed her chips on the table and slid into a chair. When the hand ended, the players greeted her by name. She offered polite, but curt greetings of her own and asked to be dealt in.

For the next half hour, Cash studied Bonnie Hart's business-like approach to playing poker. She spoke little, mostly saying just what was necessary to keep the game moving. Her face betrayed no emotion. She raised, folded, or called with the same robotic voice. As hard as he tried, Cash couldn't see any tells. It was no wonder that her chip pile soon doubled in size.

A hand ended and one of the men at Bonnie's table said, "I gotta take a piss." When he rose, two other men got up and stretched.

The banker said, "Ten-minute break?" The others murmured agreement.

Cash slid into the chair next to Bonnie. Without looking at him, she said, "That seat's taken."

"I'm not here to play. I was hoping to have a quick word with you."

She swung toward him and produced a faint smile. "Aren't you a fine-looking fella?"

Cash imagined that a lot of men had fallen for the look she was giving him. "Thank you, ma'am."

Her smile widened. "And polite too." Pointing she said, "See that whiskey on top of the fridge? Bring that over here. A cup too. One for yourself if you want some. Then we'll talk."

Cash retrieved the bottle and a plastic cup. She poured herself a drink and said, "None for you?"

"Thanks, no."

She sipped her drink. "What can I do for you?" Her voice was friendly, maybe even flirtatious. Nothing like the poker-playing robot she had been moments before.

"I want to ask you about Ralph Spencer."

The sparkle in her eyes faded into a glaze. "I don't know anyone by that name."

"He's a regular in here. Last week he won a gold coin from you."

She pursed her lips in thought. "Right. I remember him now. Lucky son of a bitch. I had an ace-high flush." Her voice had reverted to the robotic delivery.

"I was wondering where you got that coin."

"Are you a cop?"

"I'm a deputy with the sheriff's office."

She stood up. "Sorry, I don't talk to cops."

Cash rose from his chair. "Did you know that Ralph is dead?"

"Like I said, I don't talk to cops. Now, if you'll excuse me, I'm going to the ladies' room."

He watched her walk away. She was no beauty, but from the way she rocked her slender hips, Cash figured she had no trouble attracting men.

As he made his way to the door, Moreno stopped him. "What did you say to her? She didn't look happy."

"She said she doesn't know Ralph Spencer. Is that true?"

"Hell if I know."

"If she flashes any more gold coins in here, let me know, okay?" He started for the exit.

"Hey."

"What?"

"Don't forget your beer."

Cash waved a hand. "Merry Christmas."

9

Hoping to avoid conversation with Vicky, Cash kept his head down as he entered the station lobby. Her constant flirting had become tiresome. Hadn't he made it clear that he and Edie were a couple? That should be reason enough for her to let up. Plus, she was a good ten years younger than him. Just a few months ago, she was getting ready for senior prom. What kind of fool would he be to entangle himself with a kid barely out of high school?

"Good morning, Cash."

Damn. There she was. He couldn't just ignore her. "Good morning, Vicky."

"Look what Tyler got me." She fingered a pendant hanging from a chain around her neck. "It's a heart. Know what it says? 'To eternal love.'"

He glanced at it. "That's very nice."

"It's from James Avery. Tyler bought it in Kerrville. He hasn't said it yet, but I think he loves me."

"James Avery. Wow." He uttered a silent thank-you to Tyler.

"We're going dancing at London Hall this Saturday. You and Edie should come."

Cash feigned disappointment. "Sorry, we're having dinner at the sheriff's house."

"Oh." She fluttered her eyes. "Maybe another time?"

"You bet."

He grabbed a cup of coffee and made his way to the conference room. It had become Santos' habit to start each morning with a brief meeting over coffee. Given the department's small size—just Santos and two deputies—the meetings didn't last long.

Deke Conrad was already at the table when Cash arrived. "Hey, Deke."

"Morning, Cash."

"How are you feeling these days?" Cash asked. Conrad had been shot in the abdomen by Clovis Ward during his final showdown with Cash.

"The pain is almost gone. I just wish I could get off desk duty."

Cash recalled hearing similar sentiments from wounded comrades in Afghanistan. "If you rush it, you just prolong your recovery."

"You sound like my doctor."

"And here I didn't even go to medical school."

Santos ambled into the room. "Good morning, guys."

Before Cash or Conrad could respond, Keisha Hodge followed. Clad in a pristine Noble County deputy's uniform of olive-green pants and a short-sleeved khaki shirt, she looked eager for work.

"I thought you didn't start until next week," Cash said.

"I got moved in with my grandmother sooner than I thought. If I didn't get out of the house, she was going to find stuff for me to do. Meemaw doesn't tolerate anyone just sitting around."

The two new arrivals found seats. Santos said, "Other than Keisha starting today, I don't have any big news to announce. Oh, but I am going to get my ass kicked in the election."

"It's not over till it's over," Cash said.

"It might as well be. The guy knows how to work a room. He's loaded, too."

"He sounds like a phony to me. People will see right through him."

"I wish I shared your optimism." He didn't want to linger on the unpleasant prospect. "On another note, what happened at the poker club last night?"

Before Cash could answer, Vicky poked her head into the room. "Sorry to interrupt, Sheriff, but you told me to let you know if that guy called again."

Santos said, "What did he say?"

"The same as last time."

"Did you get a name?"

"No, he hung up before I could ask him."

"Okay, thanks."

Vicky left. Cash said, "What was that about?"

Santos waved a dismissive hand. "Some asshole keeps calling to complain about—" he made air quotes— "our 'woke' police force."

Cash looked at Hodge. "Hey, it wasn't me," she said.

"That's not what I was thinking."

Santos said, "Calls like that came in when I was hired. It's probably the same guy."

"We've got his number on caller ID, right?"

"No. He blocks it."

"You could get it from the phone company."

"Not worth the trouble. Now tell me about the poker club."

Cash sat up straight. "I met the woman Ralph got the coin from. Her name is Bonnie Hart. She clammed up as soon as she found out I was a deputy."

"So, are you done chasing that particular red herring?"

"No. I want to find out more about her. Something's off." He reminded Santos about his encounter with Emmett Fuller.

Santos said, "I'm still waiting to hear what crime you're investigating."

"Is there some other crime I'm neglecting?"

"Point taken. As long as you're investigating major criminal activity, why don't you take Keisha with you today?"

"Want to tag along, Keisha?"

"Sure."

"Anything else, boss?" Cash asked Santos.

"Go get 'em, Batman."

***

"Have you had breakfast?" Cash said as he fastened his seat belt.

"Just coffee," said Hodge.

"Then our first stop is the donut shop. And no jokes, they make breakfast tacos too."

Cash drove to Shelly's Donuts on the square. Inside, he grabbed a bottle of chocolate milk from the cooler and said, "What do you like on your tacos?"

"I don't know. I need to look at the menu."

Cash ordered a dozen chocolate-covered donuts and an egg, potato, and cheese breakfast taco. Hodge got the Shelly Special, with eggs, refried beans, potatoes, bacon, and cheese. They took the food across the street to a park bench. Several grackles swooped in from a nearby pecan tree and began strutting back and forth in front of them. Their shiny black feathers glistened in the morning sunlight.

"Greedy little beggars," Hodge said as she unwrapped her taco. She took a bite.

"How is it?" Cash said.

"Taco Shack is better."

"Ooh lah lah, you're a taco snob."

Salsa dribbled onto Hodge's chin. She wiped it off and said, "What's our first move to bust up this crime ring?"

"After we finish eating, we'll head over to the real estate office. Bonnie Hart is relatively new in town. I want to know more about where she lives."

"They'll tell you that?"

"There are no secrets in a small town." He held up the bag of donuts. "And Stephanie loves donuts."

Hodge tossed the rest of her taco to the birds. "All done."

***

Stephanie Granger's real estate office was located just off the square in an old house converted for office use. A metal sign in the small front yard bore her photograph and business logo. American and Texas flags hung limply from separate flagpoles protruding at an angle from the building. Cash parked in the street and, noticing the maroon Jeep Grand Cherokee in the driveway, said, "Looks like she's here."

They got out and crossed the street. Cash pointed at a sticker with the Texas A&M slogan "Gig 'em Aggies" on the Jeep's bumper. "Better not flash the 'Hook 'em Horns' sign while we're in there," he said.

Hodge said, "Only if she gives me the 'Gig 'em' sign first."

Inside, they were greeted by Granger's receptionist Charlene Higgins. Cash had gone to high school with one of her three sons. She was now a grandmother several times over. It occurred to Cash that the sheriff's office would benefit from a matronly presence like hers.

He dropped the bag of chocolate-covered donuts on Charlene's desk. "I brought you a present."

"You devil," she said, clapping her hands with glee. "I just went on a diet last week."

He snatched up the bag. "Guess I better keep these then."

"You put those right back. What's a diet without a little temptation?"

"Is Stephanie here?"

Charlene fished out a donut. "She's in her office."

The reception area had once been the house's family room. A short hall led to two bedrooms converted to offices, one on either side. Beyond that were a kitchen and bathroom. One of the office doors was open. A short, stocky woman with silver hair and bright red lipstick sat behind a desk. She waved Cash in.

"I thought I recognized that voice. Are you finally ready to sell your parents' place?"

Cash had no intention of selling. The house occupied the last two hundred acres of what had once been a thirty-five-hundred-acre ranch founded by his great-great-grandfather. He planned to restore the land as much as possible, not sell it off for a developer to divide it into two-acre house lots. Besides, his parents still owned it.

"Afraid not. I'm here on official business."

Stephanie smiled at Hodge. "Are you the new deputy?"

Hodge reached a hand across the desk. "Yes, ma'am, I'm Keisha Hodge."

"How about that?" said Stephanie, shaking hands. "We've got a Mexican sheriff and a Black deputy. It's a regular United Nations. Of course, with Mitch Eaton running for sheriff, I suspect Santos will soon be demoted. If he's not fired altogether."

Cash resisted the urge to call Stephanie out for her insensitive comment. He needed her help. "May we sit?"

Stephanie gestured at two plastic stacking chairs in front of her desk. Cash took one but Hodge remained standing. Cash registered the scowl on her face.

"Did you hear about the explosion over at Stripes?" Cash asked.

"Sure did. Charlene told me. She said somebody was killed."

"That's right. A guy named Ralph Spencer. It was probably an accident but I'm just trying to make sure nothing's been missed. That's why I'm here."

"I don't understand."

"Spencer knew a woman named Bonnie Hart. She's relatively new in town. I'm wondering if you were her real estate agent."

Stephanie stroked her chin. "Bonnie Hart. That name rings a bell. Let me check." She turned toward her laptop screen and entered a few keystrokes. "Yeah, here she is. She bought a house on a hundred acres west of town. I wanted to show her some nicer places for about the same price closer in but she said she liked the privacy of this one. She acted like she was in a big hurry. It seemed weird."

"Where is it exactly?"

She gave him the address.

"Was there anything else unusual about the purchase?"

"Not really. She blew into town on a Wednesday, and we closed the next day. I only showed her two properties. Easiest sale I've ever made."

"Was anybody with her?"

"Yeah. Believe it or not, Ralph Spencer."

Cash's ears perked up. He knew Bonnie had been lying about not knowing him.

"There was another guy, too," Stephanie said. "Big, scary-looking guy. Rode a Harley."

"Was it Emmett Fuller?"

"I never got his name. What's going on? Are they running a meth lab or something?"

"I don't know that anything is going on yet. Like I said, I'm just covering all the bases regarding Ralph's death." Cash stood. "Thanks for your help. I left a bag of donuts with Charlene."

"Charlene!" Stephanie hollered, bustling out of the office. "You better save me some."

***

"I wasn't sure she'd answer your questions," Hodge said on the way back to the station.

Cash chuckled. "Stephanie will do anything for a donut."

"But she didn't know you brought them until we were leaving."

"She must have smelled them. Besides, she's always been a chatterbox. How come you didn't sit down?"

"I didn't feel particularly welcome."

"That was indeed an inappropriate remark about the U.N."

"Rude, more like it. But I've heard worse."

At the station, Cash led Hodge to the conference room. He logged on to the computer kept there for deputy use and invited Hodge to take a seat next to him.

"What are we looking for?" she asked.

"I want to look up that address." He tapped on the keyboard. "Here it is. A hundred and three acres on Tannehill Road. Look at that. It backs up to Emmett Fuller's place."

"Maybe they know each other."

"Maybe. Anyway, Bonnie's place has a three-bedroom house and a barn. Built in 1962. She paid seven hundred fifty thousand dollars."

Cash experienced a momentary thrill when he realized that, given that price, his land and house were worth well over a million. Correction, his parents' land and house. He had talked them into holding onto it as long as he wanted to live on it, but there was nothing to keep them from changing their minds.

"Are we going out there?"

Pulled from his daydream, Cash said, "Eventually. First, we're going to go see Jeanine."

***

On the way to Farm and Ranch Credit Union, Hodge said, "Think I could ask the questions this time?"

"You just started. Be patient."

She huffed and looked out the window. "Okay."

"I'm not saying it will always be like this. I'm just saying you need a little experience first."

"I said okay." She pursed her lips. "Sheriff Santos said you've only been a deputy for a month. I was on the Austin force for two years."

"That's true. But I spent a year in Afghanistan. I questioned a lot of people who weren't all that anxious to talk. Had to use an interpreter, too."

"I won't need an interpreter around here. I speak Spanish."

"I didn't know that."

"You didn't ask.

Cash parked in front of the credit union. "Tell you what. Let me ask the questions, but when I'm done, if you think I've left anything out, then speak up."

"Deal."

They entered the small lobby. A young man stood behind one of two counter windows. The other was empty, as were the two chairs against the opposite wall. The complete absence of sound unnerved Cash. Churches weren't this quiet.

The young man smiled. "Can I help you?"

"I'm here to see Jeanine."

"Hang on. I'll tell her you're here."

The teller disappeared into a back room. Moments later, credit union manager Jeanine Jarvis emerged. A lanky, middle-aged woman who seemed to be trying to erase the years with pounds of makeup, she bounced up to them and said, "Hello, Deputy. What can I do for you?"

"Could we talk in your office?"

She led them back through the doorway into a surprisingly large room with space enough for a laminate desk, two upholstered chairs, a coffee table, and a two-seat sofa. A framed photograph of the University of Texas football stadium dominated one wall. A curtainless window with its blinds raised provided a view of Main Street.

They sat around the coffee table. Cash introduced Hodge before asking Jeanine if she knew Bonnie Hart.

"I wouldn't say I know her, but I know who she is."

"Does she have an account here?"

"I can't talk about that. It would break privacy rules."

"What about a mortgage?"

"Again, I'm not allowed to divulge that kind of information."

"I'm not asking for specifics. I'm just asking if she's a customer here. It's part of an investigation."

She shrugged. "I'm sorry. My hands are tied."

Hodge pointed at the wall. "Is that DKR Stadium?"

Jeanine turned to look. Smiling, she said, "It is. I'm a big fan."

"My parents have season tickets. Dad is a Lifetime Longhorn."

"He played for UT?"

"Yes. Back in the nineties when John Mackovic was the coach."

"What position did he play?"

"Defensive end."

Cash spoke up. "Keisha played for the women's basketball team."

Jeanine broke out a wide grin. "You're kidding! I love the Lady Longhorns!"

"I wasn't a star or anything. But I loved being on the team."

"I'm a huge fan. I don't get to very many games, but I watch them on TV."

"My parents have tickets to those games too. Maybe we could go sometime. They're good seats."

"I'd love to." She leaned back in her chair with a contented sigh. "If that don't beat all."

No one spoke. The only sound in the office was the ticking of a clock on the desk.

Jeanine sat up. "Well, I do want to help. It's just ... Bonnie Hart. You didn't hear this from me, but she took out a loan to buy a house and some land out in the country."

"On Tannehill Road, right?" said Hodge.

Jeanine's eyes widened. "How did you know that?"

"We asked around."

"I'll tell you something weird about that deal. I probably shouldn't say this but ..." She glanced at Cash. "She tried to pay the down payment with a sack of gold coins."

"Really?" said Hodge with genuine surprise.

"Really. I told her we couldn't accept gold coins. Most banks won't. Maybe some in big cities but—" she emitted a shrill laugh –"Pinyon isn't a big city, is it?"

"What did she do then?"

"She asked me if she could at least make the monthly mortgage payments in gold. Again, I had to tell her no. She came back the next day with a briefcase full of money. I never saw anyone walk in here with so much. That was for the down payment. Now she comes in like clockwork once a month with cash for the mortgage."

Hodge drew the obvious inference. "I guess she's selling the coins?"

"Yes, in Kerrville."

"How do you know that?"

"The money comes in envelopes from a coin shop there. I'm sorry, but I can't remember the name."

Hodge said, "When is her next payment due?"

"Let me check." Jeanine went to her desk and activated her computer. After a few keystrokes, she said, "Next Tuesday. She always comes in on the due date or, if that falls on a weekend –the Friday right before it."

"Thank you." Hodge turned to Cash. "Do you have any more questions, Deputy?"

They traded a smile. "I do. Do you know Ralph Spencer?"

Jeanine said, "Wasn't he the guy killed in that explosion?"

"Yes. Does he bank here?"

Jeanine's friendly demeanor dissolved. "You guys are pushing it."

Hodge said, "It ties in with Bonnie Hart. Please, it's important."

"Well ..." She put her hands back on the keyboard. "You'll tell me what this is all about someday?"

"Every last detail."

Her fingers danced on the keys. "Yes, he's a customer. Or was, I guess."

"Was he making regular deposits? We don't need to know the amount, just whether or not he was making them."

"Once a month."

"Was it enough to live on?"

"If he wasn't extravagant, yes."

"Thank you so much, Jeanine," said Hodge. "This really helps our case." She stood and looked at Cash. "Is there anything else?"

Cash's face reddened. "No."

"I guess we'll be going then."

Jeanine said, "Don't forget, we're going to a game this fall."

"Absolutely."

***

Cash put his hands on the wheel of the squad car but didn't start the engine. Looking over at Hodge, he said, "You did good in there."

"Thanks."

"That was smooth, picking up on the football stadium."

"We ran into Longhorn fans all the time in Austin. It never hurts to take advantage of that."

"What if you're talking to an Aggie?"

"I'd just bring up a game that we lost to them." She smiled. "There weren't that many, so they're treasured by Aggies."

Cash fired the ignition. "Like I said. Smooth."

10

He slapped the basketball and tossed it to her. "Game point."

He hadn't necessarily expected to beat the ex-UT player, but she was a point away from trouncing him. The score stood 9-3 in her favor and she had the ball. She was quick as a cat, her feints and lightning moves to the basket keeping Cash off-balance enough for her to make several easy layups. Even when he was able to keep her from driving, her jump shots usually found their mark. With his height advantage, Cash thought he might block a few of her shots, but her hands were always just out of reach. And his own shooting touch was rusty. Even when he was open the ball clanked off the rim more often than not. He had even thrown up an airball.

Hodge held the ball off to one side and crouched low. Cash kept his eyes glued to her waist, vowing not to fall for any feints this time. She faked a move to the basket, then jerked her arms upward as if to shoot. Cash started to leap. He caught himself, but Hodge ducked low and flew past him. He turned just in time to see her lay the ball in to win the game.

Hodge chased down the ball. "Good game," she said.

"I don't know about that," Cash said with a laugh. "You slaughtered me."

"Your shots weren't falling. Your moves were good. Clearly, you know how to play."

"I guess."

She tossed him the ball. "One more?"

"I can't. Gabe and his wife are having me and Edie over for burgers. Why don't I call him and see if there's enough for one more?"

"Thanks, but my grandmother is making pot roast. If I don't show I'll never hear the end of it."

"Okay. Guess I'll see you tomorrow."

"We'll do this again, right?"

He turned and fired up a twenty-footer. It swished through the net. "You bet."

***

Cash stepped through the sliding door onto the patio with two ice-cold cans of Packsaddle IPA. He handed one to Santos. "How are the burgers coming?"

"Almost there," Santos said as he accepted the beer. He flipped one of the patties. Grease sizzled as it hit the flames. "How did it go with Keisha?"

"She slaughtered me ten to three."

"I meant on the job."

"She'll do fine. Did you know she speaks Spanish?"

"Yeah. To test her, I conducted most of the interview with her in Spanish. She stumbled a couple of times but she's pretty good."

"You could have told me."

"Why? Did you guys run into somebody who doesn't speak English?"

"No." Cash recalled the meeting with Jeanine. "When we were at the credit union, she wanted to ask all the questions."

"Did you let her?"

"Not at first. But Jeanine didn't want to talk." He made air quotes. "Privacy concerns. Then Keisha noticed a picture of the UT stadium on the wall and mentioned that her dad played there. After that, Jeanine wouldn't shut up. If Keisha hadn't been along, I wouldn't have learned squat."

Santos held up a finger, as if giving a lesson. "Maybe you should let her take the lead from now on."

"Very funny."

Santos' wife Katrina poked her head outside. She sported a bright red apron over thigh-length shorts and a striped tank top. Her jet-black hair glistened in the afternoon sun. "Everything's ready in here."

"Perfect timing," said Santos. He removed the burgers from the grill and slid them onto a plate. Cash followed him into the house.

Edie was already seated in the dining room. Cash dropped into the chair next to her and eyed the fresh salad, pinto beans, and steaming ears of corn laid out on the table. "This looks great."

"Thanks," Katrina said as she found a seat. "Dig in."

They filled their plates and began to eat. Katrina said, "Edie, Gabe tells me you're helping with his campaign."

"Correction," Santos said. "Edie *is* the campaign. Without her, I'd be dead in the water."

Edie said, "That's not entirely true. Your husband is a very good public speaker."

"That may be, but I'm definitely the underdog."

"That's where I think you're wrong. You're the incumbent. That alone gets you some votes."

"Not enough. You saw Eaton at the Firewheel. Everybody knows him. They were fawning on him like a movie star."

"Not everybody will act like that. People at the lunch knew him. I think I made a mistake in having you start there. Most of the folks in that club are the same ones who have been running things forever. People like Virgil Hall. They're resistant to change. Eaton looks to them like the same old comfortable candidate they've always voted for."

"Say it," said Santos. "He's white."

"Some people in this town will vote against you because of that."

"I know. I met one of them at the Rotary Club."

Edie took a deep breath. "I ran into Mitch Eaton after you left. He said he needed to talk to me about something."

Santos stopped eating. "What?"

"He asked me to run his campaign."

The long silence was broken by Cash. "What did you tell him?"

"I told him thanks, but no thanks." She cleared her throat. "Getting back to *your* campaign, Gabe, we need to broaden our vision. Try to appeal to voters outside the good old boy network."

"Like who?"

"Like people who aren't used to having a say in how things are done. Kids just out of high school. Old folks out in the country. Folks like Bernadette. I'll bet she's never seen the inside of a voting booth."

Cash winced at the mention of Bernadette. A foolish one-night stand with her over a year ago had resulted in the birth of his daughter Emma nine months later. Bernadette had expressed hostility toward him when she learned she was pregnant, refusing to involve him in her prenatal care visits and later resisting his efforts to see the child. She had softened lately but still required deft handling.

Santos said, "That's all well and good, but how do I convince them to vote for me?"

"Are you kidding? Sure, Eaton's family has been in the area for generations, but he left Noble County the minute he got out of high school. He went to Tulane, an expensive private school, then moved to Waco after graduation to eventually become CFO for the largest hospital in that town. He still golfs once a week at the ritziest country club in Central Texas."

"I see what you mean," he said with some bitterness. "He sounds like such a loser."

"What I'm saying is, he is not a person most people in this area can relate to. You, on the other hand, are a decorated army veteran and the hero who took down the worst criminal this county has ever seen while saving me, Cash, and Deke Conrad in the process. Why wouldn't people vote for you?"

"My only decoration was a Purple Heart."

"Even better. You were wounded in service to your country."

"She's got a point, Gabe," said Cash. "A lot of people didn't even know I was running and, thanks to Edie, I still got thirty-one percent of the vote."

Santos finished his ear of corn and reached for another. "All right. Just tell me what to do."

***

As Cash drove Edie home in his truck, he said, "Can you believe the nerve of that guy Eaton? Asking you to run his campaign right after Gabe's appearance. Sheesh, what a jerk."

Edie didn't respond.

"What did he say when you told him no?"

"I didn't tell him no." She spoke barely above a whisper.

Cash stared at her. "What do you mean?"

"Eyes on the road, please."

He reluctantly obeyed. "What the hell do you mean?"

"I told him I'd think about it."

"What is there to think about?"

"He said he'd pay me five hundred a week." She paused. "That's a lot of money."

"There are things more important than money."

"I didn't say I'd do it, just that I'd think about it."

Cash shook his head. "I can't believe it. Why did you lie at dinner?"

"I didn't see any point in telling Gabe."

"You saw no point in telling the guy whose campaign you're running that you might jump ship to help his opponent. Yeah, I don't see how that's relevant to Gabe."

"You don't have to be sarcastic."

They rode the rest of the way in silence. Cash kept his mouth shut, not wanting to say something he'd regret. He reached her house and turned into the driveway. As she opened her door, he tried to lighten the mood. "Good night."

Instead of responding, she got out and slammed the door shut. Cash watched her march to her front door and disappear inside. As he backed into the street, he found himself wondering how well he really knew this woman.

11

Kerrville had only a handful of coin shops. Cash printed out the list and assigned half of them to Hodge. Ten minutes later, she returned to the conference room and reported she had struck out. None of the shops she called had noticed a woman coming in monthly to sell gold coins.

"I'm oh for two," he said. "Have a seat while I call this last one."

He placed the call. A man answered on the third ring. "Frederick Family Coins. This is Peyton."

Cash gave his name and occupation before saying, "I've got a coin I'm trying to identify. On one side is Queen Elizabeth; on the other, a woman holding a trident."

"What's it made of?"

He studied the evidence bag containing the coin.

"It says that it's one ounce fine gold."

"That would be a Gold Britannia. They're made by the Royal Mint."

"So they're from England?"

"Yes."

"I'm in Pinyon. Why would they show up here?"

"It's a common coin with collectors. They're popular with people that want to convert cash into gold."

"What about the other way? Converting gold into cash?"

"That too. I buy them all the time."

Cash pictured Bonnie Hart trying to convince Jeanine Jarvis to accept a sack of the coins as a down payment. "Do you ever get people coming in with several to sell?"

"Sure."

"Does anybody come in regularly, say once a month?"

"As a matter of fact, a couple has been making those transactions every month like clockwork for at least a year."

"Where are they from?"

"I don't know. They never said."

"A married couple?"

"I don't think so. At least, they don't act like it. What's more, she always sells three coins, while he sells only one."

"What do they look like?"

The shop owner described them. The man could have been Ralph Spencer. The woman was definitely Bonnie Hart. "What about the first time they came in? Did she sell a larger quantity?"

"Yeah, that time she had a whole sack of them. I had to go down to the bank for that much cash. She came back the next day."

Everything was matching up. "Any idea when she'll be back?"

"I expect her tomorrow."

"One last question. How much are these coins worth?"

"Depends on the price of gold. These days, I'm paying around two thousand bucks an ounce."

"Thanks, Peyton." Cash ended the call. "What time is it?" he asked Hodge.

"Almost nine. Why?"

He rose. "We're going to Kerrville."

***

Peyton shoved his phone into a pants pocket and returned his attention to his customer. "Hmm," he said, taking another look at the Gold Britannia coin on the counter. "That was a deputy up in Noble County calling about Gold Britannia coins."

The customer, a man in his forties, said, "That's odd. What did he want?"

"He's looking for someone who sells them in bulk." Peyton picked up the coin. "I don't have much cash on hand today. Would Venmo be okay?"

"Sure."

Peyton pulled his phone back out and tapped the screen. "What's your name?"

"Eaton," said the man. "Mitch Eaton."

***

Conrad sighed as he entered another phone number on the spreadsheet. Santos had asked him to update the department phone directory from a handwritten list he gave him. Such tedious work strained his patience to the breaking point. He hadn't joined the force to work behind a desk. Of course, he hadn't joined intending to be shot, either, but that was a risk he had accepted when he took the job. Nevertheless, until Santos deemed him completely recovered from his surgery, he'd be stuck doing scut work.

The phone rang. Grateful for the interruption, Conrad picked up the receiver.

"Noble County sheriff's office."

"When are y'all gonna hire some white folks?" It was a man's voice.

"Excuse me?"

"Don't you know affirmative action is dead?"

The man hung up. Conrad stared at the receiver in disbelief. What was that about? Disgusted, he returned to his spreadsheet.

***

Edie was on her way out the door to go grocery shopping when her phone buzzed. Because it was a number she didn't recognize, she almost didn't answer it. Her friend Julie blocked incoming calls from numbers that weren't in her contacts. For Edie, though, an occasional call from out of the blue proved to be one she wouldn't have wanted to miss. She tapped the green circle to accept.

"Hello."

"Hey, Edie, this is Mitch."

She racked her brain for a Mitch and came up empty. "Who?"

"It's Mitch. Mitch Eaton."

"Sorry. What's up?"

"Are you ready to start?"

"Start?"

"Running my campaign. Six hundred a week."

She could feel herself softening. "I thought you said five."

He laughed. "Now it's six."

Edie ran the numbers through her head. The election was a month away, which meant taking the job would bring in an extra twenty-four hundred dollars. She could use that money.

Eaton said, "I thought we could meet at Chez Abby for supper and talk strategy. On me, of course."

She weakened a little more. "Chez Abby?"

That was the one nice restaurant in Pinyon. Serving steaks, seafood, fancy pasta, and more, it had tablecloths and dressed its servers in black. On weekend nights a professional musician from San Antonio entertained diners with background music played on a grand piano. It was a place she frequented only on special occasions. The prices ensured that.

"Yeah, Chez Abby. They serve a ribeye steak as big as your face."

Edie had been telling herself she hadn't yet decided whether to accept Eaton's offer but she knew in her heart what was the right choice. "I'm sorry, I have to say no." She paused. "I just can't."

"Are you sure? What if I said seven hundred?"

She sucked in a breath. Hurrying her words to prevent herself from changing her mind, she said, "That's very generous of you, but no."

Eaton allowed an expertly timed silence before he said, "I understand. But how about we meet for supper anyway? Strictly professional. We can go over some ground rules for our campaigns."

Should she accept? Saying yes meant a swanky dinner out with a single man, and a handsome one at that. It would essentially be a date. Could she do that? What about Cash? Well, what about him? She had made him no promises. Like Eaton, she was single, so what was the harm? Besides, this would be a professional meeting. As Gabe's campaign manager, she'd be interacting with men regularly. "Could it be tomorrow? I have a commitment already for tonight."

"Sure. I'll pick you up tomorrow at seven."

"There's no need for that. I can drive."

But he had already ended the call.

***

Still thrilled with the feel of his truck on the highway, Cash used the vehicle to drive to Kerrville. On the way, he mulled over what he had learned from the coin shop owner. A man and woman came to his shop once a month to sell Gold Britannia coins. The woman had to be Bonnie Hart. Was the man Ralph Spencer? Or did Bonnie have a husband? A boyfriend?

Hodge interrupted his thoughts. "Why are you spending your own money on gas? We could have taken a squad car."

"I like driving my truck. Besides, I don't want to show up in a squad car. We're going incognito."

"Why?"

He told Hodge about Bonnie Hart's refusal to speak to him at the poker club.

"Do you think we'll see her there?"

"I think there's a good chance. Her next payment is due tomorrow. She's never been late. And she always shows up right after the credit union opens. I'm guessing she sells the coins the day before the payment is due."

Hodge nodded. "You're in uniform. Won't she refuse to talk to you again?"

"She would, but I'm not going in. She'll be talking to you."

"I'm in uniform too."

"You won't be." He pointed to a plain blue T-shirt and pair of sweatpants on the seat. "Those are for you."

"How did you know my size?"

"You dunked over me, remember? I made an educated guess."

***

Frederick Family Coins occupied the storefront at one end of a strip mall anchored by a Goodwill store. The building stretched along the Junction Highway on the north side of Kerrville. Cash parked at the far end of the building, handed Hodge the T-shirt and sweatpants, and said, "I'll look the other way."

She laughed. "You know I once ripped my jersey off after a big win in front of three thousand fans at the Moody Center."

"I gotta start going to those games."

When she was changed, Cash said, "Go see if she's there already. If so, send me a text. If not, come on back."

Hodge exited the truck and headed toward the coin shop. Watching her, Cash replayed their recent one-on-one game in his mind. The blowout loss rankled him. He should have given her a better game. He was a good player, although not good enough to play for a Division I school. Nevertheless, he averaged twenty points a game during his senior year at Pinyon High. At Sam Houston State, he played in pick-up games with players on the school's team and held his own. Maybe he could install a basket at his house and work on his jump shot. But would that help? She had played for a national powerhouse.

Hodge returned. She had been gone for less than five minutes.

"Not there, eh?" Cash said.

"Except for the owner, the place was empty. I asked him if Bonnie Hart has been in yet and he said no."

"You shouldn't have done that."

"Why?"

"We're supposed to be incognito, remember?"

"To Bonnie Hart. Not the store owner."

"We don't know that yet."

"Well, shoot. Sorry about that."

"Don't worry about it."

He took out his wallet and removed a twenty-dollar bill. Handing it to her, he said, "I see a taco shop over there. Why don't you get us something to eat and I'll keep watch. If I see her, I'll call you. I'd go, but I don't want anyone to spot my uniform."

"What kind of taco do you want?"

"Whatever you get is fine. Chocolate milk to drink."

***

The tacos were good, shredded pork with cilantro, lime juice, and avocado. The taqueria didn't sell chocolate milk, so Cash had to make do with iced tea. When they were done, they took turns catching a quick nap.

By three o'clock, Cash was beginning to think Bonnie Hart would be a no-show. Maybe Jeanine had made a mistake. Maybe Hart had already paid for the month.

He sat up when a blue GMC Terrain pulled into a parking space in front of the shop. A woman with blonde hair got out. It was Hart. He nudged Hodge and said, "Showtime."

***

Entering the shop, Hodge paused to allow her eyes time to adjust to the light. Bonnie Hart was already at the counter talking to the owner. Hodge could hear their chatter. When the owner glanced at Hodge, she pretended to study a wall of coin proofs.

The owner said, "Where's your friend?"

"He's not here," said Bonnie.

"What happened? I thought you guys always come in together."

Instead of answering, Hart laid four gold coins on the glass counter. "How much?"

"You're in luck. Gold's up a little this month."

"Hundreds if you have them."

"I'll be right back."

The owner disappeared into a back room. Hodge wandered over to lean on the counter a few feet away from Hart. "What are you selling?"

"Just some coins." Her voice was flat.

"They must be valuable if he's paying you in hundreds."

"They're nothing special."

"I don't know," Hodge said with a laugh. "Hundreds sound pretty special to me."

Hart grunted and looked away. The shop owner came back with a stack of bills. He counted them out for Hart before slipping them into an envelope.

"Thanks." She turned to go.

"Wait a second," Hodge said.

"What is it?"

"That looks like a good investment. Where can you buy coins like that?"

She jerked her head toward the shop owner. "Try him."

"I mean in bulk. Say, maybe twenty or thirty of them."

Hart forced a smile. "I wouldn't know."

***

Back in the truck, Hodge told Cash what had happened. "She wouldn't tell me anything. You'd think somebody who's into coins would be happy to talk about them."

"That's the thing," said Cash. "I don't think she is into coins. I think she had a big stash of cash that she converted into gold."

"That doesn't sound normal."

"Some people believe gold is safer than currency. The value may fluctuate slightly, but it will never crash. Of course, there could be another reason."

"What's that?"

"She doesn't want it tied up in a bank account. For whatever reason, she wants to keep it fluid."

"So if she needed it in a hurry, she'd have it."

"Exactly. Plus, no one could track how much money she has."

"There's nothing illegal about that."

"No," said Cash, starting the engine. "But this woman lied to me about knowing Ralph Spencer. Not only that, for the past year she and Spencer have been selling coins together each month. Now he's dead. Doesn't that sound suspicious?"

"I guess it does. But where do we go from here?"

Cash pointed across the parking lot at Hart's blue Terrain pulling onto Junction Highway. "To the credit union with Bonnie Hart."

***

"This time you stay in the truck," Cash said as he eased into a parking lot on the Pinyon town square. The blue Terrain was parked in front of the credit union. "There's no need for her to know you're a deputy just yet."

"What do you expect to get out of her? Clearly, she's not going to tell you anything."

"I'm just looking to shake the tree a little and see if any nuts fall out."

"That statement is just begging for a punch line."

"I'll look forward to hearing it when I get back."

Cash ambled across the street. He found a spot next to the door and leaned against the building to wait.

A few minutes later, Hart emerged into the late afternoon sun, blinking and shielding her eyes. As she started toward her car, Cash intercepted her.

"Good afternoon, Bonnie. Did you get that mortgage payment in on time?"

She turned at the sound of his voice. As recognition set in, her eyes narrowed to slits. "I told you I don't talk to cops."

"Those coins are worth what, two grand each? Twenty-five hundred?"

"I don't know what you're talking about."

"I'll bet it really pissed you off to lose one in a poker game. You must have had a great hand."

"Like I told you, that guy was lucky as hell."

Cash stepped closer to her. "From what I understand, that guy appeared regularly with you at a coin shop in Kerrville."

"Are you following me?"

"I'm just looking for an explanation. Ralph Spencer had no job and no money. Where was he getting the cash to give to his girlfriend? For that matter, where did he get the cash to play poker? Then I find out he's been going to Kerrville once a month to sell a Gold Britannia coin just like the one he won from you."

She clicked her key fob to elicit a chirp from the Terrain.

"How about a quick chat at the Firewheel? I'll buy you supper."

"I've got somewhere to be."

"We could meet at your house tomorrow. You're out on Tannehill Road, right?"

"You know where I live?"

"I investigate things, Bonnie. It's not that hard to get an address."

She thought for a moment before nodding her head. "All right. Tomorrow, ten o'clock. How's that sound?"

"That sounds fine."

"After that, will you leave me alone?"

"Of course."

She opened the car door. "Don't be late."

12

Edie had invited Cash over for supper. On his way to her house, he drooled at the thought of the meal she was making. Her great-grandparents had emigrated from a small town in southern Germany in the 1920s. She hadn't known them but was close with her eighty-six-year-old grandmother. Oma had taught her several recipes, including jägerschnitzel, breaded pork cutlets smothered in mushroom gravy that Cash couldn't get enough of. Served with creamed spinach, red cabbage, and spätzle, or homemade egg noodles, jägerschnitzel fit his notion of the perfect meal. A bowl of spätzle alone would rate a nine out of ten in his book. It was even better with the six-pack of Bock-saddle beer set beside him on the seat. Leave it to Steve to come up with an idiotic name like Bock-saddle.

Cash pulled into Edie's driveway and killed the engine. Even now, weeks later, he shuddered at the memory of dodging bullets while Edie was forced into Clovis Ward's squad car. Minutes later, he faced off with Ward and his lackey Judd Noteboom at Griff Turner's house. Ward had planned to kill Cash and Edie there and make it look like Cash had returned to the Turner house to finish off his widow, Mia. Showing remarkable courage and resourcefulness, Edie freed herself from a pair of handcuffs, lunged at Ward, and punched him in the face. That gave Cash enough time to punch Noteboom before tangling with Ward. Cash got the upper hand but Noteboom recovered enough to grab his gun. Only the timely appearance by Santos prevented the corrupt deputy from opening fire.

Cash grabbed the beer and bounded into the house like a kid who had just smelled chocolate chip cookies in the oven. He paused as he entered the kitchen. Where was the wonderful aroma of the jägerschnitzel? Why wasn't Edie standing at the stove stirring the spätzle? For that matter, where was Edie?

"Edie?"

"In the den."

He stowed the beer in the refrigerator and followed her voice. She sat on the sofa holding a baby bottle in one hand. In her other, she cradled a baby.

"That's Emma," he said, scratching his head.

"I'm glad you recognize your own child."

"But ... what is she doing here?"

"Bernadette dropped her off. She had to go help Dr. Manor with an emergency dog surgery and her mother is out of town."

Cash dropped onto the sofa next to her. "Are we still having jägerschnitzel?"

"Sorry, no. I've had my hands full with Emma."

"Son of a gun. What are we having?"

"Leftover lemon chicken soup." She swatted his arm. "I thought you wanted to spend more time with your daughter."

"I do. It's just ... spätzle." He sighed and held out his arms. "Give her to me."

She handed the baby over. Cash snuggled her for a moment before cradling her in his lap and offering her the bottle. "Is this breast milk?"

"Yeah. You should be proud of Bernadette for having it ready. I know from experience it's not easy to plan ahead like that."

As the child suck down the milk, his heart fluttered. Getting Bernadette pregnant had been irresponsible of both of them, but now that Emma was here, he wouldn't change a thing.

Edie got up and disappeared into the kitchen. Cash called out, "I've been meaning to ask you, does Bonnie Hart ever eat at the Firewheel?" Edie had previously said she thought she had seen her around town.

He heard the clank of dishes and the sound of the microwave being started. Edie hollered, "Every now and then. She likes the Cajun chicken."

"Does she ever show up with anybody?"

Edie returned to the den and eased into the lounge chair. "I saw her once with a guy about her age. He had the biggest beard I've ever seen. Dressed like a biker. He rode up on a Harley. I could hear it coming from two blocks away."

"What's his name?"

"I don't know, but he ate like a horse. I tried chatting him up, like I do with all my customers, but he wasn't in the mood for small talk. The only thing I remember him saying was when I gave him his meal. He got the Cajun chicken, too. He took a bite and told Bonnie that Cajun chicken is better in Louisiana."

"That's what you get for ordering Cajun food in the Texas Hill Country."

***

Cash spent the night with Edie. He was relieved when Emma slept straight through until morning. The last time he watched her, she had kept him awake for hours with her crying. Edie's four-year-old son

Luke did wake them up once with a loud shout from his bedroom, but Edie quickly coaxed him back to sleep.

Cash was up by six-thirty. He dished himself a bowl of homemade muesli and sliced a banana into it. With the addition of milk and a handful of blueberries, it made for a filling breakfast.

Someone knocked at the front door. The mother, Bernadette.

"How did she do?" she said as she stepped into the house.

"Great. How was the surgery?"

"It went okay. Some fella's dog got a chicken bone stuck in its throat. It took a while, but Dr. Manor got it out and the dog was fine."

"Glad to hear it."

Edie sauntered in with Emma in her arms. "I put her things in the den. She's such a sweetheart."

"Thanks for taking care of her."

"Anytime. Right, Cash?"

The disappointment of the missed jägerschnitzel flashed through his mind. "Right. Absolutely. Anytime."

After Bernadette was gone, Cash returned to his breakfast. Edie followed him into the kitchen. "Are you going to work now?"

"If it's okay with you," Cash said, finishing the last few spoonfuls. "I need to brief Gabe on what Hodge and I did yesterday."

Edie picked up on the name right away. "Speaking of Hodge, I heard she kicked your butt on the basketball court."

"Has she been bragging?"

"No, Deke Conrad told me."

"It wasn't so bad."

"Ten to three? Right."

He busied himself with putting the bowl in the sink. He gave her a peck on the lips. "Have a great day."

He turned to leave but Edie put out her arm. "There's something I need to tell you."

"What?"

"I turned Eaton down."

He kissed her again. "I knew you would."

***

On the way to work, Cash basked in the warm feelings from the morning. He had long fantasized about casual breakfasts with Edie followed by a goodbye kiss as he left for work. This morning's experience had him yearning for more. Edie seemed to enjoy them as much as he did. Not that she seemed ready to make them a daily occurrence. She had her house in town and he lived out in the country. She had made it clear that, although their relationship was firing on all cylinders after a ten-year hiatus, she wasn't ready to make it permanent. If he was honest with himself, neither was he. But he was close.

Cash strolled into the department lobby excited about the prospect of sitting down later with Bonnie Hart. Something smoldered beneath the known facts surrounding Ralph Spencer's death. He was sure of it. Not that Hart was necessarily involved, but she was holding something back.

He braced himself for a flirtatious comment from Vicky but, when she caught his eye, she pointed toward the hall and said, "Somebody's waiting for you in the conference room."

"Who?"

"Some lady. I don't remember her name."

Wondering if Bonnie Hart had decided to meet him on his turf, Cash hurried down the hall into the conference room. He found not

Bonnie Hart, but Alissa Collins, the less-than grief-stricken girlfriend of Ralph Spencer. She sat stiff-backed in a chair at the conference table, her hands wrapped around a cup of coffee with bits of powdered creamer floating on the surface. The sour look on her face suggested that it wouldn't be a pleasant meeting.

"Alissa," Cash said, taking a seat across from her. "What can I do for you?"

"I want that coin."

"The gold coin I found on Ralph?"

"Yes. I looked up gold online. It's worth a lot of money."

"It's evidence. You'll get it back, but for now, I need to hold onto it."

She gave him a steely-eyed look. "What's it evidence for?"

Cash realized he had no good answer for her. What crime was he investigating? Besides, Frida Simmons had already photographed it and brushed it for fingerprints, finding only Ralph's. And with Ralph and his income out of the picture, the coin did indeed represent a significant chunk of change for Alissa and her children.

Cash thought about it. After all, what if Ralph Spencer had a will and she wasn't in it? That wouldn't be fair. The guy lives in her house for a year and doesn't leave her anything? On the other hand, the coin was official evidence. It was signed out to him. If it disappeared, he could be accused of theft. Furthermore, if Spencer did have a will, it might indicate that the coin now belonged to someone else. He couldn't take that chance. "You make a good point," he told Alissa. "But I can't let it go just yet. And I don't have it on me. It's in evidence storage." He took out his wallet, looked inside, and saw eighty dollars. He handed it to her. "Here, this is all I have."

She snatched the bills. "Thank you." The words sounded anything but thankful.

"I'm sorry."

"I'm sure you're heartbroken." She stood up. "By the way, this coffee tastes like shit."

13

Bonnie Hart caressed the big man's back and nudged him to one side. She blew a sharp breath. "Baby, that was fantastic."

Dennis Webb let out a satisfied moan and propped himself up on one elbow. "Bless the Lord for life's earthly pleasures." He fondled one of Bonnie's breasts. "If Delilah was only half as hot as you, I can see why she was able to trick Samson."

She stroked his beard. Some women complained about their men's facial hair. Bonnie didn't understand that. She found Dennis' bushy face sexy. She loved it when he nestled it into her neck during the act. "I've been meaning to tell you something."

"What?" His breath blew hot on her cheeks.

"Do you remember that sheriff's deputy I told you about?"

"The one Emmett found snooping around the trailer? What about him?"

"He's coming to the house this morning."

Webb jerked upright. "What? Why?"

"The guy followed me to Kerrville. I thought if I got him out here and answered his questions, maybe he'd leave me alone."

"How stupid can you be?"

"Don't get all bent out of shape. He's just curious about the coin he found on Ralph."

"You shouldn't be talking to him."

"News flash, Dennis. Stonewalling didn't work. Now it's time to sweet-talk the man until he goes away."

"Goddammit, woman!" Webb looked up at the ceiling. "Forgive me, Lord." Then he returned his attention to Bonnie. "This is what happens when you don't listen to me."

Now it was her turn to be angry. "What are you talking about?"

"I told you not to carry those coins around with you. If you hadn't lost one in a poker game, this wouldn't be happening."

"And if you hadn't panicked back in Louisiana, I wouldn't be playing poker in a shithole like Pinyon, Texas."

"Watch your language."

"Watch your own."

He slapped her. She reacted as she always did, with an icy glare.

"Baby, I'm sorry," he said, hanging his head.

"One of these days, saying sorry won't be enough. You know that, right?"

"I do. I'm so sorry. It won't happen again."

Knowing the effect this would have, she got out of bed and stood naked before him. "You see this, right? You want it again, don't you?"

"I do."

"Then stop acting like an asshole."

He heaved a sigh.

Sliding into his lap and kissing him she felt his developing erection press against her leg. She lifted his hand to her breast. "How about another round?"

Moaning, Webb dropped back onto the pillow. "Thank you, Lord, for this bounteous day."

***

Cash had just left the conference room when Santos called out from his office. "Is that you?"

"Yeah."

"Can I have a second?"

Cash reversed direction and stepped into the office. Lowering himself into a chair, he said, "What's up?"

"That was Ralph Spencer's girlfriend, wasn't it?"

"Yes."

"It's time to let that go."

"I didn't invite her here. She came to see me."

"I know. Now it's time to move on. Unless you know something you haven't told me."

"There's nothing new. But I was heading out to see Bonnie Hart just now."

Santos was reaching the end of his patience. "You're kidding, right?"

"Come on, Gabe. She asked me to come." Technically, that was true.

"And I'm asking you not to go."

"Why?"

"We're stretched thin. You're wasting your time."

"I'll tell you what. If I don't learn anything out there today, I'll put it to rest. How's that?"

Santos leaned back and studied Cash long enough to make him feel uneasy. With a rap of his knuckles on the desk, he stood up. "Deal."

***

Conrad was stumped. His streak of solving the daily Wordle had reached seventeen days but, with only one guess remaining, he might not make it to day eighteen. He lacked only one letter, but he had two possibilities to choose from. Which word was more likely, stone or shone?

He entered "stone" and emitted a soft whoop when the T turned green. Success! Eighteen days in a row!

The phone rang. "Noble County sheriff's department," Conrad said into the receiver.

"I'm still waiting," a man said. The whirring of a power tool in the background made it hard to hear his voice.

"For what?"

"For more white faces on the damn force." The whirring stopped. A different voice said, "Hey, Virgil, come take a look at this."

"Who is this?" said Conrad.

The line went dead.

***

On the drive to Bonnie Hart's place, Cash reviewed what he knew so far. He had to admit it wasn't much. Ralph Spencer, an unemployed man whose only known income stemmed from the theft of diesel fuel, died in an apparent accidental explosion while pumping gas. In his pocket was a Gold Britannia coin worth over two thousand dollars. He won the coin in a poker game with Bonnie Hart. Hart tried to make a down payment on her property with a sack of similar coins. That was declined, so she was traveling monthly to a coin shop in Kerrville to sell enough coins to pay the mortgage. According to the shop owner, she usually showed up accompanied by a man fitting Ralph Spencer's description. Both Spencer and Hart were relative newcomers to Noble County, having arrived about a year ago. Spencer showed up with Louisiana plates on his truck. And Spencer's friend Emmett Fuller was reluctant to talk about him.

What was the common thread that could explain these seemingly unrelated facts? How did Hart and Ralph Spencer know each other? Where and how did Bonnie get the coins? How did Emmett Fuller fit in?

Maybe Santos was right. Maybe nothing was going on. At least nothing that concerned the Noble County sheriff's office. If that was the case, he could at least give that coin to Alissa Collins. Assuming Spencer didn't have a will that ordered otherwise.

Cash followed the instructions from his GPS and took Tannehill Road for 7.4 miles before pulling into a turnoff blocked by an electric farm gate. The gate looked new. Sunlight reflected off the gleaming aluminum bars directly into Cash's eyes, causing him to squint. He edged the truck closer and the reflection disappeared, allowing him to see a pole-mounted keypad. Next to it was a speaker, beneath which was a call button. Cash pushed it.

"Is that you, Deputy?" For the first time since he had met Bonnie Hart, her voice sounded friendly.

"Yes, ma'am."

"Come on up. Just follow the road to the house."

The speaker buzzed and the gate swung open in a slow arc. Cash drove along a weedy granite gravel road through a pasture dotted with prickly pear and immature cedar trees. The trees were tall and thick enough to limit his view to no more than fifty feet. He passed a barn and a full stock pond. A four-foot chain-link fence surrounded the latter, a precaution Cash had never seen before. Why would anyone enclose a stock pond? How were the livestock supposed to reach the water? Fifty yards farther on, he arrived at the house.

The house was a modest pale blue frame building with an unpainted metal roof. What could at one time have been well-tended flower beds along the front were now choked with weeds. The structure looked to be a hundred years old. There was no garage. He spotted Hart's blue Terrain beneath an unattached carport. Parked behind it was a cherry red Harley Road Glide motorcycle. As Cash got out of the squad car, Hart opened the front door and stepped outside. She wore jeans and a tight-fitting blouse that seemed designed to distract.

"Hello, Deputy."

"Good morning, Ms. Hart."

"Call me Bonnie. Won't you come in?"

Cash gestured at the Harley. "Do you ride?"

"That's my husband's. He's anxious to meet you."

She ushered him into a cozy den of rustic cedar furniture and cowboy-themed artwork. It reminded him of his own house.

"Have a seat. Can I get you something to drink? I made mimosas."

"No, thank you."

"Come on, it's mostly orange juice."

Cash eased into a leather lounge chair. "Okay. A small one."

She disappeared through a doorway and reappeared moments later with a drink in each hand. Giving one to Cash, she sat on a couch opposite and sipped hers. "I find these refreshing, don't you?"

"Yes, ma'am." Catching her disapproving look, he said, "Bonnie."

"So, what can I do for you?"

Cash set his drink on a coaster showing the Alamo. "I'm just trying to understand something. Why would someone try to make a down payment on a house with Gold Britannia coins?"

Her smile faded. "What's it to you?"

Before he could answer, Cash heard a noise and turned to see a giant of a man, his huge frame barely clearing the doorway, enter the room. As the newcomer ambled by the furniture in the small den, he reminded Cash of a tank rumbling past a row of jeeps. An enormous salt-and-pepper beard couldn't hide his dark scowl. He wore pressed jeans and a Texas Longhorns polo shirt big enough to shelter an elephant. Heavy ostrich boots clomped on the pine floor until he stopped next to Bonnie.

"Deputy, this is my husband, Dennis Webb."

Cash rose and reached out for a handshake. The big man's meaty paw seemed to swallow Cash's arm up to the elbow. His iron grip squeezed his hand like a steel clamp.

"What are you doing here, Deputy?" Webb asked gruffly.

"Don't be rude, Dennis," said Bonnie. "Why don't we all sit down?"

With a huff, Webb eased himself onto the couch to sit beside Bonnie. Cash returned to his seat in the lounge chair.

Bonnie said, "The deputy was just asking why I might have tried to make a down payment on a house with gold coins." She looked at Cash. "It's simple, really. We don't trust banks. Not with the way this country's been going lately. Look what happened to Silicon Valley Bank. The people that had accounts there are lucky they didn't lose everything. That's not going to happen to us. We like to keep our assets within easy reach."

"I see." It was a logical, if extreme explanation. "What was your relationship with Ralph Spencer?"

"I didn't have one."

"The coin shop owner said Ralph came to the shop with you each month."

"He's mistaken. That was Dennis."

Cash knew she was lying. The coin shop owner had described Hart's companion as clean-shaven. Cash doubted that anyone could miss what looked like a small furry animal wrapped around Webb's face.

"How long have you lived in Noble County?"

"About a year."

"Where did you live before that?"

Bonnie glanced at her husband, but his eyes remained fixed on Cash.

"Was it Louisiana?"

Webb said, "What makes you think that?"

"Ralph Spencer was from Louisiana. At least that's what Alissa Collins said."

"What else did she tell you?"

"Not much. Did you know Ralph back in Louisiana?" When Webb didn't answer, he added, "He had Louisiana license plates on his truck when he got here. That's how Alissa knew where he was from."

"We weren't exactly close friends."

"But you knew him, right?"

After a moment's hesitation, Webb nodded yes, his beard swaying like a sage bush in a windstorm.

"How did you meet him?"

"Bonnie met Alissa somewhere." Webb looked at his wife. "The grocery store, right, hon?"

"That's right."

"Alissa mentioned her boyfriend liked fishing, so I gave him a call. He took me to Lake Amistad a time or two. "

"Do you two know Emmett Fuller?"

Webb shook his head but Bonnie said, "Yes." Catching the confused look on Cash's face, she added, "Don't you remember, baby?

That's Ralph's friend. The one who went fishing with you that time at Amistad."

"Oh, right. You should have seen the bass he caught. That son of a gun was longer than your arm."

Cash didn't believe a word of this fable. "Was Alissa okay with Ralph going fishing with Emmett Fuller?"

"Why wouldn't she be?" said Webb.

"She doesn't seem to like him very much."

"I wouldn't know anything about that."

"She called him a liar. Said he told her kids he has a friend with a pet alligator."

Webb slapped his thigh and uttered what might have been a laugh. "Come with me. I want to show you something."

Cash followed Webb to a utility room, empty save for a refrigerator in the corner. From it, Webb pulled out a plastic bag filled with something large and heavy. Motioning for Cash to follow, he walked back through the den and out the front door.

Outside, Cash had to work to keep up with Webb's long strides. They marched toward the barn, but at the last second Webb veered off to the stock pond. Cash again was struck by the fence encircling it. Webb opened the gate and stopped to wait for Cash. Once he caught up, Webb waded through knee-high grass to reach the water's edge. "Come on up here. You can't see it from back there."

"See what?" This was all pretty strange.

"Just wait a minute."

Cash watched the water. He saw nothing out of the ordinary.

Webb pointed. "There it is."

This time Cash noticed a small ripple in the water. A pair of eyes poked above the surface. "That's an alligator."

"That's Bonnie's pet, Jeremiah. Like the bullfrog."

"How'd you get an alligator all the way here from Louisiana?"

"I never said I was from Louisiana."

"You never denied it, either."

Webb fixed Cash with a glare. "I used a trailer. The same one I pulled my Harley on."

"I saw that in the driveway. That's a damned fine bike."

Webb held up a finger. "Let there be no filthiness nor foolish talk. Ephesians."

Cash said nothing. Was the guy kidding?

The alligator drifted toward them. "Now here's the fun part," said Webb. He took two steps back. The reptile reached the water's edge and crawled up onto land. Webb stepped back again. He reached into the plastic bag and came out with a frozen chicken. Without warning, he tossed it at Cash's feet. Cash scrambled backward as the giant reptile lunged. After snatching the meat in its jaws, it tilted its head back and swallowed the chicken whole.

Webb broke out laughing. "Man, I thought you were gonna wet your pants."

His heart racing, Cash said, "Yeah, that was unexpected." He watched the animal slide back into the water. "What happens if that tank dries up?"

"It won't. It's hooked up to the well. If it gets too low, the pump kicks in."

"And you've got a permit from Parks and Wildlife?"

"I do. Want to see it? It's back at the house."

Cash waved him off and started toward the squad car. "Have a good day, Mr. Webb. Tell your wife thanks for the drink."

***

Eaton picked Edie up in a black Tesla Model S, which he was quick to point out was the most powerful Tesla available. "I test-drove a Model X, but it didn't have the oomph of this one, even though it costs more."

"I drive a Prius. It has plenty of pickup."

"Apples and oranges, Edie," he said with a laugh.

He laughed again when Edie flinched as he opened the falcon wing doors. "Right out of *Star Wars*," he said.

"Why have doors like that?"

"They require less space to open. Makes parking a lot easier."

Edie never had difficulty parking in Pinyon. "If you say so."

The restaurant was mostly empty as they entered. "Guess I didn't need reservations," Eaton said. The host guided them to a table by the window that looked out on the town square. As Edie studied the menu, Eaton called a server over and ordered a bottle of wine. When the server left, he said, "You'll love this one. It's a pinot from Willamette Valley."

"I don't drink."

Eaton's eyes went wide. "I'm so sorry. I should have asked." He raised a hand. "I'll cancel it."

"Don't," Edie said. "I was pulling your leg."

He grinned. "You're a sly one, aren't you?"

The server returned with the wine and poured a taste for Eaton. He nodded regally. "This will do." The server poured two glasses and took their orders. Eaton asked for the ribeye steak, cooked medium rare. Edie went with the salmon. When they were alone, Eaton said, "You know why I always get the steak?"

"It tastes good?"

"No. It's because that beef is raised right here in Noble County. There aren't a lot of salmon in the Nolina River. Who knows where it comes from?"

Edie sipped her wine. "That is good." She set the glass down, folded her hands together, and looked Eaton in the eye. "So, shall we go over the ground rules?"

"Excuse me?"

"Of our campaigns. You said you wanted to take me to dinner and go over the ground rules."

"Oh, that." An impish grin spread across his face. "There's no need. I trust you to be fair. I just wanted to get to know you better."

"So you don't want to discuss the race?"

"Come on, now. Do you think Santos really has a chance?"

A pit formed in Edie's stomach. What was going on here? "Of course I do. I wouldn't be in this if I didn't."

He smiled again. "I admire your optimism."

"You don't think the incumbent can win?"

Eaton leaned in closer and lowered his voice. "How many Mexicans do you see in county government?"

"He's not Mexican. He's American."

"Okay, how many Hispanic Americans do you see in county government?"

She knew the answer but didn't want to say it. "None except for the sheriff."

"Exactly." Noticing the look of disgust on her face, he added. "Don't get me wrong. I'm no racist. Hell, if I wasn't running myself I might vote for him. It's just…" He gestured vaguely at the other diners, all of whom were white. "Who do you think they'll vote for?"

"I think they'll vote for the best candidate."

"No," he said with a head shake. "I grew up here. I know these people. They'll vote for who they *think* is the best candidate. That will be somebody who looks like them." He paused. "Somebody like me."

Edie wanted to reach across the table and slap the smirk off his face. Yet before she could do anything she would later regret, the food came. Scowling, she picked up her fork and attacked the salmon.

They were partway through when Eaton suddenly stood up. "Well, hello there." Edie turned around to see Keisha Hodge "What a nice surprise seeing you here," Eaton said. "Are you here to eat? The steak is fantastic."

"No," said Hodge. She held up an empty casserole dish. "My grandmother asked me to return this to one of the cooks. She borrowed it last week."

"Oh."

Hodge and Edie made eye contact. An awkward moment passed. Hodge said, "I better go. Nice seeing you both."

The rest of the meal passed uneventfully. Edie tried to suppress her anger at Eaton's smugness and racist assumptions about Noble County as talk drifted to other, less confrontational topics. She had to admit that the man was a good conversationalist: funny, witty, charming even. As for looks, his score on the eye candy scale was just fine. Was he more handsome than Cash? She preferred not to think about that.

As they left the restaurant, Edie said, "I can walk home. It's not far."

"Nonsense," said Eaton. "That would be ungallant of me."

At the house, he insisted on walking her to the door. She put out a hand for a shake and said, "Thank you for the meal."

Flashing another of his beautiful smiles, he said, "That won't do." He put his hands on her shoulders, leaned in, and kissed her on the lips. "Thank you for sharing your evening with me. I had a lovely time." Before she could say anything, he spun around and marched to his car.

Too stunned to move, Edie watched his taillights fade into the distance. She should have slapped him, or at least told him off. But for what? She could have pulled back at his approach. Instead, if she was honest with herself, she had remained rooted to the ground, had even puckered her lips when he kissed her. It wasn't a kiss for the ages, but it left her feeling guilty for wanting more. It also seemed to confirm what he told her at dinner. Stacked up against Eaton's charm, good looks, and yes, ethnicity, Santos had no chance.

14

The little boy pointed. "Mommy, horses!"

Edie patted her son's head. "Yes, look at them. Aren't they pretty?"

They stood on the sidewalk in front of the Firewheel Cafe, a perfect place to watch the Noble County Fourth of July parade. Dozens of people clustered around them, all vying for a view. Cash patrolled the street, on the alert for anyone, adult or child, careless enough to attempt crossing at the wrong time. Hodge and Conrad watched the other side of the square. This was Conrad's first assignment away from his desk since being shot by Clovis Ward.

Following tradition, the Noble County sheriff rode at the head of the parade. Mounted on a chestnut horse borrowed from a local rancher, Santos looked the part of a Texas lawman with his gleaming sheriff's badge and white Stetson hat. People cheered as he waved at the crowd.

Riding just behind Santos were the color bearers, Fred Uecker and his colleague on the county commissioner's court, Peggy Galloway. Uecker carried an American flag, Galloway the lone star banner of Texas. Uecker, who had grown up in a Dallas suburb, appeared stiff on his horse. Galloway, a Pinyon native, rode with the confidence of a woman born in the saddle.

Cash caught Luke's eye and waved. Since re-establishing a relationship with Edie, he had grown fond of the boy and did what he could to put the child at ease around him. The effort seemed to be working, as Luke's face lit up when he recognized Cash. The boy tugged Edie's arm and pointed. Mother and son waved.

A series of floats inched past. First came an organization of elderly women known as the Silver Cowgirls, riding in a trailer decorated with hay bales and red, white, and blue bunting. Each cowgirl sported chaps and a pink cowgirl hat trimmed with fuzz. Children dashed into the street to pick up the candy the women tossed at them.

Behind the Cowgirls came Packsaddle Brewing. Steve, owner of the brewery, stood in the back of his antique 1963 Ford pickup truck. Steve had purchased the bright red vehicle just two weeks ago for the specific purpose of using it in the parade. Cash recognized the two women in the truck bed with Steve as servers at the brewpub. The three of them wielded large squirt guns, which they loaded from a barrel labeled "Beer" and shot into the crowd. Steve spotted Cash and nailed him across the chest. Everyone laughed, Cash included.

Next was Avi Rao driving his vintage Ford Mustang with the top down. Avi's wife rode beside him, their two young children in the back. Each child held an American flag aloft.

The crowd roared as a powder blue vintage Cadillac convertible rounded the corner. Driven by a young man wearing an enormous cowboy hat, the vehicle bore a banner hanging along its length that read, "Eaton for Sheriff!" Waving a hat even larger than the driver's, Mitch Eaton rode in the front passenger seat. Riding in the back seat were two beautiful women decked out in white gloves and sequined red, white, and blue blouses.

The Cadillac stopped and Eaton stepped onto the pavement. Shouting through a megaphone, he said, "God bless Noble County! God bless the USA!" Loud cheers erupted from the crowd. The women in the Cadillac tossed full-sized candy bars into the street triggering a mad rush of children. Eaton raised his hat over his head and shouted, "I'm Mitch Eaton and my only aim is to serve you, the wonderful people of Noble County!"

Cash approached the Cadillac. Cupping his hands and yelling to be heard over the crowd, he said, "Let's keep things moving."

Eaton held a hand to his ear. "Sorry, what?"

"Back in your car, please. You're blocking the parade."

Eaton grinned. "Is that any way to talk to your future boss?"

Cash shrugged and waved his hand to move him along. With a departing wave, Eaton climbed back into the Caddy and nodded at the driver. The car resumed its previous crawl up the street.

Irritated by Eaton's showmanship, Cash strolled to the other end of the block. As a county employee, he had to maintain a neutral stance in public, but he shuddered at the thought of working for Mitch Eaton. Surely Santos, with Edie's help, would be able to hold onto his position.

***

Across the square, Conrad spotted the man he wanted to see. He sidled up to him and said, "Hey, Virgil. Can I have a word?"

Virgil Hall turned in surprise. "Hey, Deke. Sure."

They stepped back from the parade crowd. Conrad said, "I've been wanting to talk to someone about some ideas I have. I saw you and thought, there's a community leader. He could get things done."

Virgil's face brightened. "If I can help, I'm glad to do it."

"It's about the makeup of the force. I don't know if you've noticed, but we now have a Black deputy and a Mexican sheriff."

"I have noticed." He lowered his voice. "It's a little too woke for me."

"Somebody ought to do something about it."

"I'll let you in on a secret," said Virgil. "I've been calling the department to give them a piece of my mind."

"Who did you talk to?"

"Mostly that dimwit secretary. The last two times, though, it was some guy."

"That was me."

Virgil smiled. "It's good to know my words didn't fall on deaf ears."

"I heard you loud and clear. And let me tell you something." He leaned in close. "If I hear of any more such calls, I will post your picture all over town as the asshole making anonymous racist calls to our public servants. Got it?"

Virgil stepped back, a shocked look on his face.

Conrad said, "Enjoy the parade."

***

Cash's phone buzzed. He slipped it from his pocket and held it to his ear. Thinking it would be Edie, he said, "Great parade, isn't it?"

"Yes, very nice. Why haven't you been answering your phone?" It was Hodge.

Cash glanced at his phone screen and saw he had missed three calls, all from the department's after-hours dispatcher. "Sorry, I guess I didn't feel it buzzing in my pocket. What's up?"

She said something he couldn't understand before adding, "We've got to get out there."

"Out where?"

"Alissa Collins' house."

"What's going on?"

"She's missing."

***

Cash dragged his feet as he approached Alissa Collins' house. He dreaded the thought of talking to her children. If breaking the news of Ralph Spencer's death to Alissa had been an awful task, questioning her children about their mother's disappearance was even worse. Let inside, he and Hodge found them on the den sofa, their cheeks wet with tears. Sitting next to them was the elderly woman who had greeted them.

"Deputies, I'm Gail Ramsey. I live in the house next door."

"I'm Deputy Cash." He nodded at his partner. "This is Deputy Hodge."

"Pleased to meet you."

Cash said, "Are you the one who discovered that Ms. Collins is missing?"

"Yes."

"Can you tell us what happened?"

"I was out in my yard pulling weeds when I heard screaming. It seemed to be coming from here, so I walked over to check it out. The front door was open. The children were locked in the closet, poor things. When I let them out, they said a man had taken their mother away."

"Could she have gone with him willingly?"

She shook her head. "No. She never left those children alone. Once when I wanted to show her my rose bushes, she fetched them out of the house first to come with her."

Cash was puzzled by one detail. "Where is your house? I didn't see any others as I drove in."

"I'm on the other side of the cedar trees there along the driveway. You can't see it from here but my house is about a hundred feet beyond."

"Did you see the man she left with?"

"No. A white sedan was turning onto the road when I came through the trees, but I couldn't see the license plate."

"Could you see the driver?"

"No."

"How about the make and model of the car?"

"I don't know much about cars." She hung her head. "I'm sorry. I know I'm not being very helpful."

"There's no need to apologize. You've given us something to go on. Have you seen anyone else visit the house recently?"

"Come to think of it, I have. Terry Moreno came by the day after that truck blew up at the gas station. I also saw him here about two weeks ago."

"Why would Terry Moreno come visit?"

"I don't know."

Have the children said anything yet?"

"No."

Cash turned to Hodge. "Take a look around the house while I talk to them."

She nodded and headed toward the kitchen.

The boy was maybe six years old, and Cash squatted beside him. "What's your name?"

The child didn't look up. "Isaiah."

"Isaiah, I'm so sorry that your mother is missing. I want to find her as quick as I can so she can come home to you and your sister. Do you understand?"

He nodded.

"Can you tell me what happened?"

"Me and Ginny were watching TV. I heard Mommy talking to somebody in the other room."

"Was it a man or a woman?"

"A man."

"Did they sound mad at each other?"

The child shrank back at that idea. "I don't know."

"Did you hear what they said?"

"No."

Cash tried the girl. "What about you, Ginny? Did you hear anything?"

The girl shook her head.

Shifting his attention back to Isaiah, Cash said, "What happened then?"

"Mommy came in and told us to get in the closet. She said we were going to play hide-and-seek and that we'd be it. We were supposed to count to a hundred."

"And did you count?"

"Uh-huh. Then I tried to open the door, but I couldn't." More tears flooded the boy's eyes. "I got scared."

Mrs. Ramsey said sternly, "I found a chair wedged under the doorknob. That's why they couldn't get out."

Cash patted Isaiah's knee and stood.

Hodge returned, holding up a cell phone in a gloved hand. "Does this belong to your mother?"

The boy nodded.

Signaling for Hodge to follow, Cash led the way outside.

"What do you think?" he said.

"I think she was kidnapped."

"I agree, but why her? Look at this place. She doesn't have anything a kidnapper would want."

"I don't know."

"It's too bad she left her phone. We could have used it to track her."

"I don't think she forgot it," Hodge pointed out. "Whoever took her wouldn't let her bring it."

"You're probably right." Cash wiped the sweat from his brow. "It's awfully coincidental that this happens only a week after her boyfriend's death."

"Tell me, who's Terry Moreno?" Hodge asked.

Cash explained about the poker club owner.

"I wonder why he was here," she said. "Not once, but twice."

Were more gold coins involved? "We need to find out."

"If she has no money, why would anybody take her?"

"I can think of only one reason."

She asked, "What's that?" although it looked like she already knew the answer.

"They're not after a ransom. They mean to kill her."

"Who means to kill her?" Mrs. Ramsey, who had just stepped outside, asked in alarm.

Cash said, "Right now, we don't know that anyone is trying to kill her. We're just throwing ideas around."

"You frightened me. Poor Alissa." She paused. "Tell me, what will happen to the children?"

"We'll notify the Child Protection and Family Advocacy Board. They'll find a temporary home for them until something more permanent can be arranged."

"You mean until you find their mother."

"Of course."

***

They left the Collins children with Gail Ramsey and drove to the square. The parade had ended and the crowd had thinned out. Stepping out of the car, Cash spotted Deke Conrad holding his side on a bench in front of Star of Texas Thrift Shop. He waved, "Are you okay?"

"I'm fine. Just a little tired."

"You look wiped. Go home and take a nap."

Conrad stood up. "I might do that."

When Conrad was gone, Hodge said, "He didn't look so good."

"No, he didn't. I don't think he's fully recovered yet from being shot." He gestured at the antique store. "Let's go find Moreno."

They entered the store and greeted the owner, Sadie Billings. "Is Moreno in back?" Cash said.

"Yeah. He just got in."

They found Moreno in his club sipping a beer and watching a baseball game on TV. Cash introduced Hodge and said, "What have you been up to today?"

Moreno squinted. "You didn't come here just to be social. What's going on?"

"Alissa Collins is missing." Cash looked close for a reaction, but saw none. "Her neighbor saw you there a few days ago."

"Do you think I took her?"

"I'm not saying that. Can you tell us where you were this morning?"

"At my house."

"Is there anyone who can vouch for that?"

"No, I was by myself. Cleaning bathrooms."

Cash said, "What kind of vehicle do you drive?"

"A Toyota Corolla. I've got an old pickup, too."

"What color is the Corolla?"

"Gray. Look, Cash, you're scaring me. Am I a suspect here?"

"Mr. Moreno, we're just doing our job. One last question. Why were you at Alissa's house?"

"I heard about her boyfriend's death. I went there to offer my condolences."

"You were there a couple of weeks ago, too," said Hodge.

Moreno's eyes darted back and forth between Cash and Hodge. "If you must know, we dated for a while. She broke it off when she met that Spencer guy. I wanted to see if they were still together."

"Was it an amicable parting?" Cash asked.

Moreno scoffed. "As amicable as getting dumped can be."

"Okay, thank you. That's all for now." Motioning for Hodge to follow, Cash turned to leave.

"Hey, Cash."

"Yeah?"

"I would never hurt her."

Cash nodded. "I never said you would."

***

Alissa Collins stared at the man with fear in her eyes. Correctly interpreting her look of terror, the man said, "Listen, Alissa, everything will be all right. I just want to ask you some questions, and then I'll take you back home."

The man was lying. He told himself he lied out of concern for the kidnapped woman's feelings. But he knew that was also a lie. He also knew the poor woman had done nothing wrong and didn't deserve what was coming.

Alissa blinked in the relative darkness of the barn and said, "I don't know why you couldn't just ask me your questions at my house." Her voice trembled.

"Relax. This won't take long. We'll have you home in time for supper."

The man closed the barn door. He led Alissa to a rickety round table in one corner. Nearby was a sink, a refrigerator, and a countertop holding a microwave oven. Beyond was a small workbench covered with tools. The man had Alissa sit at the table. As he studied her face, he couldn't help admiring her. What a remarkably pretty woman she was. High cheekbones, smooth skin, full lips, well-proportioned figure. How an ugly bastard like Ralph Spencer had scored her he had no idea. A pit formed in his stomach as he thought again of her fate.

"All right," Alissa said, "what do you want to know?"

The man sighed and spread his hands on the table. "Want something to eat?"

She wasn't hungry, so he launched his interrogation. He asked a series of questions, none of which elicited satisfactory answers. He got up and came around the table. "You're not being truthful."

"I am. That's everything I know."

He hit her with his fist. Not too hard, just enough to rattle her teeth and draw a drop of blood from her lip.

"Tell me the truth, damn it!" Her wide-eyed look reminded the man of a deer he had once shot and watched die. He hit her again and demanded the truth.

"I'm telling you everything I know!" She was shrieking now. Tears spilled onto her cheeks and a thin trickle of blood ran from one nostril.

The man figured she was telling the truth. She had to be. Why would she endure a beating without spilling her guts about a dead man? Poor woman. One of his employers said if she didn't know anything to take her back to the house. But that would never work. They had kidnapped her and bloodied her face. She'd go straight to the sheriff if they let her go.

The man pulled a box of tissues from the Camry and handed it to Alissa. "Here, wipe your nose."

She did so and then turned watery eyes on him. "Can I go home now?" she said through her tears. "I won't say anything about this. I swear."

The man stuck a finger under her chin and lifted it to study her face. He took the tissue from her. "You missed a spot." He wiped the blood off and pointed at an ice chest beneath the workbench. "There's food and water in there. Gesturing at a door at the rear of the barn, he said, "There's a toilet in there." He strode toward a side door.

"What are you doing?" she said, her voice choking. "You can't leave me here."

The man turned. "If I hear you scream, I'll come back. You don't want that."

15

The morning meetings held by Santos had become social gatherings. Someone, usually Deke Conrad, would show up with donuts or kolaches. Cash once brought an electric skillet to make migas for the group. Everyone brought a cup of coffee. Jokes and stories flew. They might discuss someone's favorite television show or last night's football game. If conversation lagged, Cash had photos of Emma at the ready.

This morning started no different. Conrad, the last to arrive, was still limping to a chair with a box of donuts when Santos said, "Congratulations are in order for Deputy Conrad for cracking the anonymous caller case. Deke, care to fill them in?"

Conrad told them about his conversation with Virgil Hall on the courthouse square.

Santos said, "Good work, Deke. I think we've heard the last from Mr. Hall. All right, on to more serious business. A woman is missing. Cash, bring us up to speed."

Cash filled them in on what he and Hodge had learned.

"What did Moreno have to say?" Santos asked.

"He said he was home all morning. He used to date Alissa and was evidently trying to get back with her. That's why he went to her house. Also, he drives a Toyota Corolla but it's gray, not white."

"Can anyone back up his story about this morning?"

"No."

Santos said, "Any other suspects?"

"No."

"Okay, so we know she left with a man in a white sedan. Moreno's car is gray, but maybe it looked white to Gail Collins."

"Could we search his car?" Conrad asked.

"I'll draw up a warrant for Judge Mixon but I'm not optimistic. We have nothing connecting him to the disappearance."

"Can I make a suggestion?" said Hodge.

"Go ahead."

"We could go through all the vehicles registered in the county and pull the white sedans."

Conrad scoffed. "Do you know how long that list would be?"

"The population of Noble County is only about three thousand. Not all of those people own vehicles. And a good number of those will be trucks."

"Keisha makes a good point, Deke," said Santos. "It sounds like a manageable task to me. I want you to get on it first thing."

"Why me? It's her idea."

"I watched you come in. Looks to me like you're still hurting from your surgery. We might have jumped the gun by putting you on the square yesterday."

Conrad let out an exasperated sigh. "Okay, I get it. Stick the cripple back behind a desk."

"Deke, are you refusing to carry out your assignment?"

"No. I'll do it."

"Good. Now, what else can we do?"

Cash said, "We need to know more about Alissa Collins. Is there an ex-husband? Does she owe money to anybody? Does she have an ex-boyfriend with a grudge?"

"Maybe you could go back and ask the neighbor."

"I was thinking Keisha could do that. I've got something else in mind."

"Tail Moreno?"

"No, I find it awfully coincidental that Alissa goes missing not long after I visited Bonnie Hart and her Neanderthal husband."

Santos shook his head in frustration. "Are you bringing that up again? I thought I told you to let that go."

"Hear me out. When I was at their house, I told them I knew Ralph Spencer came to Noble County with Louisiana license plates. I mentioned Alissa as the source of that information. I told them I assumed they also came from Louisiana. They didn't deny it. Maybe they're worried because Alissa gave me information they wanted kept secret. Now they're worried she might blab something else they don't want to make public."

"Are you saying they kidnapped her to keep her from talking?"

"It's possible."

Santos considered the idea. "If that's the case, they don't want ransom. They want her gone."

"I know. That's why we can't ignore the possibility."

"What do you propose?"

"I'd like to go back out there and look for tire tracks. Maybe that would give us a clue to the white sedan."

"They won't let you back on the property."

"No, but the road turnoff that leads to their gate is packed dirt. We had some rain a couple of days ago. I'm hoping the ground is still damp enough that the kidnapper left tracks."

"Okay. One question, though. Did you see a sedan when you were there?"

Cash's shoulders sagged. The only car he had seen at the house was Hart's blue Terrain. "No."

"Well, go check it out." Santos stood. "I'll go keep an eye on Moreno."

***

Tannehill Road was a lightly used two-lane ribbon of asphalt leading from Pinyon to the unincorporated community of Tannehill fifteen miles away. Deep potholes and cracks in the pavement made the drive a precarious one. Most people in Pinyon hated it. The exception was Virgil Hall, whose tire shop profited from repairing the flat tires it caused.

As Cash steered the squad car around yet another crater, he said, "Man, somebody ought to fix this road." He looked at the rearview mirror to make sure Frida Simmons was still following. He had asked her along to make casts of any suspicious tracks they found and he was reassured to see her silver Ford Fusion a hundred yards behind. He chuckled when he saw the front end of the car drop into a pothole, imagining the string of curse words Frida was now hurling into the wind.

Cash arrived at Bonnie Hart's gate. He braked to a stop in the weeds lining the road. Moments later, Frida's Fusion eased in behind it. Cash got out and crossed the pavement. The gate lay fifteen feet from the road. A strip of packed earth and gravel filled the space in between. Cash knelt and probed the soil with his fingers. The top half-inch was dry but below that the dirt felt cool and moist. He signaled to Frida. "Come take a look."

Frida squatted next to Cash and studied the ground. "When are they going to fix this damned road?" she said.

"Ask Fred Uecker," said Cash.

"Who's that?"

"One of the guys that sets your salary."

Frida pointed. "Look over there."

Cash shielded his eyes from the sun. A few feet in front of him he saw a two-foot-long tire impression. "Bingo," he said.

Frida stood up. "I'll get my stuff."

Cash stepped onto the pavement to wait for her. He called out, "Do we have a subscription to a tire tread database?"

"If not, you need to get one."

"Another item for Fred Uecker's to-do list."

The sound of an engine starting up reached their ears. Had someone seen them? "That's coming from the house," Cash said.

The engine revved. Without warning, the gate clicked and began to swing open. The engine noise grew and a motorcycle appeared in the driveway. It was heading straight for them. As it drew closer Cash recognized Emmett Fuller on his Harley. "Here comes trouble," he said with a scowl.

Taking care to avoid the tread marks, Cash advanced to the gate and raised his hands as an indication for Fuller to stop. Instead, Fuller kept coming, the motor now roaring like a jet engine. Fearful of being hit, Cash lunged to one side. At the last moment, Fuller hit the brakes and skidded to a stop. Cash hollered for him to shut the engine off, but Fuller ignored him. He revved the bike and, using his left foot as a pivot, executed a series of circles between the gate and the road. The maneuver shot a cloud of sand and gravel at them, forcing them back even more. Fuller then zipped out onto the road and killed the engine.

"What the hell are you doing?" Cash shouted. "You could have killed us."

Fuller grinned. "I'm just showing off my bike. It's a beauty, isn't it?"

"I ought to give you a ticket for reckless driving."

"The edge of the road is the property line," Fuller said with a shrug. "You can't ticket a man for riding his bike on his own property."

"You don't live here. This is Dennis Webb's property."

"We're neighbors. He's a friend of mine."

"The easement is wider than the road."

"Yeah, but it's an easement. That only gives the county the right to use the property. It doesn't give it the right to block the property owner from doing whatever he wants to on it."

Seeing no benefit in arguing the finer points of property law with Fuller, Cash said, "Where were you yesterday afternoon?"

"I don't think that's any of your business."

"Alissa Collins is missing."

"Ralph's woman? I'm sorry to hear that."

"Do you know where she is?"

"No. Of course not."

Cash stared at Fuller, fantasizing about ripping him off the bike and beating information from him. "If you see her, you'll let us know, right?"

"Sure, I'm always eager to help the law. But it's not like Ralph and I were best buds or anything. Now that he's dead I don't expect to ever see her again." He started the bike's engine. Shouting over the deafening roar, he said, "Well, folks, I gotta run. It's been real." He released the brakes. Tires spitting sand and gravel, the Harley shot through the gate and disappeared around a bend.

Frida put her hands on her hips and swore. Assessing the torn-up ground, she said, "Whatever was there is gone now."

Cash kicked his boot over the now-obliterated tread mark. "Son of a bitch is hiding something."

***

Webb slapped a hand against the coffee table, eliciting a flinch from Bonnie. "Do you see what your stupid poker game has done?" He was working himself up into a lather. "One thing leads to another, and now the sheriff's department is nosing around."

From her spot on the couch, Bonnie sipped her rum and coke and waited for Webb's flame to burn out.

Webb stood up and began pacing. "They were looking for tire treads. There's no other reason they'd stop at the end of the driveway. It's a good thing I saw them on the monitor."

"So what if they were looking for tread marks?" She took another sip. "That was the first time that car had been used in months. It's locked up in the barn. Even if they could tell what kind of vehicle they're after, it wouldn't help them any."

"Don't you get it, woman? We've been here a year without a lick of trouble and now, in the space of two weeks, lawmen are following you and poking around our property asking questions."

"A week and a half."

"What?"

"It's only been a week and a half since Ralph died."

"Don't try to distract me." He disappeared into the kitchen and returned with a glass, which he filled with rum from the ever-present bottle on the coffee table. After a quick sip, he said, "We need to come up with a plan."

Bonnie finished her drink and decided to settle Webb down. She slid onto his lap and gave him a prolonged, open-mouthed kiss. Fingering the abundant chest hair poking up from beneath his shirt collar, she said, "Come on, baby, let's go play."

16

Santos watched Moreno emerge from his house and head straight for the squad car. "Shit," he muttered.

The house was an old frame structure, well-kept with a neat yard that lacked the tall weeds in front of the house on either side. Moreno strode down the walkway and crossed the street. Santos got out of the car.

"I already talked to Cash," Moreno said. "I had nothing to do with Alissa's disappearance."

"If you did, would you tell us about it?"

"Want to see the inside of my house?"

"Sure."

Five minutes later, Moreno ushered Santos back through the front doorway and onto the porch. Santos indicated the gray Corolla parked in the driveway. "Think I could see inside the car?"

Moreno rolled his eyes. "Sure. I've got nothing to hide."

Santos wasn't putting up with any guff. "Mind standing in front of the car where I can see you?"

Moreno mumbled something unintelligible but did as ordered. Santos opened each door in turn and inspected the interior. He popped the trunk. It was empty.

"Satisfied?" Moreno said, not bothering to hide his irritation.

"Thanks for your cooperation."

***

Hodge returned to the sheriff's office to find Conrad slouched in a conference room chair. He glanced up from a computer screen as she entered the room. "What did you find out from the old lady next door?"

"Her name is Mrs. Ramsey."

"Whatever."

"How are you feeling?"

"Fine."

"I imagine it is tough to come back from being shot."

"I said I'm fine." His voice took on an edge.

"I'm not asking to tick you off. I'm genuinely interested in your well-being."

He decided she was for real. "Thank you. I'd say I'm about ninety percent recovered."

"Good. I'm looking forward to working in the field with you." She dropped into a chair. "I didn't learn anything useful. Alissa Collins was married once, to a guy named Foster Collins. He died three years ago when he tried to beat a freight train at a crossing."

"Hard way to go."

"Mrs. Ramsey didn't know of any boyfriends other than Ralph Spencer and Terry Moreno. Until he moved in with her, Collins was working at the Dairy Queen. They have a new manager who came on after she left and doesn't know her. One of the other employees remembers her but didn't recall any problems at work."

"Sounds like you got squat."

"I even tracked down a brother in Florida. He hasn't seen her since Covid broke out."

"Where are her kids?" Conrad asked.

"Mrs. Ramsey is watching them for now at her house. The Family Advocacy Board is still looking for a foster family." She pointed at the computer screen. "Any luck with the car?"

Conrad moaned. "Do you know how many white cars there are in this county?"

"No, tell me."

"Four hundred seventeen."

"And of those cars, how many are white sedans?"

"All of them. I wasn't counting the trucks."

"Shoot. I guess my idea wasn't such a good one after all."

"You think?"

Conrad stood up and stretched. "I'm gonna go get a Coke. Can I bring you something?"

Before Hodge could answer, Cash and Santos marched into the room and flung themselves into chairs. Their faces bore sour expressions.

"You guys don't look happy," Conrad said.

"We're not," said Cash. "You wouldn't believe what happened."

"What?"

Cash relayed the story of his encounter with Fuller, concluding with, "The bastard knew what he was doing."

"That would mean they're monitoring the gate with a security camera," said Hodge.

Conrad said, "Thank you, Captain Obvious."

"What did you find, Sheriff?" Hodge said to Santos.

"I've told you before, call me Gabe. Moreno let me search his house and car. I didn't see anything suspicious."

Cash's ears perked up at the sound of Edie's voice out in the lobby. Then she charged into the room and slapped a flyer on the table. "Eaton put this up in the Firewheel's window. They're all over town."

Cash rotated the flyer so he could read it. An all-caps headline read, "ARE YOU TIRED OF CRIME?" Below that was a picture of Alissa Collins. The text at the bottom gave the few known facts of the case, followed by, "Mitch Eaton vows to keep the people of this county safe. Vote Eaton for Sheriff."

"Can you believe it?" said Edie. "The gall of that man."

Cash slid the flyer across the table for the others to read.

"Well, shit," said Santos. He crumpled the flyer and tossed it at a nearby trash can. It fluttered lamely to one side.

Conrad said, "Hodge needs to give you basketball lessons."

Edie pulled up a chair. "Guys, this isn't necessarily bad news."

"Right," Santos said with a snort. "Smearing the department is a good thing."

"What I mean is, it could backfire on him. Suppose you solve this case and bring Alissa home safe and sound?"

"That's a big if," said Cash. "We're spinning our wheels right now."

"You've been in worse spots and come out okay. Look how things turned out when everyone thought you killed Griff Turner. You found the real killer and came out of it a deputy. Have faith."

"You're right." That gave him an idea. Cash rose from his chair and started toward the door. "Hodge, you want to come?"

"Where are we going?"

"To knock on doors."

***

Cash knew that Alissa Collins' front door didn't have a doorbell camera—he had checked— but they'd passed several other houses, some of them closer to the road. If they were lucky, one of them was fitted with a doorbell camera. If they were luckier still, it was in a position to capture the road.

They drove to Alissa's house and turned around. Coming back toward town, all they saw for the first two miles were pastures and stretches of mesquite and cedar growing among the sedge grass. The only road they passed was a loop that Cash knew curved toward Phil Sawyer's place before returning to the main road. Sawyer and his wife were in their eighties, so Cash figured they were not strong kidnap suspects.

As Cash steered the squad car around a curve, a brick ranch house fifty feet from the road came into view. A rusted chain-link fence surrounded the front yard. Two small dogs of indeterminate breed patrolled the fence.

Cash eased to a stop. When he and Hodge got out, the dogs began barking and lunging at the four-foot fence. Hodge extended a hand to them and, by speaking in a low, soothing tone, quieted the animals. Soon, both were licking her hand and wagging their tails.

"Where did you learn that?" Cash said.

"Dogs like me."

The front door of the house opened, and a frumpy woman with thin gray hair wearing sweatpants and a Disney World T-shirt stepped outside. "Can I help you?"

Taking a chance that the dogs would remain friendly, Cash opened the gate and entered the yard. Hodge followed, closing the gate behind her.

Without warning, the smaller of the two dogs charged and nipped Cash's ankle. "Damn it!" he said, shooing the animal away.

"Barney, stop that," the woman hollered. The dog backed up several paces and growled. The woman said, "Maybe you should talk to me from there."

Cash performed a quick check of his ankle and saw no blood. "It's okay, he didn't break the skin." Giving Barney a wide berth, he approached the woman. "I'm Deputy Cash and this is Deputy Hodge."

"She's a deputy?"

"Yes, ma'am."

The woman said nothing but folded her arms in disapproval. Cash braced himself for a racist comment but she wasn't going that far.

"We're hoping you might have a doorbell camera that would have picked up a car suspected of being involved in a kidnapping."

The woman's expression didn't change. "Somebody's been kidnapped? Who?"

"Your neighbor down the road. Alissa Collins."

"You don't say."

"Do you know her well?"

"I can't say that I do." She pointed at one of the dogs. "Barney here got out one time and she found him at her house. She made me come get him."

"Ma'am, do you happen to have a doorbell camera?"

She arched an eyebrow. "Doorbells got cameras now?"

"Yes, ma'am. For quite some time."

"Land sakes, I don't know what I'd need one of them things for."

They had struck out. "Thanks anyway," he said, starting to go.

"Hey." The woman was looking at Hodge.

"Yes, ma'am?"

"Is this some kind of equal opportunity thing? You getting hired, I mean."

Cash started to speak but Hodge raised her hand to stop him. "No, ma'am."

"We hired the best candidate," Cash said.

The woman harumphed. "Sure you did."

Back in the car, Cash said, "I'm getting tired of people saying stuff like that."

"It's not your fault."

"Still ..."

"I'll be all right." She slid her seat belt across her chest, then added, "By the way, you don't have to run interference for me. I can take care of myself."

Cash studied her face. He expected to see anger but she appeared calm, as if they were merely discussing the weather. "Okay, got it."

They passed two more houses, but both were so far from the road that Cash didn't think they'd be useful even if they did have cameras. He noted, out of the blue, "By the way, nice work with those dogs back there. Country dogs don't always settle down like that."

"Neither do city dogs. Austin had some mean critters. And he didn't exactly settle down. He bit you."

"Just a scratch."

Hodge pointed up ahead. "Look at that one."

This house had a more modern look than the rest. Judging by the window over the front door, Cash estimated ten-foot ceilings inside, and the gleaming metal roof looked like it had been installed yesterday. He turned into the smooth concrete driveway and parked behind a late-model Chevy Tahoe. "Somebody's home," he said.

At the door, Cash tapped a black rectangular device attached to the frame. "Bingo." When he knocked, a short, stooped man with white hair answered. Cash recognized him as one of the regulars at the Firewheel's domino tables. "Well, if it isn't a couple of sheriff's deputies," the man said, registering their uniforms. "What can I do for you?"

Cash said, "Hello, Mr. Fitzgerald." He explained what they were after.

Fitzgerald was glad to help. "Come inside and we'll take a look."

They waited in the entry hall while he went in search of his phone. Cash realized he had been wrong about the ten-foot ceilings. This one was at least twelve feet.

"Nice house," Cash said.

Hodge craned her neck and looked up. "How do you dust that ceiling fan?"

"You're supposed to dust ceiling fans?"

Before Hodge could answer, Fitzgerald returned with his phone. He tapped the screen and handed it to Cash. "This shows all the recent events. You can scroll down to the time span you're interested in."

Cash clicked on the first event and saw it had been triggered by a UPS truck speeding past the house. From its size he concluded that if the white sedan had come this way, they should be able to see it. He scrolled down to yesterday morning's recordings. Mrs. Ramsey had said she heard the Collins children screaming at eleven-thirty. The first event of the day happened at seven o'clock, and Cash saw a cattle truck go by. He checked several more events and came up empty. At 11:17, though, there it was, a white sedan. He didn't recognize the make and model but knew they could figure that out with the computer back at the department.

"Look here," Cash said, showing the clip to Hodge. "This could be it."

"Tinted windows, though. You can't see the people inside."

To make sure he didn't miss anything, Cash checked the rest of the clips recorded before noon. He saw no other white sedans. Handing the phone back to the house owner, he said, "Is it possible to send that clip to my phone?"

"Sure, what's your number?"

Cash gave it to him. Moments later, his phone dinged. Checking his messages, he saw that he had a video clip from an unknown number. "Got it. Thanks." He forwarded the file to Santos with an explanation.

On the way back to town, Hodge said, "What if this car is registered in another county? Or even out of state?."

"It wouldn't be on Deke's list."

"Then what?"

"Then we're screwed."

After another mile, Hodge spoke up again. This time her voice had a scratch in it, one of reluctance. "Ah, I've been debating whether or not to tell you this, but I saw Edie with Mitch Eaton last night at that fancy restaurant on the square."

"Chez Abby?"

"Yeah."

"Are you sure it was her?"

"Oh, yeah."

Cash felt like someone had punched him in the gut. "Maybe they weren't together. Maybe they just ran into each other."

"I don't think so. They were sitting at the same table." She took a deep breath. "Sharing a bottle of wine."

Cash's hands tightened on the wheel. That son of a bitch, he thought. Then he realized Eaton couldn't have forced Edie to eat with him, and his neck flushed hot. "Well, shit."

***

"It's a Toyota Camry," said Santos. He swiveled his laptop around so Cash and Hodge could see the screen. "You can tell by the trim and the shape of the headlights and taillights."

Cash studied the side-by-side images on the screen, one from an ad of a late-model Camry, the other a still from the video clip. "Did you tell Deke?"

"Yeah. He's going through his list again to find the Camrys."

"It's still not much, but it's more than we had."

"I'll update the BOLO. Maybe we'll get lucky."

Hodge said, "Is there anything else we can do?"

Santos closed his laptop and stood up. "I'm out of ideas."

"If we don't find her, Eaton will have a field day."

"Let me make something clear," Santos said, his voice harder. "Our primary concern is with the safety of Alissa Collins, not the election."

"Still, if—"

Santos cut her off with an upraised hand. "This is not a political issue. I'd rather lose the election than have us treating it like one."

"Understood."

Santos left the office in a huff. Hodge said, "Is he always like that?"

"If you mean is he always a man of integrity, then yes."

"I guess that's a good thing. What about you? Can you think of anything else we should be doing right now?"

Cash glanced at the wall clock. It was almost eight o'clock. "Go home. Eat supper and get a good night's sleep. We'll meet back here at six."

17

"Forget it," said Fuller. "It's your turn now."

"What does that mean?" Bonnie said, leaning forward to sweep his empty beer can onto the floor. "You've already killed a guy."

"Hey, knock it off. This isn't a pig sty. And I didn't kill him. He fell and hit his head when the bomb went off."

"I'm not sure a jury would go for that," Bonnie said, glancing around the trailer. Fuller did keep a neat house. With spotless furniture, clutter-free surfaces, and a kitchen area that glistened in the afternoon light, the place looked like it belonged to a clean freak. Which, Bonnie concluded, Fuller must be. She reached into a pocket. "If you're determined to be difficult..." She slapped a Gold Britannia coin onto the coffee table. "Here's a bonus for going above and beyond."

Fuller scoffed. "Just one? I don't think so."

Bonnie dug another coin from her pocket and dropped it beside the first. "That's over four thousand dollars. Just for making a phone call."

"There's a little more to it than that."

Leaning forward to give Fuller a view of her cleavage, Bonnie said, "Listen, baby. You're in this as deep as me. If I go down, you're going with me." She softened her voice. "Besides, this should be the end of it."

"You don't know that for sure."

"I think I do. Who followed me to Kerrville? Who ambushed me outside the bank? For that matter, who showed up here without an invitation? That deputy. Get rid of him and this all goes away."

Fuller reluctantly took the coins from the table. "Sometimes I wish I had never met you."

"Don't say that. You'll hurt my feelings," Bonnie said, oozing honey. She made a show of unbuttoning her blouse. "And you don't want to hurt my feelings, do you?"

Fuller stared at her chest. "No . . ."

"Good. Now let's have some fun."

***

Fuller peered through the binoculars at the distant limestone house. He lay prone beneath a large cedar tree, under low-hanging bottom branches bare enough that he could see past them while maintaining good cover. He swept his gaze across, checking each window for light, seeing none. The deputy must be asleep. At three in the morning, that was no surprise. Training the field glasses on the sleek Ram pickup parked in front of the house, he felt a twinge of remorse. It was a shame to ruin such a beautiful vehicle.

Fuller jogged to the crushed granite road that led to the house. He pulled a pair of medical gloves from his pocket and slipped them on. After popping the Camry's trunk he traded the binoculars for a spool of baling wire and a foot-long piece of PVC pipe. Earlier, he had capped the pipe at both ends after stuffing it with gunpowder collected from several boxes of 12-gauge shotgun shells Bonnie gave him. The pipe also contained a detonator wired to a burner cell phone.

Keeping his eyes glued on the house, Fuller made his way toward the truck. He kept to the grass next to the road to avoid crunching the crushed granite. He wore rubber-soled sneakers instead of boots for the same reason.

Fuller dropped to the ground behind the truck and slid on his back beneath the gas tank. He produced a small flashlight from his pants pocket and clamped it between his teeth. Using the baling wire, he secured his homemade bomb to the truck's undercarriage. When finished, he extricated himself and returned to the Camry.

Now came the boring part, setting an alarm and trying to sleep in the cramped sedan until it went off in three hours. He thought back to the previous evening when Bonnie had delivered the bomb-making components to him. One minute she was giving him instructions on how to detonate it, the next they were ripping each other's clothes off on their way to his bed. When he expressed concern that Webb would wonder why she was gone for so long, she laughed and said, "After two Ambien, he won't have a clue." He wished she were with him now to help pass the time.

***

It was still dark outside when Cash woke up and glanced at his phone. It was five-thirty. He lay in bed, listening to a flock of wild turkeys wander past the house. Their strange warbling reminded him of the reason he had returned to Noble County instead of settling in Austin near his parents. You couldn't get turkeys in their backyard.

Cash dumped a large scoop of muesli into a bowl and added blueberries, banana slices, and chunks of dried apricot. He had made the muesli himself by combining rolled oats, raisins, and roasted pecans. A generous pour of ice-cold milk was the icing on the meal.

As he munched on the cereal, Cash contemplated what he knew about Alissa Collins' disappearance. He was certain she hadn't left her house voluntarily. If she had, she wouldn't have lied to her children about playing hide and seek when she put them in the closet. Nor would she have propped a chair against the door to trap them inside. That was likely a precaution by her kidnapper.

Cash suspected that Alissa knew the kidnapper. Her children had heard nothing that suggested a struggle. The older child said, after a knock at the door, his mother opened it and let somebody into the house. His mother was alone when she came to tell him and his sister to get into the closet. Later, when the neighbor let them out, their mother was gone. The neighbor said she had left with someone driving a white sedan, which he now knew was a Toyota Camry. That seemed to exonerate Terry Moreno. Cash needed to find that Camry. But how?

Cash finished his breakfast and rinsed the dishes. As he stepped outside, a burst of satisfaction surged through him as he admired his truck. He had long dreamed of owning his own pickup. What rural Texan didn't? Taking it anywhere, anytime. Going off-road if the mood struck. Heading out on a road trip without worrying about a breakdown, like he did with his old, beat-up Ford Fiesta.

Cash climbed into the driver's seat. He pulled the door shut and smiled at the satisfying click it produced as it snapped into place. He inhaled the intoxicating new truck odor and ran his hand over the seat, his daily ritual since he drove it off the lot in San Angelo. He touched the brake pedal with his foot and pressed the start button.

The vehicle roared to life. Cash listened to the steady purring of the engine for several seconds before shifting into drive. Just as he touched the gas pedal, an ear-splitting bang punctured the soothing sound. The airbag deployed, pounding his chest as it slammed him against the seatback. Smoke poured from beneath the vehicle. Cash had a flash of Afghanistan waiting for the staccato tapping of automatic weapons fire that followed an unexpected explosion. Acting on instinct, he threw the door open, leaped from the cab, and sprinted away from the truck. Another bang split the air. The smoke cloud intensified, then diminished to a thin wisp. Cash rubbed his eyes in disbelief. What the hell had just happened?

The distant sound of a car starting up reached Cash's ears. He sprinted into the open field to give himself a view beyond the bend in the drive. He cleared it just in time to see a white sedan approaching the main road. It was too dark and the car was too far away for him to make out the license plate. The sedan turned left—away from town—and roared off. Cash couldn't determine the make and model, but his gut told him it was a Toyota Camry. He pulled out his phone and made a call.

Santos answered. "Damn, Cash, it's early. What's up?"

Cash let out a long breath and tried to ignore the pain in his chest from the expanding airbag. "I'm gonna be a little late this morning."

18

S am Caldwell, the owner of Caldwell Auto Repair, pushed a button to activate the motor operating his four-post lift. "Let's see what we got here." The motor hummed as Cash's Ram truck rose into the air. Sam, a friendly-faced man in jeans and a grease-stained work shirt, scratched his ear and said, "You say it just blew up?"

Cash fought off a cloud of gloom as he watched the truck's ascent. "That's right." He shook his head. "I've only made one payment on the thing so far."

"Keep your chin up," Sam said as he stepped beneath the truck and studied the undercarriage. "It might not be so bad. I don't see anything leaking out of her."

Cash was finding it hard to keep his chin up. His beautiful truck had just been towed into an auto repair shop, its gleaming newness a thing of the past. The spider-webbed rear window wobbled in its frame. The muffler dangled low and a back tire had blown out. Black streaks crawled up the side panels, marring the once beautiful blue finish.

Sam craned his neck and executed a slow tour of the undercarriage. "What are we looking for?"

Cash joined him beneath the truck. "Anything that shouldn't be there."

"Look at that." Sam pointed to a dent in the gas tank. "Something sure gave it a knock. The good news is I don't see any holes in it."

Cash stood on his toes as he peered at a section of cracked PVC pipe dangling from a loose wire. "What's that?" He followed the wire with his fingers up and around the pipe it was attached to. "Got any wire cutters?"

Sam fetched a pair and handed them to Cash.

Cash took a pair of medical gloves from his pocket and put them on. He didn't want his fingerprints on any evidence. After snipping the wire, he jerked the pipe free and walked out from under the truck into better light. Sam followed.

"What is that?" Sam asked.

Cash estimated the pipe was about a foot long. A crack ran along its length. One end was sealed with a PVC cap. The other end had jagged edges darkened with what looked like powder burns. Cash tipped the pipe upright and several unidentifiable plastic particles slid into his palm.

Sam let out a low whistle. "Holy crap. I've never seen anything like that before. What the hell is it?"

"It's an IED."

"An IUD? What are you talking about?"

"Not IUD. IED. Improvised explosive device. Like the Taliban used in Afghanistan."

Sam recoiled from the assertion. "It's a bomb?"

"It is."

"Jesus Christ, who put it there?"

Cash poured the plastic particles back into the pipe. "That's a good question."

"What are you gonna do now?"

"Go look at another blown-up truck.

***

Rick's Salvage Yard sprawled over two acres of fenced land a mile south of town. Rows of junked vehicles occupied most of that space. Rick had sorted the vehicles by type so that each row contained only sedans, or pickup trucks, or SUVs, or whatever other category he could think of. A large aluminum barn near the entrance gate was fitted with shelves crammed with parts: hubcaps, rims, steering wheels, carburetors, and a lot more. A hand-painted plywood sign over the gate claimed, "If it ain't here, it ain't anywhere."

Cash was familiar with Rick's, having purchased a door for his old Ford Fiesta shortly after moving to Pinyon. Rick had offered to paint the door, but Cash declined, preferring to save his meager funds for more essential items, like food. The last time Cash had seen the Fiesta, the mismatched yellow door still marked it as a beater.

Cash pulled the squad car through the gate and killed the engine. Looking worried, Rick stepped out of the single-wide trailer that served as his office. When he saw Cash climb out, though, the look dissolved into a smile.

"Hey, Cash. I thought you bought a new truck."

Cash shook Rick's hand. "I did. A Ram 1500."

"How come you're not driving it? Whenever I buy me a new car, I don't drive anything else until the new car smell is gone."

"That's what I'm here about. Do you still have that truck that blew up at Avi's place?"

"Yeah." He pointed. "It's right over yonder."

"You haven't broken it down for parts yet?"

"Naw. There wasn't much to save that wasn't burnt to a crisp. When I get around to it I'll haul it to San Antonio and sell it for scrap."

"Can I take a look at it?"

Rick led Cash around the barn to what remained of Ralph Spencer's truck. Cash agreed with Rick's assessment that the vehicle appeared worthless. He slid a flashlight from his pocket, flicked it on, and dropped to the ground.

"What are you doing?" Rick asked.

Instead of answering, Cash flipped onto his back and slid beneath the truck. Moments later, he reappeared with a length of baling wire in one gloved hand and a small piece of charred PVC pipe in the other.

Rick's eyes narrowed. "What the hell's that?"

Excited over his find, Cash headed for the squad car. "A murder weapon."

***

Santos studied the length of blackened PVC pipe inside the evidence bag. "That's an IED."

"I know it's an IED," said Cash. "That's why I'm showing it to you."

"Where did you get it?"

"From the bottom of my truck. Somebody planted it there."

"Somebody planted this on your truck?"

"That's right."

"Holy shit."

Santos sat behind his desk, Cash across from him. Santos laid the evidence bag on the desk. "Did you show this to Frida yet?"

"I did. No prints."

"Someone was trying to scare you."

"Or kill me."

"If that's the case, why aren't you dead?"

Cash picked up the bag. "Look at it. Both ends would have been capped, right? But the cap on one end got blown off. Enough of the explosion's force was released to make a big bang, but not much more."

"What's that debris in the bag?"

"I'm guessing it's what remains of a cell phone. It would have been wired to a detonator and—"

"I know how a cell phone bomb works."

"I guess you do," Cash said, recalling their shared military service.

Santos sat back in his chair and stared into the distance. Cash recognized that as wheels turning in his friend's head.

"You said you had something else to show me," Santos said.

Cash fished out the bag containing the wire and pipe fragment from Ralph Spencer's truck from his pocket. "Ralph Spencer's death was no accident. I found these under his truck. I missed it the day of the explosion because I didn't know to look for it."

"Looks like the device on your truck."

"Yeah."

"How come Spencer's bomb was lethal and yours wasn't?"

"Ralph didn't die from the explosion. He died when he was thrown to the ground. He hit his head hard enough to fracture his skull. That's what caused the brain bleed. I was in the truck cab and the airbag deployed, so I was relatively safe. Also, Ralph was stealing diesel fuel with a leaky system. Maybe the caps on his bomb were sealed better. A bigger explosion, diesel fumes, and—boom—it's the Fourth of July."

The office door burst open and Edie charged into the room. "Cash. What the hell! Your truck blew up?"

His stomach roiled at the sight of Edie. He still hadn't decided what to do about her dining out with Eaton, but this was neither the time nor the place for a confrontation. "How did you hear about that?"

"Sam Caldwell told me. I just served him at the Firewheel."

"Have a seat."

Edie hesitated, then dropped into a chair.

"It's an overstatement to say that my truck blew up," Cash said. "There's really not all that much damage."

"Was there an explosion or not?"

"Well, yes."

She knew he was beating around the bush. "What happened, Gabe?"

Santos shrugged. "A small explosive device went off under his truck. As you can see, he wasn't hurt. We were just talking about what to do about it."

"What to do about it? I'll tell you what to do about it. Find the bastard that put it there and shove a"—she made air quotes—"small explosive device up his ass."

Despite his anger at Edie, Cash couldn't help but laugh. One of the things he loved about her was her decisiveness.

Santos said, "Believe me, Edie, if we do find the guy we'll consider it."

"If?"

He threw up a hand. "Excuse me: when. Now, if you'll excuse us, Cash and I have some sheriff's business to discuss."

She frowned at him, then looked over at Cash.

Cash shrugged. "He's right."

Edie eased out of her chair. "All right, I'll get out of here." Wagging a finger at Cash, she said, "Later on, I want the full story."

After she was gone, Santos chuckled and said, "Don't ever do anything to make that woman mad."

"Amen to that."

Santos turned back to the matter at hand. "Seriously, Cash, how are we going to find this dude?"

"It seems pretty obvious to me who did it."

"Would you mind letting me in on the secret?"

"Think about it. Somebody kills Ralph Spencer. Later on, his girlfriend goes missing. That can't be a coincidence."

"I'll concede the possibility. So?"

"Who else besides Terry Moreno has seen me investigating Alissa's disappearance?"

Santos thought a moment before his eyes lit up. "Emmett Fuller."

"Right. And he intentionally destroyed the scene Frida and I were investigating with his motorcycle."

"We don't know that for sure."

Cash gave him a look. "Right."

"Can you swear he did it on purpose?"

"Why else did he come out there? Frida was about to make casts of tire treads leading directly onto that property. He must have spotted us on a motion-sensitive camera. My guess is there's a white Toyota Camry parked somewhere back there. My only question is why Fuller is the one who came out. Where was Bonnie Hart? Or that husband of hers?"

"Good question. But we can't just go waltzing in and search the place. We'd need a warrant."

"I'm aware of that. I'll write one up."

"Our case is pretty weak."

"Are you telling me not to try?"

Santos leaned on his elbows and sighed. "No. Go ahead. Let me ask you this, though. Have you dealt with Judge Mixon before?"

"No."

He cocked a finger and fired. "Good luck."

19

With its twelve-foot ceilings and heavy use of oak trim, Judge Barbara Mixon's office in the historic Noble County courthouse building looked like a movie set from an old John Wayne Western. Paramount had even filmed scenes in *The Shotgun Sheriff* in the building. Little had changed since the film shoot. Cash imagined he might even be sitting in the same padded ladder-back chair that the Duke had used. Judge Mixon, with her crisp bun and wire-rimmed glasses, added to the Old West aura. The only thing missing was a rack of shotguns and Winchester rifles next to the mounted deer head on the wall.

Cash fidgeted as he waited for Judge Mixon to finish reading the search warrant he had prepared. He didn't know her well and couldn't predict her response. She was as old as his grandmother, and she had the stern look of someone who enjoyed telling people no.

The judge rustled the warrant and said, "This looks like a fishing expedition to me."

"With respect, Judge, we have strong reason to believe we'll find the car we're looking for on that property."

"Then why didn't you write that reason down?" Her eyes bore into him like he was a third-grader caught cheating on a spelling test. "All I see here is speculation."

"It's not speculation. He intentionally destroyed the scene we were documenting."

"And you know for a fact he did this deliberately."

"Of course I—" Cash stopped and forced himself to rein in his rising agitation. "It's the only logical conclusion. Call it a gut feeling."

"You're asking me to sign a search warrant based on a gut feeling."

"Ma'am, a woman's life is at stake."

"I'm sympathetic to that fact. But nothing in this request justifies waiving the property owner's right to privacy."

"Ma'am...I...I..." Cash stuttered as he searched his mind for something he could say to change her mind. Stymied, he fell back in his chair and blew out a hard breath. "I can't believe this."

"You can't believe what?" the judge said, her voice sharp enough to pierce steel. "That I'd follow the law? You're not doing yourself any favors here, Deputy."

"I thought we were on the same side."

The judge scoffed. "So did I."

Cash returned her hard stare. He wanted to tear the glasses from her face and snap them in two. "Yes, ma'am. I'm sorry, ma'am." He made little attempt to hide his frustration.

"I'll choose to respond to your words, and not the tone in which they were delivered." She handed him the unsigned warrant. "Find a reason based on evidence, not a gut feeling, and I'll reconsider."

"Yes, ma'am." He snatched the warrant from her hand. "Thank you for your time." He rose and turned to leave.

"Deputy."

"What?"

"If you really consider us to be on the same side of the law, you'll follow the rules. You just stepped a toe over the line that should never be crossed. Don't do it again."

***

Cash returned to the squad car in a mood foul enough to strangle puppies. Barbara Mixon had lived up to her reputation as a hardass. The woman's arrogance and patronizing demeanor enraged him. She had all but spanked him on his way out of her office. How did she expect law enforcement to protect the community if she was going to be so nitpicky? And what about Alissa Collins? Didn't Mixon care that the poor woman's life hung in the balance?

Cash checked his phone and saw that he had five messages, all from Keisha Hodge. He called her number. She picked up on the first ring and said, "Where have you been? I've been looking all over for you."

"Sorry, I've had a hell of a morning."

"I heard. Santos just filled me in. Did you get the warrant?"

"No, Mixon wouldn't sign."

"Well, crap. Any ideas on what we do now?"

"Other than egg Judge Mixon's house? No."

"I got Alissa listed on all the missing-persons databases I know of."

"Good thinking."

"Maybe we could get the FBI involved."

Cash had entertained the same thought and dismissed it. "They won't take a case unless the disappearance is suspected to be the result of foul play."

"You don't think she was kidnapped?"

"I do, but we haven't turned up anything specific to suggest that. For all we know, she locked her kids in the closet and went to Acapulco with her lover."

"What about the Texas Rangers?"

"Again, she's a missing person, but not a definite kidnapping victim."

"What about Ralph Spencer? That's a murder case."

Cash fought to control a rising sense of annoyance. Was she suggesting the task was beyond his abilities? "Why are you so anxious to pass the buck on this case?"

"I'm not. It just seems like we need some help."

"I get it. We're just a bunch of small-town hicks so we better bring in somebody who knows what they're doing."

That stopped her short. "Point taken. What now?"

"Go get some lunch. I need to think. I'll see you back at the department."

As Cash pocketed his phone, his stomach rumbled. He could use some lunch himself. He climbed out of the squad car and crossed the square to the Packsaddle. The noon crowd was thinning out and he had several empty tables to choose from. Cash took a four-top near the window. Seconds later, a young woman appeared with a menu. He waved it away and said, "I'll have the smoked brisket sandwich with sweet potato fries."

"Anything to drink? There's a special on the Avocado Ale."

Cash winced. Another foul concoction dreamed up by Steve. Countless barrels of the nasty stuff were probably stored in the basement. "I'll bet there is. Just bring me an iced tea. Unsweetened."

As Cash waited for his food, his mind returned to Alissa Collins. The thought that Emmett Fuller might be holding her against her will tortured him. If he could only sweat the guy a little more, maybe he'd learn something that would help him crack the case. But he saw little chance of another interview with Fuller. Even before Alissa's disappearance, the jerk had made clear his unwillingness to cooperate.

But what about Bonnie Hart? Fuller's property abutted hers. Unlike her husband, she regularly ventured out, if only for the weekly poker games and monthly trips to the coin shop. Today was Thursday. She might show up at Terry's tonight. Maybe he could catch her there.

"Take a look at this." Steve, slapped a flyer onto the table and slid into a seat. "Somebody taped it to my window. I took it down."

A grainy photograph of Alissa Collins appeared below the headline "Have You Seen This Woman?" Beneath the photo was a smaller headline that read, "The Noble County Sheriff Hasn't." Still smaller font spelled out the details of Alissa's disappearance, ending with "As your sheriff, I will make sure the people of Noble County are safe. That's a promise from me, Mitch Eaton."

"Son of a bitch," Cash said, crumpling the flyer into a ball.

"Somebody should punch that guy."

"He could end up being my boss."

"Let's hope not." Steve gave a look of horror. "On another note, are you guys having any luck with your search?"

Cash shook his head. "No. Judge Mixon just shot down my best chance of finding her."

"How so?"

"I think I might know where the vehicle that took Alissa Collins away is. I asked Mixon to sign a search warrant and she shot me down."

"Why?"

"She said I didn't have enough cause. She's next in line for a punch after Eaton."

"Do you?"

"Do I what?"

"Have good cause."

Cash threw his friend a dirty look. "Good enough."

"What does that mean?"

"It means I need to search that property."

"So ... you don't."

"Fuck you. Whoever it was blew up my truck."

The server showed up with the food. As if sensing the tension created by Cash's last comment, she plopped it on the table and scurried away.

Before Cash could stop him, Steve grabbed a fry and popped it into his mouth.

"Do you mind?" said Cash.

"Relax, I'll get you more if you want. And don't be so testy. Mixon can be a hardass, but she has a duty to go by the book."

"Screw the book."

"All I'm saying is that there are rules. Everybody has to follow them, especially law enforcement. Without that, the whole system breaks down. And before you tell me to fuck off again, take a bite of your sandwich and think on it. Because you know I'm right."

Cash checked his urge to bite his head off and chose the brisket instead. "The meat's tough."

"Admit it," said Steve as he poached another fry. "I have a point."

Cash made a show of chewing the meat. "You do. But what am I supposed to do now?"

"You come at it from a different angle."

The server approached with a drink. She set it down and said, "Here's your tea. I forgot to bring it with the food." She turned to leave.

Steve said, "Hang on, Riley."

"Yes?"

He grabbed a handful of fries. "Bring that man another plate of fries on the house."

20

The man set the plate of food on the ground to open the barn door. Retrieving the plate, he stepped inside. Out of nowhere, a blow from a shovel knocked him to his knees. The plate shattered when it hit the concrete floor, red beans and rice flying in all directions. He registered a blur as Alissa Collins sped past him through the open doorway.

The man hauled himself to his feet, staggered a bit, and lumbered outside. There she was, thirty yards ahead of him and heading for the road. Alarmed, he sprinted after her. When she was still well short of the gate, he caught her by the hair and yanked her with a vicious twist to the ground. She tried to get up and he pushed her back down. She tried again and he hit her, holding nothing back. She gave a short yelp and collapsed.

Fighting to catch his breath, the man grabbed an arm and jerked Alissa to her feet. "Why are you doing this?" she said, her voice plaintive.

"Shut up, bitch."

She tried to wrench her arm free but he wrapped an iron hand around her neck. "Try it again and I'll snap you in two."

Back at the barn, the man shoved Alissa inside and pointed at the food strewn about the barn floor. "There's your lunch," he said. "Eat it."

As the man turned his back to leave, Alissa grabbed a hammer from the workbench and swung it at him. He ducked but still caught a glancing blow to the temple. Alissa attempted to squeeze past him through the doorway, but he whirled and caught the side of her head with his fist. As she reeled backward, she slipped on the beans and toppled to the floor. Her head hit the concrete with a sickening thud. When she tried to climb to her feet, the man picked up the hammer and, holding it sideways, smashed it against an ear. She dropped and lay still.

"Maybe now you'll stay put!" the man shouted. When she didn't react, he nudged her legs. "Get up."

She still didn't move. The man knelt and lightly slapped her cheek. Nothing. He felt her wrist for a pulse and didn't find one. Dropping an ear to her chest, he listened for the sound of her breathing. He heard only his own panting breaths.

The man stood up and kicked her lifeless body. "I guess you'll stay put now, won't you?"

***

Bonnie shrugged. "You caught her, didn't you?"

"Yeah."

"Then I don't see what the big deal is."

"She's dead."

Bonnie nearly shrieked. "What? How did that happen?"

"She hit me with a hammer. I hit her back and when she fell, she cracked her skull on the concrete."

"That wouldn't kill her."

"Are you forgetting Ralph?"

Bonnie could see that he was lying. "What really happened?"

Fuller folded his arms. "I hit her with the hammer."

Bonnie stared at him for a long while. She stood up and crossed the den. Using both hands, she searched Fuller's scalp. "There's a cut, but it doesn't look deep. Not much blood either. I don't think you'll need stitches."

"That's not the point. What do I do with her now?"

Bonnie let out a long sigh. "I have an idea."

***

An hour later Bonnie watched Fuller click off the reciprocal saw. Such an unpleasant task, cutting up a human body. At least Alissa had been a small woman, weighing little more than a hundred pounds.

Fuller removed the twelve-inch blade from the saw and rinsed it with a hose. After disconnecting the saw from its power supply, he rinsed it as well. The water would ruin the tool, but that didn't matter. He would bury it along with the blade in a remote corner of the property.

Fuller attached a spray nozzle to the hose and directed the powerful water stream down at the bloody ground of his workspace. He didn't stop until all traces of blood had been obliterated. Once the area dried, he'd turn the soil over with a spade, dig a hole, and plant the five-gallon Spanish oak sapling he had purchased at a San Antonio Home Depot.

A gust of wind carried the odor of Alissa Collins' remains to Bonnie's nostrils. She grimaced and recited a prayer Dennis often used. "Father, grant me the strength to complete this task. I am your instrument and humble servant. Amen." It didn't relieve her revulsion.

The body parts lay scattered on a large tarp. Fuller had saved the head for last, flipping the limbless torso face down so they wouldn't have to look at the face. It had been a messy job. His clothes and work gloves were spattered with blood. He had forgotten to change work boots and now had to burn his best pair along with the gloves and clothes. First, though, he had one final unpleasant mission to carry out.

Fuller dragged the tarp to the edge of the stock tank. Floating motionless in the water, the alligator tracked his approach. "Come on out of there, Jeremiah," Fuller called. "I got something for you." When the reptile didn't move, Fuller tossed one of Alissa's feet at its snout, creating a splash a foot in front of the huge beast. The animal glided forward. Its powerful jaws sprang open. With a flip of its head, it brought the fresh meat onto its tongue, snapped its mouth shut, and swallowed.

"Come on, boy, there's more where that came from," Fuller said. The gator slid forward again until its front feet rested on dry land. Fuller tossed the other foot in its direction. It disappeared in an instant.

Telling himself this was no different from tossing frozen chickens to the gator, Fuller continued feeding the beast until only the woman's head remained. With a shudder, he grabbed it by the hair and rolled it toward the alligator's open mouth. The animal squeezed its jaws until the skull shattered with an audible crack. Sickened, Fuller turned away. He turned back to see the reptile heave its body back into the pond and slide beneath the surface.

Fuller headed for a primitive stone fire pit Bonnie had assembled for the occasion. He slipped off his boots and tossed them in. Next came his socks, jeans, and shirt, followed by the work gloves. After dousing everything with kerosene, he lit a match, tossed it, and watched the heap explode in flames.

Bonnie approached the fire and watched the flames consume Fuller's clothes. "She didn't deserve that."

Fuller spat. "You're gonna buy me another pair of boots, right?"

21

Cash's lunch with Steve hadn't done anything to improve his sour mood. First, Judge Mixon had handed him his ass on a platter. Then, Steve delivered a lecture on why she was right to do so, all while eating most of his fries. What really stung was that, deep down, Cash knew both of them were right. Steve was his best friend. He had only been trying to help. And if Judge Mixon honestly believed the warrant request was out of bounds, then it was her duty to deny it. Still, how was he supposed to solve a case unless he could follow the leads where they took him?

Still grumbling, Cash strode into the department lobby trying to think of his next move. Vicky looked up from her computer and caught his eye. For once, her cloying smile was absent. She jerked a thumb toward the back offices.

"Sheriff Santos is waiting for you."

Cash paced down the hall. He found the sheriff behind his desk in conversation with an older man wearing khaki pants, a starched white shirt and green tie, and the shiniest black cowboy boots Cash had ever seen. A white cowboy hat sat in his lap. Pinned above his shirt pocket was the round shield of the Texas Rangers.

Santos and his visitor rose when Cash entered the room. Santos said, "Cash, this is Captain Clete Borden of the Texas Rangers. He's here to help us with the Alissa Collins case."

Cash and Borden shook hands. Everyone sat.

"This is a surprise," Cash said. "Was this Hodge's idea?"

"As a matter of fact," said Santos, "it was mine. Is there a problem?"

Cash stole a furtive glance at Borden. The Ranger's face remained impassive.

"No, I just didn't think we needed help yet."

"You're at a dead end," said Borden. "A fresh perspective can only help."

Cash didn't like Borden's patronizing tone. "I'm not at a dead end. I think I know where the car that took her away is."

Borden huffed. "Your sheriff told me about that. You're never getting on that property with what you have. Shoot, I can't believe you even gave that a try."

Cash's face flushed hot as anger and embarrassment flooded his brain in equal measures. "What's your brilliant plan, Captain Borden?"

If Cash's sarcasm annoyed Borden, the Ranger didn't show it. "Simple. I'll watch that ranch. Fuller's place too."

"You can't watch two places at once."

"One of your sheriff's deputies will help." He paused. "Maybe it will be you."

"What do you expect to see?"

"I wasn't finished. I'll also have every Ranger in the state looking for a man and woman in a white Toyota Camry. And when I leave here, I'll drive to Alissa Collins' house and go over it with a fine-toothed comb."

A brilliant plan. How many white Toyota Camrys were there in Texas? And he doubted Borden would find anything useful at Alissa Collins' house. He and Hodge had already searched it thoroughly.

"May I make a suggestion?" Cash said.

"Go ahead," said Santos.

"This is Thursday. That means Bonnie Hart should be at the poker club tonight. I'll meet her there and pump her for information."

"And she'll tell you where this woman is?" said Borden with an eye roll. "I heard she doesn't talk to cops."

Cash stood up. "Such a pleasure to meet you, Captain. Good luck at the ranch."

***

Edie set a bowl and spoon in front of Cash. "Sorry that it's only leftover soup. I didn't know I'd be having company tonight." She disappeared into the kitchen.

Cash picked up the spoon and dipped it into the steaming liquid. "I thought I better come by and explain about my truck." He wanted to discuss another matter too, but that could wait. He swallowed a spoonful of soup. "Hey, this is good. What is it?"

Edie returned with another bowl of soup and a plastic children's plate. She placed the bowl on the table opposite Cash and slid the plate in front of Luke. "Chicken nuggets and peas for you, buddy." She took a seat. "It's mulligatawny. I hope there's not too much curry."

"No, it's great," Cash said, wiping a drop of soup from his chin. "That's a unique flavor."

"That's the apple chunks. You add them just before you serve it. It gives it a tang to offset the curry."

"I take it Luke's not a fan."

The child shoved a piece of chicken into his mouth. "I like chicken nuggets."

Edie said, "All right, tell me about the truck."

Cash explained the morning's events, from climbing behind the wheel and hearing the bang to seeing smoke and hustling away from the vehicle. He omitted the moment of gut-wrenching terror when he felt transported back to Afghanistan.

Edie said nothing. She lifted a spoonful of mulligatawny to her mouth and blew on it.

"Aren't you going to say anything?" Cash asked.

"I'm thinking." She blew one last time and swallowed the soup. "How bad do you want to work in law enforcement?"

"What?"

"That's the second time in just a few weeks that somebody has tried to kill you. So, I'm asking, how bad do you want to be a sheriff's deputy?"

"That's not accurate. The first time I wasn't a deputy yet."

"Yes, but it wouldn't have happened if you hadn't run for sheriff."

"You don't know that for sure."

She slapped her spoon on the table. "Cash, I spent four years sweating bullets while you were in Afghanistan, sick to death thinking that I could hear about you getting killed at any time. Now you've been a deputy for what, three weeks, and somebody plants a bomb on your truck? I don't know how much of this I can take."

Cash's mouth hung open in surprise. "You were worried about me in Afghanistan? We weren't together then."

"That doesn't mean I didn't care about you."

"I had no idea."

"You haven't answered my question."

Cash felt blindsided. Edie had known for years of his goal to work in law enforcement. Now that he had finally achieved that goal, she was questioning it? "I don't know what to say. Me going into law enforcement isn't a surprise."

"I know that. It's just ..." She glanced at Luke. "What if that bomb had done what it was meant to do?"

"Are you saying you want me to quit my job?"

She didn't speak for what felt like an eternity. She spooned more of the mulligatawny into her mouth. Swallowing, she said, "Do you want some bread with your soup?"

"Thanks, no." The soup was terrific, but Cash had lost his appetite. "There's something else I wanted to talk to you about."

"What?"

Cash winced. She sounded angry already. His next words came out in a rush. "Someone told me they saw you and Eaton together at Chez Abby."

"Who told you that?"

"That doesn't matter."

She cocked her head and frowned. "It was Hodge, wasn't it?"

How did she know that? "Yes."

"She should mind her own business." When Cash didn't say anything, she said, "Okay. He asked me to meet him to discuss ground rules for the sheriff's race."

"Over a bottle of wine?"

Her face darkened. "Yes, over a bottle of wine. Is there something wrong with that?"

Cash didn't know what to say. On the surface, people did have a glass of wine with a nice meal. But wine could indicate more than a business meeting. Too much wine certainly would. "Will you see him again?"

"You're jealous, aren't you?"

Cash felt lightheaded. Of course, he was jealous. He was jealous enough to punch a hole through the wall. He didn't want to admit it, though. "No."

"If you're going to lie, at least make it plausible."

"All right, I'm jealous. Are you happy?"

"Hell no, I'm not happy. What business is it of yours what I do when I'm not with you?"

"We're going together, aren't we? Doesn't that mean we don't date other people?"

Her eyes sparkled with fury. "If we're going together, that's news to me. What I remember us telling each other is that we'd see how it goes. Do you remember something different?"

He had to admit that he didn't. "No."

"And it wasn't a date. It was a business meeting."

"If you say so."

"I do say so."

A lengthy silence followed, during which Edie resumed eating. Cash stared at his soup. His chest tightened and it felt like someone was squeezing his head. He felt the need to break something. He stood up. "Thanks for the soup." He waited for her to respond. When she didn't, he spun around and left the house.

***

Cash sipped iced tea at an outdoor table at the Firewheel and directed his attention to Star of Texas Thrift Shop across the square. There were several open parking places. Bonnie would likely park in one of them if she showed up for Thursday night poker at Terry's. Ten minutes later, his assumption proved correct when her blue Terrain rolled into one of the spots.

After one last sip of tea, Cash was starting toward the vehicle when a black Tesla braked behind it and honked. Bonnie hopped out of the Terrain holding a cardboard box, grinned, and waved. Cash changed direction and kept walking until he could see the driver. It was Mitch Eaton.

He and Bonnie had what appeared to be a friendly conversation. Bonnie took something out of her purse and handed it to Eaton, but Cash couldn't see what it was. After they were finished, she gave a farewell wave and strutted into the store, swinging her hips like a supermodel on a Parisian runway. Cash could almost see the drool coming out of Eaton's mouth.

Eaton wiped the slobber from his lips and roared away in the Tesla. An interesting new connection, Cash thought.

He jogged across the street and went in. The place was empty. A door in the back opened and closed and he knew Bonnie had gone into the poker club.

Cash pushed through the door himself. No one paid him any attention as he nodded a greeting at Terry. The club owner put up a hand to stop him. Leaning in and speaking in a low voice, he said, "Are you harassing me?"

"Relax, I'm not here to see you."

"Just don't piss anybody off."

"Who have I pissed off?"

"Bonnie. She's been bitching about you ever since you questioned her during a game."

Cash pushed past Moreno. "No promises."

Bonnie Hart had already taken a seat at the table. Cash walked up behind her and tapped her shoulder. "May I have a word?"

Bonnie's head swiveled in surprise. "My goodness, Deputy, you startled me." When Cash said nothing, Bonnie smiled and added, "Is there something I can do for you?"

"You can step outside and talk to me."

Bonnie gestured at the four players around the table. "We were just about to start our game."

"It will only take a moment."

"Excuse me, boys," she said to the four men at the table. With an exaggerated sigh, she picked up the box at her feet and followed Cash back into the store.

Cash said, "Does your husband know what good friends you are with Mitch Eaton?"

"What do you care?"

"He's a handsome man. Might make your husband jealous."

She gave him her best Southern woman smile. "Again, is that any concern of yours?"

"I suppose not. What's in the box?"

"Why, Deputy, that's none of your business."

"Where's Alissa Collins?"

Her expression didn't change. "How should I know? I hardly know the woman. I heard what happened, though. I do hope she's all right." She sighed. "Those poor children."

"What kind of car does your husband drive?"

"He prefers motorcycles," she said with a shrug. "If he needs a car, he uses my SUV."

"Was he ever in the service?"

"You mean like the army?" She laughed. "Goodness, no. I have to ask, though, why are you asking me all these questions?"

"One last question and you can get back to your game. Where did you and your husband live before you came to Noble County?"

She pressed her lips into a line. "I think we're about done here."

She tried to leave, but Cash blocked her way. "We're not finished."

"I think we are," she said, pushing past him.

"Somebody tried to blow me up in my truck this morning."

She gave him a long, expressionless look. "Now why would you feel the need to tell me that?"

"I think it has something to do with Alissa Collins' disappearance."

"Again, why tell me?"

"Bonnie, a woman's life is at stake."

She spun around and headed toward the club. "I'm gonna go play poker."

***

Edie was reading a mystery novel in her living room when she heard a vehicle turn into the driveway. She peeked through the blinds to see Mitch Eaton step out of his Tesla. Puzzled, she watched him approach the house. The doorbell rang.

"Hello, Mitch," Edie said when she opened the door. "What can I do for you?"

Eaton held up a manila folder. "I brought some campaign flyers by to show you."

She laughed. "Thanks, but I don't need them."

"Of course not. They're not for you to keep, although you could if you wanted to. I'm bringing them by as a courtesy."

"Okay. Come on in."

He followed her inside. She gestured for him to sit on the sofa, chastising herself for allowing him to kiss her the other night. "Want something to drink? I've got water, iced tea, and juice boxes."

"I can't pass up an offer like that," Eaton said with a chuckle. "I'll take a juice box. Apple, if you have it."

"I do."

Edie went into the kitchen and returned with the fruit juice. She saw that Eaton had opened the folder and laid it out on the coffee table. He patted the couch cushion and said, "Have a seat."

She handed him the juice and perched on the cushion, ready to jump out of reach. Eaton turned the folder so she could read it. When she was finished, she fixed him with a glare and said, "You're slinging mud already."

"This isn't mudslinging. It's a picture of a missing woman whose life is in danger."

"'Have you seen this woman? The Noble County Sheriff hasn't.' That's as muddy as it gets."

"I don't see it that way. Mud would be a grainy black-and-white picture of Santos with a headline accusing him of pedophilia."

Edie closed the folder and held it out. Eaton took it and tossed it on an end table. "There's something else I wanted to talk to you about."

"What?"

He scooted closer. "I really enjoyed our dinner together. I'd like to do it again."

"I don't think so."

He took her hand. "You're a beautiful woman, Edie. Not only that, you're smart. Not to mention feisty. I like that in a woman."

She pulled her hand back. "I think you should go."

"You can do better than Adam Cash."

"Get out."

"I don't know why you're settling for that loser."

"He's not a loser. And I'm not settling." She surprised herself with her next words. "I love him."

He stroked her arm. She swatted it away.

"Like I said, feisty." With a lightning move, he pivoted and thrust himself at her, pressing her into the back of the sofa. Before she could react, his hand was behind her head and his lips were pressed against hers. She tried to turn her head but his grip was too strong. After what seemed like an eternity to Edie, he pulled his head back. "Come on, Edie," he said. "You only live once."

She punched him. She didn't put everything into it but did use a closed fist with enough force to snap his head back. "Get out. Now."

Rubbing his chin, Eaton stood up. "You're lucky you didn't break my jaw."

"So are you, you jerk. Now get the hell out of my house."

"Cash can have you." He strode to the door. Nodding at the folder, he said, "You can keep that."

Edie stood up, grabbed the folder, and hurled it at him. "Thanks, but I'm all stocked up on toilet paper."

***

As Cash rolled up the driveway in the squad car, he instinctively veered to the right to avoid parking where his truck had been that morning. Soot stains on the crushed gravel still formed a rough outline of the vehicle. The sight caused the hair on the back of his neck to stand up. He had been lucky.

Inside, he grabbed a can of cherry-flavored fizzy water from the refrigerator and fired up the laptop on the kitchen table. Steve was right: he needed to approach the case from a different angle. The search for Alissa Collins, though ongoing, was at a standstill. Maybe if he dug more into Ralph Spencer's past he'd find a clue that would break the case.

What did he know about Spencer? Not much. He had lived with Alissa for about a year. She claimed he was from Louisiana. He had a connection with Bonnie Hart, given their regular trips to the Kerrville coin shop. And he had been pilfering diesel fuel at the time of his death.

Cash typed "Ralph Spencer Louisiana" into the search bar and hit enter. An obituary for a Ralph Spencer Granger in Shreveport came up, but there was nothing helpful in the article. Several public record sites claimed to have information about Ralph Spencer. Cash clicked on the first one. The site listed 187 people by that name in the United States. Only one lived in Louisiana and he was eighty-nine years old.

Maybe he'd been Ralph Spencer, Jr. Cash paid the fee to obtain the phone number and called it.

A woman answered. "Hello?"

"May I speak to Ralph Spencer?"

"Just a minute."

A man came on the line. "This is Ralph."

"Mr. Spencer, this is Adam Cash of the Noble County Sheriff's office in Pinyon, Texas. I'm calling about your son Ralph, Jr."

"I don't have any sons. Just daughters."

"Sorry to have disturbed you."

Cash tried switching the search terms around and got no additional results. He put quotes around the name and again came up empty. He changed the spelling, replacing the "c" in the last name with an "s." Nothing.

What was he missing? When Spencer first met Alissa, his truck bore Louisiana license plates. Cash hadn't asked her about it; she had volunteered the information. Surely, it was accurate. But if that was the case, he should be able to turn up something on Spencer from his life in Louisiana. Unless...

Cash placed another phone call.

"This is Rick."

"Hey, Rick. This is Cash. I didn't think I'd catch you there this late."

"Late? Hell, it's only...what...seven? What can I do for you?"

"Can you get me the VIN for that truck that blew up?"

"Sure. I record the VIN on every vehicle coming in. Avoids problems down the line."

"Text it to me, will you?"

Five minutes later, Cash's phone dinged with a message from Rick. He logged into the department website, accessed the VIN lookup site, and entered the number Rick had sent. A name popped up. Cash stared at it before snapping his drink open and taking a sip. "I'll be damned. Ralph isn't Ralph."

22

“**H**is name isn't Ralph Spencer. It's Landry Fontenot. He's from Slidell, Louisiana.”

Hodge said, "Isn't that near New Orleans?"'

"Yeah. Just across Lake Pontchartrain."

Following a knock on the conference room door, it opened and Vicky slid into the room. She dropped a box onto the table. "Sheriff Santos' wife dropped off kolaches."

Conrad bolted upright in his chair, opened the box, and grabbed three of the pastries.

"Damn, Deke," Hodge said. "Save some for the rest of us."

"Sorry. I haven't had breakfast."

"That's enough for lunch and dinner too."

"Maybe for a beanpole like you."

"I'd rather be a beanpole than a fire hydrant."

Conrad flexed his biceps. "That's pure muscle, baby."

Cash smiled at their exchange. The friendly tone of the barbs suggested a growing relationship between the two deputies.

Santos said, "Vicky, would you like one?"

"Well..." She leaned past him and picked one out of the box. "Maybe just one."

Vicky left. Santos wiped peach filling from his chin and said, "So, Landry Fontenot. What do we do with that information?"

Cash said, "We need to find out everything we can about the guy. He did something to get himself murdered. If we can solve that crime, maybe it will lead us to Alissa Collins."

"I'm sure you tried googling him."

"Yeah, there wasn't much. Two speeding tickets and an arrest three years ago for drunk and disorderly conduct. He punched a bartender who refused to serve him."

"Social media?" Hodge said.

"Nada."

Santos said, "Why did he change his name?"

Cash plucked a cherry kolache from the box. "That's the question, isn't it? He had a Texas driver's license in the name of Ralph Spencer, so the name change was a deliberate move. Yet there's no record of anyone named Landry Fontenot changing his name to Ralph Spencer, either in Louisiana or Texas. He did it on the sly."

"He must have had help," said Hodge.

"I agree. From whom?"

"Yet another question," said Santos. "Deke, I want you working on the name Landry Fontenot. Check all the states around Louisiana for that name change. If you don't find it, keep looking in other states."

"You got it," said Conrad, his lack of enthusiasm obvious. "You know I love desk work."

Santos ignored the remark. "Hodge, I want you with Borden's man this morning. If you see anything, I want to know about it right away."

"Okay."

"Cash, let's put you on—"

Cash held up a hand. "I already know where I'm going."

"Where?"

"Slidell, Louisiana."

Santos pursed his lips. "We're not looking for Landry Fontenot. We're looking for Alissa Collins."

"I know that. But I just said I think his death and her disappearance might be tied together.

"There's no proof of that."

"That's why I'm going to Slidell. To look for proof."

Santos drummed his fingers on the desk. "No, I want you here with Hodge and Borden."

"Do you think that's necessary? Borden doesn't need me holding his hand." He glanced at Hodge. "Neither does she."

"No, but she doesn't know this county like you do."

Cash wasn't persuaded. "Come on, Gabe, that's overkill."

"It may be, but that's my decision," Santos said, his gaze hardening.

"You're pulling rank on me?"

"I'm doing my job. You've stated your case and I don't buy it. End of discussion."

Cash's mouth fell open. He had never seen his friend act so imperious.

Santos stood up. "We'll meet back here at four-thirty."

Face flushing hot, Cash watched Santos leave. A long silence was broken by Conrad. "I guess I better get to it." He stood up, grabbed another kolache, and left.

Cash rested his chin in his hands. He tried to think of something he could say to Santos to change his mind. But he knew that would be impossible. During his stint in the army, how many times had he witnessed an officer issue an edict and stride away? Dozens. How many times had he seen a subordinate change an officer's mind, even with a logical argument? Zero.

Hodge cleared her throat. "We should probably get going."

His pulse still racing from the exchange with Santos, Cash said, "You go on. I'll catch up to you."

"I can wait."

Cash hit her with a hard glare. "I said go on."

"Cash, I think you should come with me. You heard what Santos said."

"Damn it, Hodge, there's a thread somewhere that ties all of this together. That thread might be in Slidell. And somebody tried to kill me. I'm not going to sit around and wait for our new friend Dudley Do-right to find out who it was."

Hodge smiled. "Who's Dudley Do-right?"

"Didn't you watch cartoons as a kid?"

"Yeah. Normal ones."

"His cartoons were on with Bullwinkle's."

"Who's Bullwinkle?"

"It doesn't matter," Cash said, his voice rising. Calming himself, he said, "Dudley Do-right is a Canadian Mountie."

"A Canadian Mountie?" Hodge scoffed. "Clete Borden is a Texas Ranger. I wouldn't let him hear you calling him Canadian."

Hodge left the room. Cash sucked in a deep breath and let it out slowly. He knew what he had to do. He was going to Slidell. He already knew his reason for Gabe when he came back. What would happen in the election if the department produced a big fat zero? That sure was the way it was looking right now, Rangers or no Rangers.

***

Cash begged Steve for the use of his truck for the drive. As Steve handed him the key fob, he said, "I think you've put more miles on it over the past few weeks than I have."

"I owe you, buddy."

"Just don't get it blown up."

Cash had already looked up everything he could find on the internet about Landry Fontenot. He had lived in Slidell for at least a few years, judging from the dates on the two addresses he had discovered. But that was it. Cash found no record of employment, no spouse, no social media accounts. He had even searched the name paired with each of the other forty-nine states and come up empty.

After giving up on Fontenot as a search term, Cash had searched Bonnie Hart and Dennis Webb. Once again he drew a blank. He wondered if they had also changed their names. If so, why? Cash had no trouble believing that a sleazebag like Fontenot had been involved in shady dealings before moving to Noble County. Maybe the same was true for Hart and Webb.

On the way out of Pinyon, Cash called Edie. He still felt sick about how he had left her house after their argument. The call went to voice mail. Annoyed, Cash entered the number again. This time, she picked up after the third ring. "Screening your calls?" he said.

"I don't know if I want to talk to you."

Cash took a breath. This was already going south. "Edie, I called to say I'm sorry. I've been thinking about it and you were right. We never said we were going together. Even if we were, you have every right to have dinner with someone who invites you out for a business meeting. I should have believed you. I should have trusted you."

"Thank you. I'm glad you came to your senses."

Cash could hear his heart thumping as he waited for her to continue.

"I thought it over, too, and realized I should have told you about it myself as soon as it happened. I'm sorry."

"Apology accepted."

"There's something I need to tell you."

"What?" He braced himself for bad news."

"Mitch Eaton came to my house. He kissed me."

Cash couldn't speak. Where was this going?

"I socked him on the jaw."

Relief flooded Cash's senses. "Sounds like he had it coming."

"Can I ask you something?"

"Yes."

"Would you like to be my steady boyfriend?"

Cash wanted to leap through the phone. "I would."

"Okay. I guess we're going together."

"That is great news," he said, his heart pounding against his ribs. "There's something else I called about." He updated her on his plan to go to Slidell.

"Will it be dangerous?" she asked.

"No, just some routine police work. Chatting with the local sheriff, interviewing people who knew Fontenot, that kind of thing."

"Are you taking your gun?"

"I'm a sheriff's deputy. Of course I'm taking a gun."

She didn't seem to like that much, because he had to wait until she said, "Come back safe. I love you."

"I love you, too."

Cash ended the call feeling giddy. She loved him. She had said so. He loved her too. They hadn't admitted such feelings for each other since their senior year in high school.

Cash shook his head and tried to focus on his trip. He was using his own money to go to Slidell. He had to, given Santos' refusal to grant permission. How much would the trip cost? More than he felt comfortable spending, especially since he hadn't yet paid the deductible for his truck repairs.

The fastest route to Cash's destination involved heading east on I-10, following that road down to San Antonio, then on through Houston and Baton Rouge before reaching Slidell. On the way out of Pinyon, Cash stopped at Shelly's Donuts on the square and filled his thirty-two-ounce vacuum flask with coffee. He also bought a sack of cherry kolaches and two pints of chocolate milk. He'd hit a Whataburger in San Antonio for lunch, then reach Slidell around supper time. After a night in a cheap hotel, he'd get to work.

***

A wearying ten hours later, Cash took the Gause Boulevard exit in Slidell and followed GPS directions to the Pennywise Lodge off the interstate. Relieved not to see an evil clown logo on the entrance sign, he turned into the parking lot. He sighed when he entered the room. A lumpy-looking bed dominated the cramped space. A threadbare carpet stretched from the door to the bathroom, its seams curling up in multiple places. A quick tour revealed mold in the bathroom shower and mouse excrement on the soap dish beside the sink. Cash hadn't been seeking luxury but hadn't expected squalor either. Still, what could he expect for sixty-five dollars a night?

Cash plopped his duffel bag on a small desk in one corner and checked the bed for bedbugs. Satisfied on that count, he sat and thought about supper. His stomach rumbled at the notion of food. Too tired to drive anywhere, he performed a quick internet search on his phone and entered a number.

"Gator Pizza," said a gruff voice.

Cash lay back and stretched his aching legs. "Do you guys deliver?"

***

Tammany Parish Sheriff Slater Bouvette clasped his meaty hands behind his head and leaned back in his leatherette chair. He rocked as he contemplated Cash's question, eliciting a soft squeak with each forward motion. "Fontenot, eh?" he said, staring at the ceiling.

"Yes," said Cash. "Landry Fontenot. Forty-three years old. Medium height and build. Brown hair, brown eyes."

Bouvette leaned forward and dropped his elbows onto the faux wood desk. "Do you know how many Fontenots there are in these parts? A lot."

"But surely there aren't too many Landry Fontenots."

"You'd be surprised." The sheriff popped open the laptop on his desk. "Give me a second and I'll check our arrest records."

Cash held his tongue while Bouvette tapped on the keyboard. The sheriff had close-set eyes that straddled a hawk-like nose. His thick blonde hair was combed in a perfect coif.

Bouvette stopped typing. "Here we go. He's had a few speeding tickets, which he paid. One arrest for being drunk and disorderly." He studied the screen. "Nothing else."

"Anything about stealing gas? Diesel, in particular."

"Nope."

Cash clicked his tongue in disappointment. "Okay, thanks. I'll get out of your hair. There are a few people I want to talk to."

Bouvette squinted so that, to Cash, he looked like the actor Owen Wilson. The sheriff said, "What people?"

"I found two addresses where Fontenot used to live. Maybe somebody remembers him."

"Well," said Bouvette, an edge to his voice. "Knock yourself out. Just don't stir up any trouble in my town."

Trouble? Cash was in Slidell to investigate a murder, and the local sheriff was worried he might cause trouble? "I won't."

Bouvette stood up. "I'll take your word for it. But I'm not real fond of outside lawmen working in my parish."

"I'll be as discreet as I can."

The sheriff extended a hand. Cash shook it. Bouvette said, "He must be a real crime lord for you to come from Texas all the way to Slidell. What's he wanted for anyway?"

"He's not," said Cash. "I'm after his killer."

"He was murdered?"

"Yep."

"Back in Pinyon, right?"

"Right."

"I'd be looking back there if I was you."

After Cash left, one of Bouvette's deputies, a twenty-year veteran named Red LeBlanc, encountered Bouvette on his way back to his office. "What did that guy want?"

"He's on a wild goose chase," said Bouvette. "Somebody got killed in Texas and he's looking for answers here."

"Where in Texas?"

"A pissant little town by the name of Pinyon. Ever hear of it?"

"Can't say that I have."

"Yeah. Me either."

LeBlanc waited until Bouvette disappeared back into his office. Then he strolled outside, drawing an involuntary breath as he hit a wall of heat and humidity. He pulled out his phone and opened his contacts. Scrolling, he found one labeled "Preacher" and tapped the call button.

"What's up?"

"There's something you ought to know."

"What?"

"Have you forgotten our deal?"

"So much for family, eh? All right, I'll put a Benjamin in the mail. Now tell me what you know."

"Two Benjamins."

"Don't be greedy."

"Two or I hang up."

"All right. Two. Now what's your news?"

"A sheriff's deputy from Texas just left the building."

"Yeah, so?"

"He's from Noble County, Texas."

There was a long silence. "Thanks. The Benjamins are on their way."

***

Clumps of weeds poked through the parking lot. The Marina Grove Apartments was a two-story building of dirty brick and flaking wood siding in a rundown neighborhood. Cash parked the truck in front of a sign reading "Office" and killed the engine. Exiting the vehicle, he stepped into a puddle of what looked like green vomit. He swore and found a patch of weeds to wipe his boots clean. Noting the humming of the soft drink machine he passed, he made a mental note to slake his thirst on his way back. Reaching the office door, he turned the handle, but the door stuck. He thumped it with his shoulder and it flew open with a bang.

Cash stepped inside. A noisy window air conditioner was doing little to ease the intense heat in the room. A faded green sofa that looked like it had been scavenged from a dumpster sat opposite a metal desk. On the wall behind the desk was a handwritten sign reading "Rent due the first of the month—NO EXCEPTIONS!"

A prune-faced woman with thinning hair stepped out of a back room. A cigarette dangled from her cherry-red lips. "You scared me half to death, young fella," she said in a raspy voice. "Busting through my door like that." She sucked on her cigarette and glared at Cash as if he had walked in on her in the bathroom.

"Sorry about that, ma'am." Cash reached into his pocket for identification. "I'm with the Noble County, Texas sheriff's department and I was hoping you could tell me about one of your former tenants."

He showed her the ID. She studied it and said, "Sonny, you must be lost. You crossed the state line about four hours ago."

"I know that. Your sheriff gave me permission to come here."

She sniffed and exhaled a cloud of smoke. "Is that so? How do I know you ain't lying?"

Cash stepped back from the nauseating smoke. The room smelled like a chimney. "You could call him if you like." He dropped onto the sofa. "I'll wait."

The old lady frowned. "No, I ain't got time for that. What do you want?"

Rising from the sofa, Cash said, "You had a tenant awhile back named Landry Fontenot. I was wondering if you remember anything about him."

"Fontenot, eh? Another damn Cajun, I guess."

"Is that a Cajun name?"

"You're dang right that's a Cajun name. Ain't there any Cajuns in Texas? Shoot, maybe I ought to move there. We're crawling with them here."

"Do you remember him?"

She shook her head and puffed on her cigarette. "Can't say that I do. Let me check something." She sat at her desk, eliciting a loud squeak from the ancient chair. She yanked a bottom drawer open and pulled out a thick binder. After leafing through it, she said, "Here he is. Landry R. Fontenot." She sounded each word out as if she was reading a foreign language. "Moved here in August 2018 and left the following June. Says here he left the place a mess. Cost me three hundred dollars to have it cleaned. His deposit was only two hundred and fifty."

"What can you tell me about him?"

The woman snapped the binder shut and returned it to the drawer. "I just told you everything I know."

"Are you sure?"

She muttered something under her breath. "Can't you understand English? I don't know nothing."

"Sorry. Thanks for your help."

Cash reached for the door handle.

"Young fella."

Cash turned.

"If you see him, tell him he owes me fifty bucks."

***

Cash held out higher hopes for the second address on his list. According to his internet search, Fontenot had moved out a year ago, roughly the time he showed up in Noble County. Also, this neighborhood looked much nicer than the one he had just left. At the very least, a nicer apartment complex should keep better records.

A fashionably dressed woman walking her dog waved at him as he turned into the parking lot of the Pine Forest Apartments. Cash followed the signs for the office through a maze of two-story buildings, each bearing a different letter of the alphabet. Stopping at building K, he killed his engine, took a final sip of his Dr Pepper, and hopped out of the truck. The sweet scent of honeysuckle that greeted him contrasted sharply with the stench at Marina Grove.

Cash found the office and opened the door. The cool air that greeted him provided welcome relief from the sauna outside. A professionally dressed woman behind an immaculate desk rose to greet him. "Good morning. Welcome to Pine Forest. I'm Amanda, the manager."

"Nice to meet you, Amanda," said Cash, producing his ID. After introducing himself he explained the purpose of his visit.

"I remember Mr. Fontenot," said Amanda. "He was rougher than our usual tenants."

"How so?"

"It was the way he talked, like he wasn't very educated. His clothes were always dirty and the truck he drove stood out from the other cars in the parking lot."

"Do you know what he did for a living?"

"I'm afraid I don't."

"Did he have visitors? Family? A girlfriend, maybe?"

"Again, I can't help you. I'm sorry. All I know is he paid his rent on time and didn't cause any trouble."

Cash heaved a frustrated sigh.

"I'm really sorry."

"Don't worry about it. One more question. Can you think of any reason that somebody might want to kill him?"

Amanda's eyebrows shot up. "My goodness, no. Like I said, he never caused any trouble. And he was a religious man."

"How do you know that?"

"When he was leaving, he came by for his deposit. I mentioned something about my church and he reached into his duffel bag and gave me a Bible."

Finally, a clue. "Do you still have it?"

"I think so." She opened a desk drawer and rummaged through it. "Here it is."

Amanda handed the book over. About the size of a hardback novel, it had a faux leather cover and the title "Holy Bible." Cash thumbed through the flimsy pages. "May I keep this?" he asked.

"Of course. I don't know why I've held onto it this long."

"Thank you." He extended his hand. "And thank you for your cooperation."

They shook. When Cash started to pull his hand back Amanda grasped it more firmly. "Why don't we grab some lunch together? I know a great Mexican place."

The invitation startled Cash. Amanda looked older than him, but not by much. And she was indeed an attractive woman. He smiled and said, "I'd be tempted if I didn't already have a girlfriend."

She stroked the back of his hand with her thumb. "I'm not looking to be your girlfriend, honey. Just looking for a little fun."

Cash pulled his hand free. "I'm flattered, but no."

With a wan smile, she said, "Well, if you ever come back to Slidell, you know where to find me."

23

Bonnie rotated the crystal bourbon glass in her hand and watched it sparkle in the light. "Emmett, do you know why your uncle recommended you?"

Seated on the sofa opposite her recliner, Fuller smirked. "Do tell, sweetheart."

"He said you were ruthless." Bonnie slammed home the bourbon and leaned forward. "That you'd do whatever it took to get the job done. The bomb didn't work. You'll have to use a more direct approach."

"What happened to all that holier-than-thou crap? I thought you guys were members of the God squad."

"That's Dennis. I just play along to keep him happy."

"How convenient." Fuller stood up, feeling her pressure, and paced the floor. "Look, this is serious shit. I agreed to stick that bomb under his truck because there's not much chance of them tracing it back to us. But this is different. I'm not going to prison for the rest of my life for you. I don't care how good of a lay you are."

Bonnie laughed. "It's a bit too late for that, isn't it? If he figures us out, how long do you think it would be before he's on to you too?"

"You bitch," Fuller said, red-faced, his eyes shooting lasers. "Are you threatening to rat me out?"

"No," said Bonnie, putting up her hands. "I'm just saying that the cops aren't stupid. If they find me don't you think they'd go snooping around the guy that lives in the trailer next door?"

Fuller dropped back onto the sofa. "Why are you so hot to get rid of this guy? There's other people in that department, too."

"He's the one that keeps showing up. Do you know what he's doing right now? He's over in Slidell poking around about Fontenot."

"Who?"

"Ralph Spencer. You might remember him. You blew up his truck."

He saw her point. "Are you sure there's no other way to get him to stop?"

"He's got a kid. I'm gonna get to know her mother. Maybe we can use her. But the only surefire way is what I've already said."

Fuller let out a sigh and laid his head back on the sofa. Bonnie refilled her bourbon glass. "No guns. Unless you can get ahold of one that's untraceable."

"I can't do that without making people wonder why I'd need it."

"A knife then. Cut his throat."

"That would be a bloody mess. Look, they would investigate the hell out of a deputy's death, maybe even call in the FBI. And they wouldn't stop until they found the killer."

"Okay, then you tell me. What *are* you willing to do?"

Fuller stalled for time. "I'll think on it and let you know. But you're gonna owe me."

"I already paid you."

He grinned. "I'm not talking about money."

"What *are* you talking about?"

It was Webb, who had slipped into the room unnoticed.

Fuller's eyes went wide with fear. Bonnie said, "Nothing, baby. He's just joking around."

Webb frowned. "I don't like that kind of joke." He looked at Fuller. "Am I clear?"

"Sorry. It won't happen again."

Bonnie said, "Baby, you need to relax."

"I am relaxed," Webb said. "He's the one who's getting a hard-on."

Bonnie sauntered up to him and rubbed his chest. "There's only one dick in this room that interests me. Got it?"

A smile slowly spread across Webb's face. He put an arm around Bonnie and tugged her toward the hall. Glancing back at Fuller, he said, "Go on, get out of here. My wife and I could use a little privacy."

***

Cash popped another piece of spicy Cajun popcorn into his mouth and sighed. He had come to Slidell in hopes of uncovering the mysterious Landry Fontenot. Instead, he had encountered a local sheriff who saw him as a nuisance, a wrinkly apartment manager who offered no help, and another apartment manager who, while more cooperative, seemed more interested in undressing him. All he had to show for his gas and hotel money was the cheap Bible that Fontenot had left with Amanda. That and a bag of spicy Cajun popcorn.

Cash could feel his eyelids sagging to oblivion. He shook his head and snapped them open. He had gotten up at four a.m. for the ten-hour drive back to Pinyon. Now he was cursing himself for starting so early. How had he expected to stay awake on such a boring drive? If Interstate 10 between the Louisiana state line and Houston wasn't the most tedious stretch of highway in the country, it had to make the top five.

Just before Beaumont, Cash exited the highway and pulled up to a gas station convenience store. He needed caffeine. He bought a large cup and downed half of it on the way back to the truck. As he settled into his seat, he glanced at the Bible next to his popcorn. He hadn't really taken a good look at it yet. As he opened it, an inscription on the title page caught his eye. It read, "For Landry, who has helped this ministry more than he can know. Keep the good word of the Lord in your heart. With Christian love, M."

Who was M? Did M stand for a first name or a last name? Probably a first name. Was he—or she, since M could be a woman—a relative? A friend? A boss? And what ministry had Fontenot helped "more than he can know?"

Finding the inscription brightened Cash's mood. Maybe his trip hadn't been wasted after all. It wasn't much of a clue, but it could be unraveled.

Two bathroom stops later, Cash arrived at the Pinyon exit. He guided the truck down the ramp, turned right toward town, and swore. An enormous billboard loomed next to the road. On it was a black and white picture of a scowling Gabe Santos beside the words, "For your family's safety, give this man the boot. Vote Eaton for Sheriff."

***

Webb fingered the battery-operated miniature camera in his pocket as he pushed open the door to Fuller's trailer. Inside, he marveled at the immaculate room. He never would have pegged Fuller for a neat freak. A blue lounge chair faced a television set on a glass-topped stand. The spotless glass beneath the TV gleamed in the sunlight let in by dust-free Venetian blinds. Three hunting magazines arranged in a neat fan pattern covered one end of a faux wood coffee table. To his right was an immaculate kitchenette. To his left past the lounge chair was a double bed with two fluffed pillows at its head. A wrinkle-free comforter lay over the turned-down sheet.

Webb walked to the bed and assessed the ceiling above it. The array of two-by-two white gypsum tiles was perfect for the job.

Given his height, Webb had no difficulty nudging a tile directly over the bed to one side. He slid four AA batteries into the camera's power pack and slipped the pack through the gap in the tiles. After attaching the power cord to the camera, he returned the tile to its original position and wedged the camera between two tiles. He lay down on the bed and studied his handiwork. He could see the camera, but only with difficulty. He figured that neither Bonnie nor Fuller would detect it. At least not while engaged in a workout.

Webb got up and smoothed the bed cover. He still had the camera app on his phone from when he had used it to spy on Ralph Spencer in Louisiana. Back then, he had been surprised to learn that Spencer was honest. Only later, when the bastard got greedy after their move to Texas, had he become a problem. After all, greed was a deadly sin.

Webb opened his phone's settings and navigated to the Wi-Fi connections. If he was lucky, Fuller hadn't changed the password since Webb had arranged to have the system installed. He typed in "Rednecksrule." The appearance of a blue checkmark next to the network name told him that Fuller hadn't.

Webb opened the camera app. He tapped on the live feed icon and saw an overhead view of himself pop onto the screen. Holding the phone close to his ear, he counted out loud. His voice came through the phone's speaker in a crisp, clear tone.

Satisfied, Webb exited the trailer. On the way back to the house, he asked himself what he would do if his suspicion that Bonnie was cheating on him with Fuller proved correct. The Bible was clear: adulterers were to be stoned to death. Could he do that to Bonnie? Probably not. Fuller, though, was a nice big target.

***

Bonnie Hart closed her eyes and listened to the rhythmic thumping of Webb's heartbeat. *Lub-dub. Lub-dub. Lub-dub.* She imagined herself a fetus inside a mother's womb. Floating gently in the amniotic fluid. No stress, no worries, blissfully unaware that worries even existed. Alive, yet free of all burdens, even the need to breathe. With everything provided through the umbilical cord, the magic lifeline connecting it to its mother that brought food, brought oxygen, brought life. *Lub-dub. Lub-dub. Lub-dub.*

A snort from Webb broke into her reverie. She opened her eyes and saw the big man's chest rise and fall. Inhaled the sweaty odor of his armpits. Felt the hair on his chest scratching her cheek. She still heard the heartbeat, but it had lost its ability to soothe. She was back to her wretched existence. Back to hiding, lying, doing whatever it took to survive. Including, she was beginning to believe, betraying the man who had hauled her out of the morass into a life of luxury.

At first, she had thought Webb handsome. His strong jaw, muscular physique, and thick beard had sucked her in. Lately, though, that relentless deputy's activities had dulled the big man's physical attraction. No matter how good the sex might be, she had no intention of going to prison for Dennis Webb. No man was worth that. Let him go up in flames by himself.

***

An hour later, Bonnie was making herself a sandwich in the kitchen when Fuller rapped on the laundry room door and let himself into the house. She didn't look up as he entered the room. "Are you hungry?" she said.

He grabbed her from behind and pulled her in tight. "You bet. But not for no damn sandwich."

She twisted out of his grasp and turned around. "Stop it. He might see us."

Fuller snorted. "Right. This late in the evening? I'll bet he's halfway through a bottle of Jim Beam right now. Which means he'll be out like a light until morning."

Bonnie removed a slice of Swiss cheese from its package and slapped it onto a piece of bread. "Maybe. But we still have to be careful."

"We are careful."

"Then don't grab me like that in the house."

Fuller opened the refrigerator and found a beer. He popped the can open with a loud snap. "I can't help it, babe. Every time I see you I get a King Kong-sized boner." He took a long pull from the can. "I thought you liked that."

She sidled up to him and rubbed a hand across his chest. Lowering her voice, she said, "You know I do." She patted his crotch. "Tell you what. Let me eat this sandwich and I'll meet you back at your trailer. That will give me a chance to make sure he's really out."

Fuller produced a face-splitting grin. "Me and King Kong will be ready."

24

Cash stepped into the building hoping to see Conrad so he could ask him about his internet research on Ralph Spencer, a.k.a. Landry Fontenot. Instead, Vicky sat alone in the lobby pecking away at her keyboard. Instead of her usual flirtatious grin, she greeted Cash with a frown.

"Hey, Vicky."

"He's awfully mad at you."

"Who?" Cash said, feigning ignorance.

"The sheriff. He told me to tell him the minute you got in."

Cash sighed. He had hoped to face Santos only after speaking with Conrad and Hodge. "Is he in his office?"

"Yeah."

Cash started past her desk. "Cash?" Vicky said, concern in her voice. "Are you in trouble?"

He waved her off. "This isn't high school, Vicky."

He found Santos at his desk going through a thick stack of documents. He didn't look up as Cash eased into a chair.

"You went to Slidell, didn't you?"

"Yes."

"I told you not to."

"I'm aware of that."

"Then why did you go?"

Cash tugged at his collar. Santos was going to play the hardass. "I wanted to learn more about Ralph Spencer."

For the first time, Santos looked up. "And did you?"

"Not really."

Santos stood up, stepped past Cash, and shut the door. He returned to his seat. "I can't believe I'm having to tell you this, but when I give an order, I expect it to be followed."

"I'm trying to save your ass in the election."

Santos continued as though Cash hadn't spoken. "There's a chain of command here, just like we had in the service. And like it or not, I'm at the top of that chain."

"It's true I didn't learn much, but we had to check it out. Landry—"

Santos cut him off. "How far would you have gotten arguing with Sergeant Malkoff about an order you disobeyed?"

Cash didn't want to answer. "Not far."

"So how much do you think I care about your reasons for going to Slidell when I told you not to?"

"Not much."

"You're goddamned right, not much."

Cash flinched at the fury in Santos' face. He had gone for the right reasons, but he had to admit it. He had made a mistake. "You're right, Gabe. I'm sorry."

Santos relaxed. "Thank you. Now, would you like to hear what the rest of us have been up to?"

"Yeah."

"Deke has been digging into Ralph Spencer, aka Landry Fontenot but not making much headway. I just don't think we're going to find anything on the man. Hodge and Borden are watching Dennis Webb and Bonnie Hart's place."

"Have they seen anything?"

"Not yet."

"I guess I haven't missed much."

There was that furious look again. Cash said, "Sorry, bad joke."

"And, with your results—or lack thereof—in Slidell, we're no closer to finding Alissa Collins."

Cash held up a finger. "There is one thing."

"What's that?"

He told Santos about the Bible and the inscription. Santos was unimpressed. "Sounds like we all wasted our time," he said. He stood up. "I'm gonna go grab a late lunch. Want to join me?"

"Thanks, no."

Santos started for the door, then stopped. "One more thing."

"Yeah?"

"We're friends, Cash, and I want it to stay that way. But don't cross me again."

***

Cash found neither Hodge nor Conrad at the station, so he drove to the Packsaddle to see Steve. He wanted to probe his friend for ideas about the Bible he had brought back from Slidell. An outside-the-box thinker like Steve might give him a fresh perspective.

It was midafternoon on a weekday, so the brewpub had only a handful of customers. A middle-aged couple shared a pizza at one of the tables. There were three people at the bar, all men. Two of them sat together watching a baseball game on the wall-mounted television. A third man drank alone.

Cash approached the bar and took a harder look at the solo drinker. Tall, clean-shaven, with muscles that Superman would envy. It was Emmett Fuller. Cash dropped onto the stool next to him.

Fuller glanced sideways at Cash and spotted the uniform. "I didn't know sheriffs could drink."

"I'm just a deputy. I'm here to see my friend. He's the owner."

A grunt from Fuller indicated that the conversation was over. Cash said, "I know you."

Fuller sipped his beer. "No, you don't."

"I do. And I think you remember me. You're the guy who burns during a fire ban."

"Are you here to give me a ticket?"

"No. But let me ask you something. What really happened to Landry Fontenot?"

Fuller's face twitched involuntarily. "Who the hell is Landry Fontenot?"

"When he died, he was going by Ralph Spencer."

"That's news to me," said Fuller, recovering from his tell. He took a long pull. "All I ever called him was Dickhead."

"How did he die, Fuller?"

Fuller drained the rest of his beer and set the glass on the bar. "Why don't you go play cops and robbers somewhere else?" When Cash said nothing, Fuller tapped his chest. "Go on. Take a hike."

"Don't touch me."

Fuller tapped him again, harder this time. "Or what?"

Cash braced himself. He knew he had touched a nerve in Fuller. "I'll let it go twice, but not a third time."

Fuller turned and moved to shove Cash from his stool, but Cash was ready. In a lightning move, he sprang to his feet, grabbed Fuller's arm, and pulled the big man past him. Fuller's momentum carried him forward and sent him crashing into a chair. Both he and the chair tumbled onto the concrete floor.

"Get up. You're under arrest," Cash said.

Fuller clambered to his feet and squared off in a fighter's stance. Cash tensed. Fuller was slow, but those powerful arms could do a lot of damage if he wasn't careful.

The big man feinted right, then charged left. Cash sidestepped, wrapped an arm around his neck, and slammed his face against the bar. "Don't move," he said through clenched teeth.

Steve dashed out from the kitchen and froze. "What's going on?"

"I'm arresting one of your customers." Fuller swung an ineffective punch. Cash tightened his hold. "Do you really want to do this? Every second you fight will only make things worse for you."

Instead of relenting, Fuller jerked his head and shoulders back and twisted out of Cash's grip. Before Cash could react, Fuller threw a quick jab into his jaw. Seeing stars, Cash bounced off the bar and dropped to his knees.

Fuller moved in for another shot, but Steve swung a beer bottle that crashed into his skull, dropping him like a shot hog. Cash scrambled onto the fallen man's back and snapped on a pair of handcuffs.

As Cash hauled Fuller to his feet, Steve caught the other two men at the bar staring. "Thanks for the help, fellas."

One of the men shrugged. "Ain't our fight."

Cash glanced at the table at which the couple had been sharing a pizza. They had fled, leaving half of their pie untouched.

"Need anything else?" said Steve.

"No."

"You're welcome."

Still panting, Cash said, "I had him." He grabbed Fuller's arm and frog-marched him toward the exit.

"Hey!" said Steve, throwing out his hands in a what-the-hell gesture. "What about his tab?"

***

Hodge slid her mouth around a forkful of macaroni and cheese and moaned with pleasure. "Meemaw, your mac and cheese is the best in the world."

Hodge's grandmother, a thickset woman old enough to recall whites-only water fountains at the Junction bus station, clicked her tongue. "Of course it is, baby. You think Big Momma would let me make it for Juneteenth if it wasn't?"

"You know Big Momma can't dress herself anymore, much less cook the mac and cheese."

"Hush. Even before she lost her mind, that woman said mine was better than hers. The secret is the hot sauce. Just enough to tickle the tongue but not enough to let you know what did it. Now, don't fill up on nothing but mac and cheese. I didn't make that meatloaf for the dog."

Hodge took a bite of the meatloaf. As usual, she found it much too salty. She would have preferred to make a supper entirely of mac and cheese but didn't want to offend her grandmother.

The two of them sat at a table that Hodge's grandfather had fashioned out of an old wagon wheel. After welding together a support stand, he had ordered a top of tempered glass from a shop in San Antonio. Hodge had been eating on it ever since she could remember.

Meemaw said, "How do you like being a sheriff's deputy? Are they treating you all right?"

"They're treating me fine."

"Nobody's giving you trouble on account of you being colored?"

"Black, Meemaw. Nobody says colored anymore."

"I say it and I'll keep on saying it if I want."

Hodge sighed. They had held such conversations many times. They always ended the same, with her grandmother launching into a diatribe against the younger generation. "Yes, ma'am. Like I said, they're treating me fine."

"I find that hard to swallow. White folks have been in charge around here forever. Why would they want to let you boss them around?"

"I don't boss them around. Besides, the sheriff is Mexican-American."

"I don't care if he's Chinese, he ain't one of us."

"Don't worry. He might not be sheriff for long."

"Are you talking about the election?"

"Yes. That guy Eaton is probably going to win. People know him around here better than they do Sheriff Santos. And he's got way more money to spend on his campaign."

Meemaw snorted. "People may know him, but that man's broke."

Hodge reared her head up. "What are you talking about?"

"I'm saying he doesn't have two nickels to rub together."

"How can that be? He has a three-thousand-acre ranch."

"That ranch is bleeding money, honey. Nobody makes a living by being a rancher no more."

Hodge was calculating what this meant. "How do you know this?"

"How would I not? Going back at least five years, he never paid your granddaddy one cent. I hear tell he owes every other store in the county, too."

A familiar ache developed in Hodge's chest at the mention of her grandfather. Before his death, the man Hodge called Chief had owned a profitable feed store in Pinyon. Until prostate cancer claimed him a year ago, they had been close. His absence still hurt. "So you're saying that Mitch Eaton has no money."

"That's exactly what I'm saying."

"What about all the money he made in Waco? Hospital administrators are paid pretty well."

"Whatever he made, he spent that and more. I hear he likes to gamble."

Wait until everyone heard this. "I'll be damned."

"You watch your mouth, Keisha Hodge. Now go on and finish your meatloaf."

She reached for the mac and cheese. "No, thanks. Here's what I want."

***

Conrad unlocked the cell door and swung it open. "All right, Fuller, you can go."

Fuller stepped out of the cell. "That deputy is a maniac. You guys ought to rein him in."

"He says you started it."

"He's a lying sack of shit."

"Yeah, right."

Conrad fed his badge into the exit door slot and waited for the click. As he led Fuller into the lobby, he said, "Next time you take a poke at a law enforcement officer, you might not be so lucky."

"Like you said, yeah right."

When Fuller was gone, Conrad caught Vicky's eye. "What time is it?"

She checked her phone. "Eight oh five."

"I better hurry."

He bolted past her and strode down the hall to the conference room. Santos, Cash, and Hodge were already seated.

Santos said, "They'd crucify you in the army, Deke."

"Good thing we're not in the army then," said Conrad, sliding into a chair.

"Don't be so sure," said Cash, immediately regretting the sarcastic remark. He glanced at Santos, but he didn't react. Instead, he rapped the table.

"Let's get started," Santos said. "Has anyone learned anything I don't already know about the Alissa Collins case?" When no one spoke, he added, "So, we've still got diddly squat."

Cash raised a hand. "Don't forget the Bible."

"What Bible?" Hodge said.

Cash explained about the book he had brought back from Slidell, concluding with, "If I can figure out the inscription, that might tell us more about who Ralph Spencer really was."

"Which doesn't help us one bit," said Santos.

"You're forgetting about Emmett Fuller. He knows something. I'm sure of it."

"I've said this before. We're not investigating Ralph Spencer's death. We're trying to find Alissa Collins."

Cash forced himself to keep his voice down. "I'm aware of that. As *I've* said before, I think there's a connection between Spencer's death and Alissa's disappearance. And now that we've got Fuller in jail, we might be able to get him to talk."

"Is that why you punched him out in the Packsaddle yesterday?"

"I didn't punch him out. He assaulted me and I defended myself."

Santos pulled out his phone. "That's not how he tells it. And he's got two witnesses that say you hit him first."

"That's bullshit." This time Cash's agitation was obvious.

"Want to see?"

He slid his phone to Cash. Cash picked it up and tapped the screen to start the video. The clip began with Cash locking his arm around Fuller's neck and slamming him against the bar. It ended with Cash straddling Fuller and locking the handcuffs. Cash said, "This doesn't show the beginning."

"Which is why I had to let him go this morning." He looked at Conrad. "He's gone, right?"

Conrad nodded. "That's why I was late."

Cash said, "You can't really believe I started that."

"I don't. But there's no proof that he did. Lars said that without a witness to support your story, there are no grounds for prosecution."

"Who's Lars?" Hodge asked.

"Lars Newsome. He's the county DA. Anyway, Fuller has two witnesses to back him up." He took his phone back. "Plus the video."

Cash's neck flushed hot. Without him realizing it, his fingers curled up to make fists of both hands. "So that's it? Fuller walks and we just give up on Alissa Collins?"

Santos said nothing.

Hodge spoke up. "Maybe we could ask the FBI for help."

"No," said Santos. "Alissa Collins is missing, but they'd want proof she was kidnapped before getting involved."

Cash let out an exasperated gasp.

Santos said, "Anyway, we still have the Rangers on board."

"By the way, where is Borden?" said Cash. "Why isn't he here?"

"He's watching Webb's gate."

"All right, Boss, what do you want me to do?"

"Go join him."

***

Cash had no intention of wasting his time with Clete Borden. He had been planning to go see Emma and now, when he had nothing better to do, seemed as good a time as any. He drove to Bernadette's trailer and knocked on the door.

Bernadette appeared and said, "What are you doing here?"

"I came to see Emma. Can I come in?"

She hesitated and then pulled the door open the rest of the way. "Okay."

Cash stepped inside. A familiar blonde-haired woman sat on the sofa. She cradled Emma in her arms. Bonnie Hart.

"Hello, Deputy," Bonnie said.

Cash turned to Bernadette. "What's she doing here?"

"I met her at work. She brought her dog in to see Dr. Manor."

Bonnie patted the couch cushion. "Have a seat." When Cash remained standing, she said, "Come on, I don't have cooties."

Cash lowered himself onto the sofa. Bonnie handed Emma to him. "Here you go, darling," she said. "Your daddy is here."

As usual, Cash's heart melted with Emma in his arms. He made a face at his daughter to elicit a laugh.

Bonnie said, "I can tell she likes her daddy."

Cash tickled the child's belly, bringing forth another squeal of laughter. He kissed her cheek and stood up. Handing Emma to her mother, he said, "I'll be right back. Bonnie and I have something to discuss." He motioned to her and walked outside. She followed him onto the small porch and closed the door.

"What are you really doing here?" He didn't bother hiding his anger.

"Bernadette and I met at the vet. We got to talking and she invited me over to see Emma. She's a beautiful child, although I must say she looks more like her mother than you."

"Bullshit. That's too much of a coincidence."

"It's a small town."

"I've been to your house. You don't have a dog."

Bonnie pointed at her SUV in the driveway. "Sure I do. There he is."

Cash looked over at the vehicle. A medium-sized spaniel mix stared at him through a rear window.

"What's his name?"

"Buster."

"And now you and Bernadette are best pals."

"I don't know about best, but yeah, we hit it off right away."

Cash worked his jaw. Yes, Pinyon was a small town, but he couldn't believe that Bonnie had run into Bernadette by chance. The woman was up to something.

"Here's what's going to happen. I'm going back inside and you're going to get in your car and drive away."

"Not without saying goodbye to Bernadette. That would be rude."

He stepped between her and the door. "Try and get past me."

Bonnie smiled and stepped off the porch. "No, thank you. She likes you, you know. She said she didn't at first, but now she does. Says you're trying real hard to be a good daddy to Emma."

"None of this concerns you."

"The question is, how much do you like her?"

"What does that mean?"

"Am I not speaking English?"

"I want you gone. Do I need to drag you to your car?"

She smiled again. "Don't be silly. I know when I'm not wanted." Her voice was overly sweet.

Cash watched her get into the SUV and went back inside. Bernadette looked at him with innocent eyes. Cash said, "Don't ever let that woman in the house again."

***

Bonnie drove to the Tractor Supply and pulled around the store to the empty field in the back. Pulling the rear door open, she said, "Go on, get out of here."

The dog bounded to the ground and looked at her expectantly.

"Shoo. Go away."

The dog didn't move.

She swore and fished in her purse to find one last dog treat. After showing it to the dog, she hurled it into the field. The dog sped away after it.

Bonnie climbed behind the wheel of the SUV and started the engine. "Mangy mutt probably got fleas in my car."

25

Bonnie rolled onto her back and opened her eyes. She felt her chest rise and fall with each panting breath. Her body tingled with post-coital pleasure as she brushed a hand against the man beside her in bed. "You're a beast."

Fuller blew out a long, slow breath. "That's the best sex I've ever had."

"Amen to that."

Bonnie had once thought it would be tough to beat Webb's prowess between the sheets. Then she met Emmett Fuller. As good as Webb was, Fuller took her to heights she hadn't thought possible. She lost all concept of space and time when she was with him, an exhilarating sensation she had never felt with Webb. He made her feel like a giddy sixteen-year-old experiencing a man's body for the first time. Bonnie couldn't get enough.

She rolled to her side and stroked Fuller's hair. He jerked his head away. "Ouch."

"What's the matter?"

"That's where that guy clocked me with a beer bottle. It hurts like hell."

"Maybe you shouldn't pick fights with county deputies."

"It would have turned out different except for that bartender."

"Anyway, he won't be bothering you much longer, will he?"

Fuller sat up. He stuffed a pillow behind his back and scooted against the headboard. "I've been thinking about that. Why should I stick my neck out? If I'm going to risk a life sentence, why not do it for myself? For us?"

"I'm not sure I catch your drift."

"What if, instead of taking out that deputy, I take out Webb? Then you and me get all those gold coins and do whatever we want without a member of the God squad breathing down our necks."

Bonnie thought about that. Her life had taken an upswing since hooking up with Webb, but there were plenty of negatives. To start, his pious, holier-than-thou schtick was wearing thin. Don't cuss, don't cheat at cards, don't lie. At least, don't lie to him. He didn't seem to care that she had lied plenty on his behalf.

Furthermore, what good was all that money if they couldn't use it? She wanted a lifestyle that involved country clubs, fancy restaurants, and travel to exotic locales. She wanted to watch the cliff divers at Acapulco, view Paris from the Eiffel Tower, and see *The Lion King* on Broadway. Instead, she was holed up on a shitty little West Texas ranch near a shitty little town whose residents thought a Backyard Bacon Ranch cheeseburger at Dairy Queen was fine dining. Webb had even objected to her playing poker at the club in town. He relented only after a shouting match that culminated in her threatening to leave him. With Webb out of the picture, she and Fuller could ditch this godforsaken place and start fresh somewhere far away.

"How would you do it?" she asked.

"With a gun. I'd shoot him in the head when he's asleep, then put the gun in his hand and shoot it again."

"Why shoot it again?"

"Don't you watch TV? They can do tests to see if someone has fired a gun. If they see that he did, they'll think it was suicide."

"Do you have a gun?"

"I've got a few."

"I thought you said no guns."

"For the deputy. This is different."

She rolled over and laid her head on his chest. The soothing sound of his heartbeat dismantled whatever objections she still had. "When?"

"The sooner the better."

"Where would we go?"

"Wherever you want."

She liked the sound of that. Webb had never asked her if she wanted to come to Texas. She lifted her head and kissed Fuller. "Acapulco."

***

Dennis Webb removed the headset and leaned back in his chair. A knot formed in his gut as he processed what he had just heard. Not only was Bonnie, a woman he had risked everything for, cheating on him, she was plotting his murder. And Fuller—what a rotten traitor he turned out to be. Webb had given him so much and now the filthy dog was turning on its master.

Bonnie's betrayal stung the most. The woman he had planned to spend the rest of his life with was just another Athalia, the evil biblical queen who murdered her grandchildren to secure the throne. She didn't love him, she loved his money. And to get it, she would kill. Which meant he would have to strike first.

Could he kill Bonnie? Even though she deserved it, he wasn't sure. Fuller was another matter.

Would God forgive him? He had to believe He would. Sometimes he wondered what his life would be like if he hadn't found the Lord. Born in Covington, Louisiana as Maurice Trahan, the man who now called himself Dennis Webb grew up in a house with little religion. His parents dragged him to church every Christmas and Easter, but young Maurice didn't see that it had much effect on how they led their lives. His father was away from home for two weeks a month, working on an offshore oil rig. When he was home, he spent most of his time drinking and playing video games.

Maurice's mother, a housekeeper at Covington's Lakeview Hospital, spent the time her husband was away entertaining a string of men friends at the house. On weekend evenings she'd toss a sack of fast food on the table, call it his supper, and head out for a night of partying. She'd get home late, usually drunk, with a male companion who'd smile at him, give him five bucks, and call him a good kid. Throughout the night Maurice would hear them moaning and rocking the cheap pine bed in his parents' bedroom.

Maurice dropped out of school midway through his junior year to work on the offshore rigs. He bought a used motorcycle and began riding with a gang calling itself "The Harley Hellraisers." Over the next few years, police arrested him four times for assault before catching him trying to sell twenty grams of cocaine. He spent five years locked up at Oakdale Federal Correctional Institution. That's where the Lord entered his life.

His spiritual guide was a fellow inmate named Tuck Barchus, an older man serving twenty years for robbery and assault. Maurice began attending Bible study sessions with Barchus. Soon he was leading them himself. By the time of his release, he considered himself reborn.

Not long thereafter, Maurice met Landry Fontenot at a Kawasaki dealership while admiring a Ninja H2 R, the most expensive model in the Kawasaki line. Neither of them could dream of owning such a beautiful machine. Fontenot was struggling to make a living as a wedding videographer. Maurice had returned to the offshore rigs. He asked Fontenot to help him create and post YouTube videos of him preaching the good news. One of his videos went viral, and soon he had over a million followers.

Calling himself the Bible Biker, Maurice began hawking merchandise at the end of each sermon. He made a small fortune selling Bibles that he had "personally blessed and signed." Soon came crosses, autographed pictures, and T-shirts showing him shaking hands with Jesus. He reassured his buyers that "every dime of profit goes straight to the Lord."

He hired a woman named Tammy Edwards to keep his books. What she really did was find ways to launder the income stream generated by merchandise sales and divert it for Maurice's personal use. A former beauty queen at Slidell High School, Tammy began sharing time on camera with her boss. Soon she also shared his bed. Shortly thereafter, they became man and wife.

By now the money was coming in by the truckload. For appearance's sake, Maurice made small donations to various charitable organizations. He used most of the cash to purchase Gold Britannia coins. He squirreled these away in a safe concealed behind a false door in the walk-in closet of his new house.

All was going just dandy until he met Jessica Patrice at a biker rally in New Orleans. Dinner and drinks led to suggestive comments, which in turn led to a trip upstairs to his hotel room and a night of wild sex. They began meeting at least once a week after that, sometimes at Jessica's house in Slidell, other times in Fontenot's apartment.

Tammy learned of Maurice's infidelity and ordered him to end the relationship. He refused, telling her his heart was big enough to love two women. When she threatened to go public with what she knew of his finances, even if it meant her going down with him, he caved. He promised her he would never see Jessica again and that he'd rededicate himself to being a good husband.

Instead of reforming himself, though, Maurice made plans to get rid of Tammy. Since their wedding, she had let herself go and now weighed well north of two hundred pounds. But divorce was out of the question. Tammy knew too much to risk having her spill her guts to the IRS. A friend from prison days created new, false identities for him, Jessica, and Fontenot. These identities came with forged birth certificates, driver's licenses, and miscellaneous other paperwork they would need in their new lives. Thus, Maurice became Dennis Webb, Landry Fontenot became Ralph Spencer, and Jessica Patrice became Bonnie Hart.

Maurice sent Fontenot and Jessica to Texas with a sack of gold coins, which they used to buy a place in out-of-the-way Noble County. A month later, after promising a romantic getaway in the country, he drove Tammy to a remote spot on the Tchefuncte River and strangled her. As his fingers dug into her neck she stared at him with bulging, uncomprehending eyes, unable to speak, clawing at him with feeble strength. Just before her light went out, Maurice apologized. He told her he loved her and that soon she'd be with God.

Landry Fontenot waited nearby. He sliced the skin of Tammy's arm with a box cutter and dabbed one of her blouses in the blood. Maurice did the same with his own blood and a pair of his pants. They tossed the items into Maurice's car and pushed the vehicle into the water. Local law enforcement didn't find it for two months. When they did, they pronounced Maurice and Tammy dead and told reporters their bodies had been eaten by alligators.

Maurice, now Dennis Webb, loaded his Harley onto a trailer and hitched the trailer to Bonnie's GMC Terrain. The trailer also held a long tube sealed at either end by a steel grate. Inside the tube was an alligator that had been lurking in a pond behind Webb's house. To trap the enormous reptile Webb tossed the looped end of a rope around its head and threaded the other end through the tube. By pulling on the rope, he was able to coax the animal to crawl into the device. After securing it next to the Harley, he hitched the trailer to the SUV and drove to Noble County. Bonnie followed in a newly purchased white Toyota Camry. Fontenot, now known as Ralph Spencer, wrapped Tammy's body in a plastic tarp, strapped it to his truck bed, and covered it with a load of 2x4s. When he arrived in Noble County, he helped Webb cut it up and feed it to the gator.

Thereafter, Webb stayed hidden on his remote property as much as possible. He ventured out only for occasional fishing expeditions with Spencer and Spencer's new friend Emmett Fuller. To relieve her boredom, Bonnie played poker in Pinyon once a week.

Webb continued to consider himself a man of God. In his mind, whatever sins he had committed were necessary to keep spreading the Holy Word. He had apologized to Tammy. He had begged for and received forgiveness from the Lord. If God could forgive him one more time, he'd do everything in his power to live a righteous life thereafter. First, though, he needed to deal with Emmett Fuller.

Webb opened the desk drawer and removed the Ruger LCP he had purchased on the black market in Louisiana shortly after his prison release. He kept it loaded, never knowing when he might need to make a quick escape, but he checked the magazine anyway. Satisfied, he slipped it back into place, chambered a round, and tucked the gun into his belt. Let that bastard Fuller come for him. He'd be ready.

26

Cash lowered the squad car window and punched in the gate code he'd been given that morning over the phone. The impressive barrier swung open, with each half sweeping a silent arc from the limestone pillars on either side. As Cash eased the car through the opening, his phone buzzed. He braked to a stop and answered the call. "This is Cash."

"Hey, Cash, this is Sam. I've got good news for you. Your truck is ready."

"Great. What did you find?"

"The good news is I went over the chassis from head to toe and didn't find much to worry about. Just a dented fuel line that I replaced. There were no leaks, though. Oh, and I pulled some rocks from the wheels that would have sounded like Armageddon if I hadn't found them."

"How much will this set me back?"

"I'm not finished. Two hundred bucks will cover the fuel line. Then there's the airbag and the rear window. The bag is six hundred, the window seven. I gave you a deal on the labor. Only charged you four hundred. So, the total is nineteen hundred dollars."

Cash gritted his teeth. "Shit."

"You've got insurance, don't you?"

"Yeah."

"Then you'll get some of that back."

"Yeah."

"By the way, I didn't take the streaks off your paint job. You'll need a body shop for that."

"Understood. Thanks, Sam."

Cash pocketed his phone and swore. Forcing himself to calm down, he followed the crushed granite driveway to a one-story frame house shaded by two towering live oaks. Its light blue paint appeared fresh and the exposed portion of the metal roof gleamed in the late morning sun. He killed the engine. As he stepped out of the car, sweat formed on his brow. He knew it wasn't caused by the heat. He had not come with good news.

A woman no older than him answered his knock on the front door. Dressed in knee-length shorts and a sleeveless brown shirt, she gave him a pleasant smile and invited him to come inside. "Thank you for coming, Deputy," she said. "The kids have been anxious to see you."

Cash gulped, knowing he was about to disappoint them. "It's my pleasure, Mrs. Uhler."

"Please, call me Jordan."

"Of course. Jordan."

"What news do you have?"

"I'm afraid we haven't found their mother yet."

Jordan bit her lip. "Oh. That's too bad." Her voice conveyed sadness, but her expression was neutral. "Well, I'll go get the kids."

Cash had a moment of panic when he realized he couldn't recall the children's names. Jordan saved him. "Isaiah, Ginny, come into the den, please. Deputy Cash is here to see you."

The two children emerged from a hallway. Ginny bounded up to Cash and said, "Did you find Mommy yet?"

Cash knelt so he could look the little girl in the eye. "Not yet. But we haven't given up."

"Do you promise you'll find her?"

He gulped. "I promise that we'll do the very best we can."

No one spoke. Isaiah finally broke the awkward silence. "Miss Jordan, can we go finish watching the movie?"

"Sure," Jordan said, and they disappeared down the hall. She turned to face Cash. "They really miss her."

"Of course they do."

"Will you be able to find her? Please be honest."

When his mind froze trying to come up with an answer, Cash could see that Jordan already knew what he would say. He cleared his throat. "I don't know."

"If you don't …" He waited for her to continue, but she turned away and wiped her eyes. When she turned back, Cash saw a damp spot on her cheek. "If you don't, would they be placed for adoption?"

"It's way too early for that."

"I know. It's just …" The words stuck in her throat. "Kirby and I have always wanted children. He married me knowing that I couldn't ever have any of my own. I've always felt guilty about that."

Cash suddenly felt light-headed. This was not a discussion he wanted to have with a woman he had just met.

She continued. "It was P.I.D. That stands for pelvic inflammatory disease. I was sixteen."

"I should get going." He took a step toward the door.

She kept talking as if she hadn't heard him. "They're good kids, you know. Isaiah's a little headstrong, but if you stick to your guns he'll do what he's asked. And Ginny's a sweetheart. She told me she's always wanted a dog. I'm thinking of getting one."

Cash edged closer to the door.

"Anyway, that's the only reason I'm asking. In case it does come to that."

Cash glanced at the door, praying that she wouldn't say anything else. This talk of adoption made him uneasy. The need for that would only come about if they—he—failed. One more step and he was close enough to the door to pull it open. "Goodbye, Mrs. Uhler. I can see that the children are in good hands."

"Goodbye."

When he was halfway to his car, he heard the front door open. He braced himself for another uncomfortable monologue.

"Deputy?"

"Yes."

"It's Jordan."

He smiled. "Of course. Goodbye, Jordan."

***

Santos stared at his laptop screen and swore. Another damn form to fill out. Why had he wanted this job? Some days it seemed like all he did was sit at his desk and try to make the bureaucrats happy. The phone rang. Thankful for the distraction, he jerked it from its receiver. "Sheriff's office."

A man's voice said, "Are you the sheriff?"

"Yes, this is Sheriff Santos."

"I'm calling about that missing woman."

"What about her?"

"You ought to search that poker club. The guy that owns it knows what happened to her."

"Terry Moreno? What does he know?"

"Just go take a look."

"What am I looking for?"

"You'll know it when you see it."

"Who is this?"

The line went dead.

***

After picking up his repaired pickup from Sam, Cash drove it to Interstate 10. Holding his breath, he pushed the speed up to seventy-five miles per hour. The motor hummed beautifully. Despite Sam's warning, he hadn't missed any loose gravel in the wheels. Relieved, Cash reversed direction and drove back to Pinyon.

He eased into a space in front of the Firewheel Café and killed the engine. Although he had called Edie to let her know he was home safe and sound, he hadn't seen her yet. His spine tingled as he recalled their last phone conversation.

Cash maneuvered around the domino players on the patio and entered the café. Only a few customers were sprinkled around the dining room. He spotted Edie taking an order from two men in biker gear. When she caught his eye he gave a small wave, but she ignored him and disappeared into the kitchen.

Cash followed her through the swinging door and waited while she gave the order to Jerry, the cook. She turned and sauntered up to him.

"What's up?" Cash said.

Without warning, she grabbed his head and planted a lengthy kiss on him. "It's official now. We're going together."

Cash grinned. "Excellent."

From the grill, Jerry said, "Get a room, guys."

Cash blushed. "Sorry."

Jerry waved him off. "I'm kidding. It's good to see you guys together."

Edie said, "I have to get back to work. Do you want something to eat?"

"I thought you said it wasn't busy."

"Do you want something or not?"

He did. He was starving. "A Swiss mushroom burger and fries."

"And chocolate milk?"

"If you have it."

"You know we don't. But I can mix you some up."

"Thanks."

He found a seat against the back wall. He couldn't stop grinning. He and Edie were officially in a relationship. As he waited, though, his mind wandered to the topic of Jordan Uhler.

The woman was smitten with Alissa Collins' children. She would be disappointed if she had to give them up. *When* she had to give them up, he corrected himself. He still intended to find Alissa alive. Although after the department meeting this morning, Cash was beginning to see Santos as more of an obstacle than an ally. The sheriff refused to consider a link between Ralph Spencer's death and his girlfriend's disappearance. Nor was he impressed by the gold coin found on Spencer. A coin he had won from Bonnie Hart in a poker game. Bonnie Hart lived with Dennis Webb, who was tight with Emmett Fuller, who had been a fishing buddy of Ralph Spencer's. Cash was convinced that somebody in that relationship web held the key to the case. But Santos had released Fuller, thereby killing their best chance so far of finding it.

Cash's meal came, delivered by a pimply teenager wearing a Rolling Stones T-shirt. "You like the Stones?" Cash said, pointing a finger at the big red tongue. "My brother's band covers some of their songs."

"I've never listened to them," said the boy as he plopped the burger plate before Cash. "My grandpa gave me this shirt." He set a glass of milk and a squeeze bottle of chocolate syrup on the table. "Edie said to give you this."

The burger turned out to be overcooked and dry, a defect the ketchup and grilled onions couldn't quite overcome. The fries were undercooked, mealy, and unappetizing. But thanks to the chocolate syrup he was able to flavor the milk just the way he liked it. And it was ice cold, adding to its perfection.

Cash finished his meal and stopped at the cash register to pay on his way out. "Was everything all right?" the cashier asked.

He saw no point in complaining. "Perfect, as always." As he pulled out his credit card, he noticed a flyer bearing Alissa Collins' picture taped beneath the glass. He leaned in for a closer look.

"You guys still haven't found her, have you?"

Cash flinched at the unexpected voice. Looking up, he saw Mitch Eaton looming over him. "Hello, Mitch," he said, straightening to bring himself to eye level with Eaton. He wanted to strangle the bastard for kissing Edie.

"That poor woman," Eaton said in a somber tone. "And she's got two kids, right? What's going to happen to them?"

"They're being well cared for."

"Just not by their mother." He snatched Cash's credit card from the cashier and handed it to him. "I've got the check."

"You don't have to do that."

"I know. But we'll be working together soon. And I want to keep my deputies happy." When Cash didn't respond, Eaton went on.

"From what I can tell, Cash, you're a good man. Your job is safe. I'm looking forward to having you on my team. Together, we'll get things done."

What, was the guy trying to do a sales job on him? "Things are getting done now."

"Tell that to those kids." Eaton handed several bills to the cashier. Reaching into his pocket, he said, "Hold on, I want to get rid of some change." He slapped a fistful of coins onto the counter. Cash didn't miss, amid the pile, the shiny Gold Britannia coin. Before he could say anything, Eaton deftly plucked the coin from the jumble and stuck it back in his pocket.

"Where'd you get that?"

Eaton ignored the question. "I'll be seeing you, Cash," he said. "It will be a pleasure working with you."

***

Cash was both annoyed and intrigued by his encounter with Eaton. Annoyed at the man's arrogant assumption that he had already won the election. Intrigued by his possession of the same unusual coin that Ralph Spencer and Bonnie Hart had.

As he laced up his basketball shoes, he watched Hodge grab a ball, dribble beyond the three-point line, and throw up a shot that swished through the net. She retrieved the ball, returned to the arc, and swished another. Cash considered himself a good shot, but Hodge was a robot. She never missed. How could he compete with that?

The answer was, he couldn't. After squeaking by in the first game 10-8, Hodge won the next three games by a combined score of 30-13.

As the ball fell through the net to clinch the finale, Cash said, "I gotta hand it to you. You're better than me."

She wiped her face on her sleeve. "You play a good game. Once you get those jump shots to fall, I'll be in trouble."

"Only if I figure out a way to stop you."

They showered and met outside the women's locker room. "Want to grab a beer?" Cash said.

"Sure. I'll buy."

"But you won."

"Okay, you buy."

They drove in separate vehicles to the Packsaddle. Cash paid for two Tartan Reds, a Scottish ale that was one of his favorites. He raised his glass. "To a great basketball player."

"To a great deputy and a good friend."

"I'm a good friend?"

"So far."

Cash took a long drink and wiped foam from his lip. "What did you and Borden find out today?"

Hodge scoffed. "You mean what did I find out? I was flying solo."

"Where was Borden?"

"I wasn't there five minutes before he split. He said he wanted to check out a hot lead."

"What lead?"

"He didn't say. I figured he'd come back after a while, but he never did."

"Weird."

"What did you do all day?"

Cash shrugged. "I went to see Alissa Collins' kids." He told her about Jordan Uhler. "She'd adopt them if she could."

"She does know we're still looking for their mother, doesn't she?"

"She does. I also ran into Mitch Eaton. He told me he looks forward to having me" he made air quotes "on his team."

"I don't trust that guy."

"Neither do I. Know what I saw?"

"What?"

He told her about the Gold Britannia coin in Eaton's pocket. "That can't be a coincidence."

"You'd think a guy with gold coins in his pocket could pay his bills," she said.

"Of course he can pay his bills. He's rich."

"That's not what my grandmother told me. When my grandfather died a year ago, Eaton owed his feed store a lot of money. Evidently, Gramps wasn't the only one getting stiffed by the guy."

Cash was mystified by the news. "I don't know how that can be. His ranch is huge. And isn't he a big shot in Waco? I hear he belongs to the most exclusive country club in the area."

"Maybe so, but from what Meemaw was saying, he's not paying his dues."

Cash stared into his beer, deep in thought.

"What's on your mind?" said Hodge.

His phone buzzed in his pocket. "Hang on, I've got a call." He fished out the phone and put it to his ear. "This is Cash."

"This is Gabe. You've got to get over here."

"What's up?"

"Alissa Collins is dead."

Cash's heart sank. They were too late. "How do you know?

"We found the murder weapon."

***

Cash and Hodge burst into the department lobby and strode past Vicky without saying hello. They found Santos in the conference room conferring with Conrad and Borden. On the table was a hammer inside a large evidence bag and a driver's license in a smaller one. "Tell us about this murder weapon," Cash said, interrupting Santos mid-sentence.

Santos said, "Captain Borden, can you fill them in?"

A smug grin spread across Borden's face. "Your sheriff received an anonymous tip today about an important piece of evidence we'd find at Jerry's Poker Club."

"Terry's," said Santos.

"Excuse me, Terry's. Acting on this, he and I went to the club. We found the hammer you see here in a box beneath the bar."

"And that?" Cash said, pointing at the smaller bag.

"It's a driver's license. We found it in Alissa Collins' purse, which was also in the box. That's why we think the hammer is connected to her death."

"It's just a hammer. How do you know it's connected with anybody's death?"

Borden slid the hammer to Cash. "Take a closer look."

Cash leaned in to examine the bag and saw a steel claw hammer with a black rubber grip. The head was smeared with what looked like hair and dried blood.

"We'll give this to your medical examiner so she can have the blood tested," Borden said, "but, given that we found her purse with it, I think I know what he'll find."

"She."

"What?"

"The medical examiner is a woman. Her name is Frida Simmons."

"Okay, she. I think I know what *she'll* find."

Something about this super neat setup didn't ring true to Cash. "If Collins was murdered, who did it?"

Borden laughed. "It's obvious, isn't it? That club owner."

"Terry?"

"Right."

Cash clasped his hands in thought. He had known Terry most of his life, and the man he knew was shady but not a killer. "That doesn't make sense."

"Does murder ever make sense?"

"Did you have a warrant to search the club?"

"Didn't need one. We asked the guy if we could come in and look around, and he said yes."

"Does he know about Moreno's car?" said Hodge, eliciting a blank look from Borden.

Santos said, "Alissa Collins left her house in a white Toyota Camry that was being driven by a man. Moreno drives a gray Corolla. Which I searched and found nothing in."

"Why didn't you tell me that earlier?" said Borden.

"I did. I guess you forgot."

Cash watched as the gears turned in Borden's head trying to process the information. He could almost hear the sound of grinding metal.

"Here's another thing," Cash said. "How stupid would Terry have to be to bring the murder weapon back to his club? Not to mention his victim's purse."

Borden scoffed. "Prisons are full of stupid people."

"What do you think, Gabe?"

Santos grimaced and clicked his tongue. "As implausible as it sounds, I think we have to follow this up. I'm asking Judge Mixon for a warrant to search Terry's house. Hopefully, Borden and I can do that later today. If not, then first thing in the morning. Hodge, you head back out to watch that ranch gate. Cash …" He hesitated, as if about to say something unpleasant. "You go tell those kids about their mother."

"No," said Cash with a shake of his head. "I'd rather wait for Frida's findings about the blood on the hammer."

"Fair enough."

"And I need Hodge for something later."

"What?"

Cash told Santos about the gold coin in Eaton's pocket. He also relayed what Hodge had told him about Eaton's finances.

"So you're going to talk to Eaton?"

"Yes. But first I want to see Bonnie Hart."

27

As Cash eased the patrol car to a stop outside Dennis Webb's gate, Hodge said, "What good is this? They won't let us in."

"I have an idea."

Cash pulled a pen and notepad from his pocket and scribbled something down. He showed it to Hodge.

"Telling them that Alissa Collins is dead will get us inside?"

"Trust me."

He stepped out of the vehicle and approached the gate. "I'm guessing there's a motion-sensitive camera mounted somewhere. That's how Fuller was able to get out here so fast when we were looking for tire tread marks." He pointed at a small device attached to a T-post five feet inside the fence. "There. That camera allows him to see anyone at the gate." He faced the camera, pushed the call button, and held up the notepad.

They didn't have to wait long. Within a minute, Dennis Webb's voice came through the speaker. "I'm sorry about that, Deputy. But why come all this way to tell me? I hardly knew her."

"The owner of the poker club killed her. I'd like to ask your wife some questions about him since she's a regular there."

With a brief buzz the gate swung open. Cash motioned to Hodge. "Let's go."

As they neared the house, Cash pointed to the fenced stock pond and said, "They keep an alligator in there."

"No shit?"

"Not a good swimming hole."

Webb was waiting for them in the driveway. He shook Cash's hand and turned to Hodge. "I don't believe I've had the pleasure."

Cash introduced them and said, "Can we go inside?"

Webb led them through the front door and a foyer into the den. "Have a seat. I'll get Bonnie."

They settled into the sofa as Webb disappeared down the hall. Cash spotted a Bible on the end table and picked it up. It was identical to the one given to him by the apartment manager in Slidell. He opened it. On the fly leaf, someone had written, "To my darling Jessica. Nothing is impossible with the man upstairs. All my love, Maurice."

His mind raced to connect the dots. Maurice. The inscription in the Bible from Slidell had been signed by "M." Were M and Maurice the same person?

"Do you read the good book, Deputy?" It was Webb, returning with Bonnie in tow.

"Every chance I get," said Cash as he returned the Bible to the end table.

"I'm happy to hear it."

When Webb and Bonnie were seated, Bonnie said, "Dennis tells me Alissa was murdered."

"That's right," said Cash. "By Terry Moreno."

Bonnie produced a loud gasp. Too loud, Cash thought.

"That's a surprise. He always seemed so nice."

"You never know, do you? I'm here to ask you about something else. Does Mitch Eaton play poker at the club?"

"How would I know? I'm not there every night."

"Have you ever seen him there?"

"No."

"I saw him at the Firewheel in possession of a Gold Britannia coin just like the one Ralph Spencer had." When she didn't say anything, Cash added, "Just like the ones you sell at the coin shop. Do you know why he might have that?"

A look of genuine surprise flashed across Bonnie's face. Recovering, she said, "I really have no idea."

"Can you take a guess? That's not a common coin to see in Pinyon."

Bonnie glanced at her husband. His face was a stone mask. "Maybe he plays at the club when I'm not there. He could have won it from Ralph. Ralph was a terrible player."

"He couldn't have been too terrible to win a gold coin from you."

"I'm still embarrassed about that."

An awkward silence followed. Webb said, "Will there be anything else, deputies?"

Cash stood up. "Thanks, no. We'll be on our way."

***

Webb refilled his tumbler from the half-full bottle on the end table. After downing most of the glass' contents, he grabbed the remote. "What do you want to watch tonight? *Seinfeld* reruns or that movie *Oppenheimer?*"

"*Seinfeld,*" said Bonnie. She dropped beside him on the sofa. "I need a laugh."

"Rough day?"

"Yeah. I could use some of that bourbon, too."

"Here, take this one." He poured the rest of the bottle into the tumbler and handed it to Bonnie. "I'll get some more." He went to the kitchen and filled a clean tumbler with iced tea. Returning to the den, he settled onto the sofa and scooted up close to Bonnie. Raising his glass, he said, "Cheers."

"Cheers."

Bonnie edged away and sipped.

"What's the matter?" Webb said.

"Nothing." She flashed a wan smile and brought her legs up onto the couch. "I just want room to stretch out."

Webb grunted and said nothing. He sipped the liquid in his tumbler and licked his lips. He had never liked the taste of tea, at least not without ice and several spoonfuls of sugar. But he wanted a clear head for what was coming. More bourbon would have brought its familiar fog. He also wanted Bonnie to think he'd be sound asleep later.

He still hadn't decided what to do with her. She deserved the same fate he would mete out to Fuller, but he wasn't sure he could commit the deed. Just a few days ago he had felt secure in the knowledge that she loved him. He had loved her, too. He supposed a part of him still did. Despite her treachery.

Halfway through a second episode of *Seinfeld*, Webb got up from the sofa. He stretched and faked a yawn. "I'm going to bed. Are you coming?"

She kept her eyes on the screen. "No, I'm going to stay up for a while."

"All right. Good night."

"Good night."

***

Fuller removed the Kimber K6s .357 Magnum from his pocket and checked the load in the dim light of the overhead porch light. He had selected this gun for the job because it was the one weapon in his arsenal he didn't mind disposing of. It held only six rounds and the snub-nose barrel made it look like a toy gun. Fuller had long regretted buying it. He intended to bury the murder weapon after shooting Webb, so he wanted to use a gun he didn't mind getting rid of.

Satisfied that the gun was fully loaded, Fuller twisted the doorknob. The door was unlocked, just as Bonnie had promised. He nudged it open and stepped into the house.

Treading as silently as his steel-toed boots allowed, Fuller made his way to the den. Bonnie lay stretched out on the sofa, her hands tucked beneath the pillow supporting her head. Her cleavage peeked through her unbuttoned blouse. The sight aroused him. In other circumstances, he would have slid his jeans off and joined her. But he would have plenty of time for that after he took care of Webb.

He touched her shoulder and her eyes slid open. Snapping to alertness, she opened her mouth to speak, but Fuller put a finger to his lips. She glanced toward the bedroom and nodded.

Fuller crept down the hall and nudged the bedroom door open. He smiled at the thought of banging Bonnie in the asshole's bed after he took care of business. It would be a final middle-finger salute to the big jerk. Then they'd dump his carcass, and he and Bonnie would jet away to a Mexican beach.

Fuller listened at the doorway for the sound of Webb's breathing. He heard nothing. The room was dark, but enough moonlight light leaked through the blinds that he could see the outline of Webb's body in bed. Time for action. He raised the Kimber and squeezed off four shots. Hurrying to the bedside, he fired two more rounds into the head.

There. He had done it. It had been easier than he thought it would be. Harder than blowing up Spencer's truck but not by much.

The bedroom light flicked on. Fuller turned, expecting to see Bonnie. "Hello, Emmett." It was Webb, pointing a Ruger at his chest.

"Webb."

"Surprised to see me?" He gestured at the bed. "I'm supposed to be under those covers, right?" Keeping the gun trained on Fuller, he advanced to the opposite side of the bed and pulled the covers back. "That's too bad. You ruined some of my favorite pillows. But at least I'm safe and sound."

Fuller took a step back and tightened his grip on the Kimber. If he was quick enough, maybe he could raise it and shoot before Webb reacted. "It's not what you think."

"It's exactly what I think, you idiot. You and Bonnie want to take my money and go live the good life in Acapulco. Or was it Cancún? I can't remember. Anyway, you came here to get rid of me. But I'm smarter than you gave me credit for." He motioned with the Ruger. "Let's go outside. I don't want to mess up my carpet."

Fuller's eyes flitted back and forth searching for an escape route. To Webb, he looked like a dog caught going through a trash can. What a loser.

Fuller's hand jerked up. A loud click sounded as he squeezed the Kimber's trigger.

"That's a six-shooter," Webb said with a chuckle. "You've used them all."

Bonnie appeared in the doorway. Her relaxed posture indicated calm, but Webb saw fear in her eyes. "I heard shots."

Webb said, "That was your boyfriend trying to kill me."

"What are you talking about?"

Fuller said, "Cut the act, Bonnie. He knows."

"Knows what?"

Webb fired the Ruger. A neat hole appeared in Fuller's chest. He fired again and Fuller spun sideways, bounced off the dresser, and hit the floor. A spreading pool of blood blossomed beneath the body.

Webb trained the gun on Bonnie. "Looks like we'll need a new carpet, after all."

***

"I'm telling you, Dennis, I had no idea he was going to do this." Her voice was pleading, desperate. She caressed his shoulder. "Thank God you're okay."

Webb tapped her nose with the barrel of the Ruger. "What did he mean when he told you to cut the act?"

"He was desperate. He knew you were about to kill him." She kissed him, but he received it like a statue.

"So you still love me."

"Of course I do." She threw her arms around him and kissed him again. "Baby, I'll never stop loving you."

Webb put his hands on her shoulders and nudged her away. "Do something for me, will you?"

"Anything."

"Have a seat at my desk."

She wrinkled her forehead. "Why?"

"Just do it."

The strange request put her on edge. "Okay."

"Now open the laptop and turn it on."

"Dennis, I don't know what this is—"

He rapped her skull with the Ruger. "Open it."

She flipped the laptop open and waited.

"Turn it on."

"I don't know your password."

"There isn't one. Now turn it on."

Her finger trembled as she pushed the power button. The screen lit up.

"See that file there? The one that says Revelations? Open it up." He waited. "Now click on the audio file."

She clicked. After several seconds of silence, she heard herself say, "How would you do it?"

Fuller's voice sounded through the speaker. "With a gun. I'd shoot him in the head when he's asleep, then put the gun in his hand and shoot it again."

Webb said, "He wanted to make it look like suicide. Only the moron fired all six shots in the gun, so that wouldn't have worked." He reached around Bonnie and shut the laptop. "You sure know how to pick them, baby."

"I do love you, Dennis." Her voice shook.

"Save it."

"He forced me."

"No, you were an eager participant."

"What are you going to do?"

He grabbed her hair and yanked her to her feet. "Not me, you. You're going to bury your boyfriend."

***

Webb found a plastic tarp in the garage and used it to wrap Fuller's body. After tying off both ends, he had Bonnie drag it out of the house and load it into the back of a utility vehicle. The owner had conveyed it with an excavator attachment, which Webb fitted to the front of the UTV. He kept a close eye on Bonnie while he worked. She had nowhere to go if she broke and ran, but chasing after her in the dark would present an unwelcome distraction.

Webb shoved Bonnie into the passenger seat and steered the UTV a half mile along a narrow dirt path that ended at the base of a steep hill. Bonnie tried to stroke his arm as he drove, but he slapped her hand away. After rolling Fuller's body onto the ground, he used the excavator to dig a hole deep enough to keep coyotes from clawing it up. He turned to Bonnie, quivering in the UTV. "Get out."

She didn't move fast enough to please him, so he grabbed her arm and dragged her to the edge of the hole. "Get in."

"Dennis, please. Don't do this."

"I said, get in."

Sniffling and choking back sobs, she lowered herself into the hole. Webb hopped in after her. He raised the Ruger. "Turn around."

She threw herself against him, wailing and clawing his chest. "Please don't. I'll do anything. Please." A snot bubble popped out of one nostril.

Webb slapped her with an open palm, knocking her against the side of the hole. He grabbed her shoulders and forced her to her hands and knees. Kneeling behind her, he raised her nightgown and unbuckled his pants. Her sobbing drowned out the noise of the UTV's motor.

Webb stuck the gun barrel in her ear. "Shut up." The sobs intensified. With a grunt, he grabbed her hips, thrust his pelvis, and took his revenge.

28

J eanine Jarvis reached into the bag and pulled out a burnt orange basketball jersey. "Oh, my God! Is this real?"

"It is," Hodge said. "It's from my sophomore year."

Jeanine squealed. "And it's signed." She held it up for inspection. "Is this everybody on the team?"

"Everyone except Mina Reed. She was home with the flu."

Studying the signatures, Jeanine said, "Even the coach signed it." She dropped it back into the bag. "This is so generous of you. You hired a good one, Cash."

"I agree."

"Keisha, I don't know if I can ever repay you. Thank you."

"I'm glad you like it."

Cash cleared his throat. "There is one other thing, Jeanine. It's not the reason we came to see you, but I have a quick question about Mitch Eaton."

She looked like she was being played for a sucker. "I swear, Keisha was planning on giving this to you anyway. I tagged along for the ride. On the way over, I realized this is a question right up your alley."

"Go ahead," she said, crossing her arms.

"I heard a rumor that Eaton is broke. Is that true?"

"Who told you that?"

"I'd rather not say."

"You're not trying to dig up dirt on him for the election, are you?"

"No. As a deputy, I have to remain neutral."

"But surely you have an opinion."

"I promise this has nothing to do with the election."

"Well ..." She stared out the window and sighed. "I guess there's no harm in telling you, given that it's common knowledge among some people in the community. Yes, he's on hard times. Don't ask me for any numbers, though."

"I won't. When you say hard times, do you mean it would be hard for him to fund his election without help?"

"You said this didn't have anything to do with the election."

"It doesn't. I'm just using that as an example."

She crossed her legs and her knee brushed against the bag. After a quick peek inside, she said, "Unless he's got a secret stash of gold bars buried on his ranch, he can't afford a Happy Meal."

***

Cash and Hodge emerged from the credit union into bright sunshine. Cash said, "I'm sorry you had to give up your jersey."

"It's no big deal. I have so much crap from those years that I can't keep track of it all. There's only one thing I'll never get rid of."

"What's that?"

"Sometimes the coach would take us to visit sick kids at the children's hospital. There was one girl I really hit it off with. Her name was Melody. She had leukemia. She was on her high school basketball team until she got sick. Anyway, she drew a picture of me shooting a jump shot that just blew me away. I had it framed. It's hanging in my den."

Cash asked cautiously, "What happened to her?"

"The chemo worked. She was able to return to the team for her senior year. She went on to play at Abilene Christian."

"Nice."

Gesturing for Hodge to follow, Cash started down the sidewalk. "Let's go. I don't want to be late."

"Explain to me again why we're having lunch with Mitch Eaton."

"I want to make him sweat a little. See if he knows anything. In particular, I want to see how well he knows Dennis Webb."

"If he does, I don't know why he'd tell you that."

"If he does and there's nothing fishy going on, I don't know why he wouldn't."

***

Cash slipped off his sunglasses and held the door open for Hodge. The lunch crowd was already beginning to fill the Firewheel Café. He spotted one last empty table and led Hodge to it.

Across the room, Edie finished taking an order and headed in their direction. Cash stood up at her approach. "Hey, babe."

"Hey." She delivered a quick kiss.

"Have you seen Mitch Eaton? He's supposed to meet us here."

Edie's eyebrows shot up. "Really? Are you guys pals now?"

"Of course not. I might be working for him soon, though."

"Don't say that. I have faith in Gabe."

"If only because you're running his campaign, so do I."

"Anyway, I haven't seen him."

She took their order and hustled away. Hodge said, "I like your girlfriend."

"I'm rather fond of her myself."

A booming voice rose above the buzz of conversation in the room. "There you guys are." It was Eaton. He grabbed a chair and shook Cash's hand, then Hodge's. "I'm glad you got a table. The place is hopping today."

Edie returned and set glasses of iced tea in front of Cash and Hodge. "Hello, Mitch. What can I get you to drink?"

"Maybe I shouldn't tell you," he said with a laugh. "You're working for the enemy. You might put poison in it."

She forced a smile. "So, nothing then?"

"How about some water?"

"You got it."

When Edie was gone, Eaton flashed a wide grin. "I'm sure this is the first of many lunches we'll share. I can't wait to work with you guys."

We may have to wait and see about that. Cash said, "Thanks for buying my lunch the other day."

"No problem."

"I couldn't help but notice that coin you had on you. What was that?"

A corner of Eaton's mouth twitched. "That? It's a souvenir I brought back from London. A good luck piece."

Cash kept his voice neutral. "It looked like a Gold Britannia coin to me."

"Hell if I know what it's supposed to look like. It's not worth anything."

"Oh, I don't know about that. A real one would fetch a couple thousand bucks."

"You know your coins."

Cash sipped his tea. "I know that coin. A woman right in our small town has been cashing them in to pay her mortgage. Her name is Jessica."

Eaton's mouth twitched again. "Can't say that I know anyone in town by that name."

"She's married to this guy named Maurice."

"Is that so?" Eaton took a deep breath and leaned forward. "This is all very interesting, but I was hoping we'd get a chance to talk about the department I'll be running."

"If you win the election."

"Right. If I win the election." He slipped a phone out of his pocket and looked at the screen. "Well, shoot. This is my ranch manager. I forgot somebody was coming by to look at one of my bulls." He stood up. "Sorry. I have to scoot."

When he was gone, Hodge said, "I didn't hear his phone buzz."

"Neither did I."

She gave him a quizzical look. "What was that all about? Who's Jessica and Maurice?"

"That's the big question, isn't it?"

***

Back at the station, Cash and Hodge ran into Santos and Borden charging out of the hallway. "What's the big hurry?" he said.

Santos said, "Judge Mixon came through with a warrant. We're going to go search Moreno's house."

"Come on, Gabe. Do you really think Terry Moreno is a murderer?"

"It's the only lead we've got right now."

"I think it's bogus."

Borden said, "You're out of your mind." When Cash didn't respond, Borden turned to Hodge. "Want to come?"

Hodge and Cash exchanged glances. "Go on," said Cash. "There's nothing else happening at the moment."

"Yeah, come with us. We'll leave Deputy Cash here to pursue all the hot leads he's got."

Hodge scowled, but followed the two men out of the building.

Cash watched them go with a sour taste in his mouth. He hadn't been wild about Borden at their first meeting and since then, his opinion of the Ranger captain had only gone downhill. Let him search Terry's house. He wouldn't find squat.

Cash hurried to the conference room and used his cell phone to call the sheriff's office in St. Tammany Parish, Louisiana. After being transferred by a receptionist, he heard Sheriff Bouvette's gruff voice. "This is Bouvette."

"Sheriff, this is Deputy Adam Cash in Noble County, Texas."

"Oh, yes. Did you catch your man yet?"

"Not yet, but I'm getting closer. I have a couple of questions for you."

"Fire away."

"I have reason to believe that Landry Fontenot was involved with a guy named Maurice."

"Maurice who?"

"I don't have a last name."

Bouvette laughed. "Do you know how many guys there are in Cajun country named Maurice? You'll have to be more specific than that."

"He's married to a woman named Jessica."

"Sorry. That doesn't ring any bells."

"All right. Thanks anyway."

He ended the call and logged onto the conference room laptop. A search for "Jessica and Maurice Louisiana" returned nothing of use. He tried again with "Jessica Maurice St. Tammany Parish" and again was disappointed. When he added the term "Slidell," though, he received a single hit with the heading "Bible Bikers Barbecue." Clicking on it brought up an article about a picnic being planned for the group at the Fritchie Park pavilion. Anyone interested was asked to call Maurice Trahan or Jessica Patrice for information.

Cash called Bouvette back. "I found the last names. It's Maurice Trahan and Jessica Patrice."

"I've heard of Maurice Trahan," said Bouvette. "But he won't be able to help you."

"Why not?"

"He's dead."

Cash paused, caught off guard. "Are you sure?"

"As sure as I can be. He and his wife drove their car into the swamp one night a year or so ago. We found their bloody clothing in the vehicle. There were no bodies. Everybody assumes the gators got there before we did."

"So they're both dead?"

"No, Trahan and his wife are dead. Her name was Tammy. I never heard of Jessica Patrice."

Cash pondered the information. Either Dennis Webb and Maurice Trahan were different people or Trahan had survived the accident. And if that were the case, why did Bouvette think he was dead? "What do you know about this Trahan?"

"Seems like every sucker with a Bible knew him. He was an ex-con who found the Lord while he was in the can. Started some bogus ministry that posted YouTube videos telling people to donate and he'd lead them to Jesus. I only know that because my mother watched him all the time. She even sent him money until I put a stop to it."

"Are those videos still online?"

"I wouldn't know. I *can* tell you that he looked to me like a pretty slick operator. I wouldn't trust him as far as I could throw him, if you know what I mean. That's why I told Mom to quit sending him money. Fact is, I wouldn't be surprised if he didn't fake his death."

Bingo. "Why do you say that?"

"Like I said, he was a slick operator. And I always wondered how, if we found a pair of his pants, we didn't find any part of him in it. As far as I know, alligators don't undress a man before eating him."

"Why would he have faked his death?"

"I've wondered if he didn't kill his wife and stage the accident to cover his tracks. And here's the other thing. His YouTube channel brought in millions, but his assets when his car was found totaled only about three hundred grand. Most of that was his house."

"Wouldn't the money have gone to his ministry?"

"It should have. My mother always said that's what he was doing with it. Giving it to charity. I called a couple of them she mentioned. Yeah, he gave them money, but it was peanuts compared to what people were sending in. And he didn't leave a will."

"Maybe he spent it."

"On what? He had a house and a nice car, but that was about it. Do you know how much was in his bank account? Eight hundred bucks. He took in seven figures through that YouTube channel. And get this. He sold the house two days before he disappeared."

"Interesting." With all those red flags, Cash wondered why somebody wasn't pursuing Trahan more aggressively. "Okay, Sheriff, thanks for your help."

"No problem. Good luck with your investigation."

Cash thanked Bouvette and ended the call. Were Webb and Trahan the same person? Did Trahan kill his wife and fake his death? And what happened to all that money? Is that where the gold coins came from?

Cash performed an internet search for "Maurice and Tammy Trahan" and found a short newspaper article about the car being found in the swamp. It confirmed what Bouvette had told him, including the assumption that both occupants were presumed to have died in the crash. He next pulled up YouTube and searched for Trahan. Nothing came up. He tried with the name Dennis Webb and again got no hits. He then tried every permutation of the two names, along with one or both of the names Jessica and Tammy. Nothing.

Cash scratched his head. According to Bouvette, Maurice Trahan had regularly posted YouTube videos with a religious theme. Now those videos were gone. Somebody must have intentionally taken them down. And how did Jessica Patrice fit into the picture?

Cash performed another internet search and began making phone calls. Forty-five minutes later, he hit paydirt with Blair Precious Metals, a coin shop thirty miles from Slidell, in the neighboring town of Covington. The owner told Cash that until a year ago a woman had come in regularly to buy Gold Britannia coins "by the truckload." When Cash asked him to describe the woman, he said, "That's the thing. At first, it was a heavyset gal but the last couple of times it was somebody different. A blonde, if I remember correctly."

"What makes you think they were connected?"

"I don't know for sure that they were, only that when the first one stopped coming, the blonde started showing up. I tell you what, I wouldn't mind seeing either one of them again. They made me a lot of money."

"Okay, thanks."

Cash killed the call. He thought he could guess what happened to the first woman. He also thought he knew where Bonnie Hart's gold coins had come from. Then he thought about the coin in Mitch Eaton's pocket. Eaton claimed it was a worthless trinket, but Cash knew it looked exactly like the one he found on Ralph Spencer. Which could only mean that Eaton had lied when Cash asked about it. Cash didn't have answers to the many questions swirling in his head but he knew one thing for sure. He needed to talk to Mitch Eaton again.

29

"What are we looking for again?" Hodge said as she snapped on a pair of medical gloves.

"Anything that links our suspect to the victim." Borden's disdain for the question was obvious.

Santos said, "Keisha, you take the bedrooms and hall bath. We'll handle the kitchen and den."

From his place on the sofa, Terry Moreno said, "Please don't break anything. If you need to look inside something, I'll help you open it."

"Thanks," Borden said dismissively. "We'll keep that in mind."

Seated next to Moreno was his lawyer, Dawn Huber. She cleared her throat. "I'd rather you all stay in the same room so we can watch."

"I'm sure you would."

Moreno said, "It's okay. I trust the sheriff."

Hodge entered the first bedroom. It had once been used by Moreno's son Hector, the pediatrics resident in San Antonio. Most vestiges of Hector's childhood had long since been removed. Only a Little League photograph and a San Antonio Spurs pennant remained on one wall. Hodge recognized a younger version of Moreno standing behind the boys and girls in the photograph. She had never seen Hector and couldn't pick him out.

Hodge needed only a couple of minutes to complete her search. She finished the second bedroom and the hall bath in the same amount of time. Returning to the den, she nodded at Moreno and waited by the front door.

Moments later, Santos joined her. "Borden's still at it," he said.

A loud crash sounded in the kitchen. Huber bolted from the couch and went to investigate. When she came back, she said, "He dropped a drawer full of flatware."

Hodge said, "Sheriff, can we talk outside?"

Motioning for her to follow, Santos opened the door and stepped onto the porch.

Hodge shut the door. "Do you believe that Moreno killed Alissa Collins?"

"No, but we have to rule it out."

"What happens when we don't find anything?"

"We wait for the DNA results from the blood found on the hammer. If it belongs to Alissa Collins, we start looking for a body."

She jumped to the next question. "How did the hammer end up with Moreno?"

"Moreno said he'd never seen it before. He thinks one of his customers planted it."

"Bonnie Hart is a customer."

The door opened and Borden joined them. He placed his hands on his hips. Through clenched teeth he said, "The son of a bitch is hiding something. I say we arrest him."

"For what?" Hodge asked.

Borden rolled his eyes. "What do you think, Deputy? Murder."

"We can't call it murder without a body. And we don't even know for sure that's Alissa's blood on the hammer."

"She's right," said Santos.

"Technicalities."

"Big ones, though."

Borden leaned over and spat. "Do you guys want to solve this case or not?"

Santos started for the car. "Let's go back to the square," he said, sounding pretty dismissive himself. "I could use a kolache."

***

Cash turned off the highway and drove the patrol car through the biggest ranch gate he had ever seen. Set inside two massive pillars, the wrought iron bi-parting gate was at least twenty feet wide. The top bars curved upward from the pillars in a graceful arc to meet in the middle ten feet above the ground. Centered in each panel was an oval surrounding a silhouette of a buck sporting an antler rack that deer hunters only dream of. A wrought iron sign reading "Eaton" spanned the pillars above the gate.

A potholed asphalt road led Cash up a gentle slope for a quarter mile before he could see the house. Another minute brought him to a circular driveway in front of a two-story colonial structure. Cattle were conspicuous for their absence.

The front door opened before Cash could knock. "I'm so glad you called. We didn't get to talk about my plans for the department at lunch."

"We didn't get to talk about much of anything. How did the bull work out?"

"The bull? Oh yeah, the guy didn't need it, after all." Eaton opened the door all the way. "Come on in." He led Cash into a spacious den with a balcony that wrapped around the upper floor. Mounted whitetail deer heads hung from the railing. "Want something to drink? Wine, beer, bourbon?"

"No, thanks."

At Eaton's invitation, Cash sank back into a cowhide sofa worn through in several spots. Eaton sat in a leather recliner.

"How was the food at the Firewheel today?" said Eaton.

"If you don't mind, I'd like to get right to my questions."

Eaton gave a dismissive shrug. "Shoot."

"How well do you know Dennis Webb?"

"Who?"

"Dennis Webb."

"Sorry, I don't know him at all."

"He used to go by Maurice Trahan."

Eaton blanched and eased forward in his chair. "Again, I don't know him."

"What about Tammy Trahan? Or Jessica Patrice?"

"What is this, Cash? Do you suspect me of something?"

"I'm just gathering information."

"If I didn't know better, I'd say you're trying to dig up dirt on me."

Cash shook his head. "Like I told you, I'm neutral in the election." He switched his approach. "I told you about the Gold Britannia coin that Bonnie Hart cashes in to pay her mortgage. That was no trinket in your pocket. That's a gold coin identical to hers."

"You're mistaken."

"May I see it?"

Eaton placed his hands on the armrest and leaned back in his chair. After considering, he let out a loud breath and stood up. "I think we're done here."

Cash rose.

"I'm disappointed, Cash. In three weeks I'll be your boss. I'd suggest you remember that before you waste my time with any more of this crap."

The answer to all of his questions was: yes. "I'll let myself out."

***

Webb tapped on the hollow-core bedroom door. He unlocked it and nudged it open with his foot, staying back in case Bonnie tried something stupid. But she was sitting docilely on the side of the bed, her hands in her lap, her face contrite. Was her contrition sincere? Time would tell. Until then, she'd stay in this room.

"I brought you something to eat." He set the tray on the dresser. Beef stew, a salad, and a glass of merlot. She had always liked his beef stew. Perhaps a kind approach would bring her around sooner.

She perched motionless on the bed.

"Do you have anything to say?" he asked.

"Thank you."

"I meant about what you did."

"Yes. I'm sorry."

He grunted and turned to go.

"You didn't have to kill him."

Webb whirled around so fast she flinched. "Of course I had to kill him." His voice spit venom.

"You could have just made him leave."

"And have him come back someday to try for me again? Don't be stupid."

"Thou shalt not kill."

He threw his head back and let loose a throaty laugh. "That's rich, coming from you. What about 'Thou shalt not commit adultery'? For the Lord says, 'Let marriage be held in honor among all, and let the marriage bed be undefiled, for God will judge the sexually immoral and adulterous.'"

"You committed that sin when you met me. Or did you forget?"

"That I did." He moved in close and wagged a finger in her face. "I fell prey to a vile temptress. 'For the lips of a forbidden woman drip honey, and her speech is smoother than oil.' That could have been written about you."

She hung her head. Webb prayed she wouldn't start crying. He knew that tears provoked him quicker than sharp words, and a man could rein in his temper for only so long.

She stood up and caressed his arm. He cringed as if she carried a contagious disease. Leaning her head against his chest, she said, "I love you, Maurice. Please forgive me."

"I told you never to call me that."

"I love you, Dennis." She nudged a leg between his thighs. "I want you."

Webb shoved her back hard enough that she bounced when she hit the mattress. "You've said that before. Then you spread your legs for Emmett Fuller."

"I was afraid of him. He threatened to kill me if I didn't help him."

"Liar! Did you forget about the recording? That was not the voice of a frightened woman."

She pulled her legs onto the bed. Locking eyes with him, she pulled off her T-shirt and undid her bra. When Webb didn't react, she slid her shorts and panties off. Lying back on the bed, she rested her head on one arm and waited.

The sight of her naked body melted Webb's anger like ice cream on a summer day. He undressed himself and lay down beside her.

"I want to make it up to you," she said.

He rolled on top of her. "You will."

30

C ash left Eaton's place and drove to the Packsaddle. He found Steve behind the bar. "What'll it be?" Steve said.

"Just an iced tea," said Cash. "I'm on duty."

Steve poured the tea and set the glass on the bar. "I ran into Edie out on the square this morning. She says she hardly sees you these days."

Cash sighed. He knew he had been neglecting Edie.

"Don't take that woman for granted. She'll move on."

"Says the world's greatest expert on long-term relationships."

"Make fun of me all you want, but she didn't sound happy."

"I'll keep that in mind."

Steve grunted and disappeared into the kitchen. Cash turned his attention to a ball game on the wall-mounted television. The Astros were leading the Angels 6—1. He watched them hold the lead over the last two innings and stood up to leave.

Steve wandered out from the back. "Don't forget what I said."

"Don't you have ketchup to water down?"

"You know I'm right."

Cash left the Packsaddle and drove to the station to fill Santos in on his meeting with Eaton. As he entered the lobby, though, Eaton emerged from a back hall. He ignored Cash and marched out the door.

Cash caught Vicky watching him. "What was he doing here?" he said.

"Nobody tells me anything."

He wandered down the hall into Santos' office. "Just the man I wanted to see," Santos said as Cash took a seat.

"Was that Mitch Eaton I just saw in the lobby?"

"Indeed it was."

"What the hell did he want?"

"He wanted to hang you from the nearest tree. Says you were at his house harassing him."

"That's bullshit. I was asking him questions pertinent to the Alissa Collins case."

Santos folded his hands. "And what, pray tell, does Mitch Eaton have to do with the Alissa Collins case?"

Cash filled him in on the coin in Eaton's possession, as well as his newfound knowledge about Webb and Bonnie Hart. "They changed identities, Gabe. They were stockpiling Gold Britannia coins. Doesn't that tell you something?"

The skeptical look on his face had lit with new interest. "You may be on to something."

"I think I am. Why would a man fake his death unless he has something to hide?"

"What's Webb hiding?"

"I believe he murdered his wife."

Santos pondered the accusation. "It would make sense."

"Damn right, it would make sense."

"How does Eaton figure in?"

"I checked, and Eaton went to school in New Orleans. He and Webb both ride Harleys. I suspect they knew each other in Louisiana and that's the reason Webb came to Noble County. Eaton is broke.

I confirmed that with Jeanine at the credit union. Maybe Webb is funding his campaign for sheriff. Wouldn't a wife killer love to have a friend as sheriff?"

The skeptical look had returned. "That all makes sense but we need something concrete. Keep digging."

"What about the complaint?"

"Let me handle Mitch Eaton."

***

"Where's Bonnie?" Eaton asked as he settled onto the familiar couch.

"Out running errands," Webb lied. "Why are you here?"

"Adam Cash."

"The deputy? What about him?"

"You've got to do something about him."

Webb fingered the cap of the whiskey bottle on the end table. He wanted a drink, but the glasses were in the kitchen and he wanted to keep this visit short. Maybe he could just take a swig from the bottle. "Tell me about it. The guy is a pest."

"He's more than a pest. He knows your real name."

Webb nearly jumped in his seat. "That's impossible."

"He asked me if I knew Maurice Trahan."

Webb forgot all about the whiskey. "How does he know that?"

"I don't know. He also mentioned Tammy Trahan and Jessica Patrice."

A drumbeat sounded in Webb's brain. He had planned everything so carefully. The identity changes. The gold coins. The land in Texas. Tammy's death. How had this hayseed deputy figured it all out? He stood and paced back and forth.

"I'm telling you, it won't be long before he finds out what happened to Tammy. Ralph Spencer, too. Did I mention that he found a coin in Spencer's pocket?"

"That's old news."

"Yeah, but he saw one on me, too."

Webb's brain all but exploded. He fixed Eaton with a laser-like glare. "How did that happen?"

"I was paying his tab at the Firewheel—you know, schmoozing my future employee—and it was mixed in with the other coins in my pocket."

"You stupid son of a bitch! You're not supposed to carry them around with you. You're supposed to get your ass to a coin shop as quick as you can and convert them to cash."

Eaton had always been a fool. Webb dropped back into his chair and massaged his temples. No, this was Bonnie's fault. It all started when she lost that coin to Spencer in a poker game. He should never have agreed to let her go to that club. That aside, how could somebody as smart as Eaton be so stupid as to pull out a coin in front of the deputy? "Mitch, we go back a long way. Hell, you were one of the original Bible Bikers. But I can't have this."

"Like I said, you have to get rid of that deputy."

"*I* have to get rid of him?" Webb closed his eyes to give himself time to think. He did want this Cash guy gone. He just didn't want to catch the heat for killing a county deputy. "Do you want to do it? I can give you a gun."

Eaton's silence was answer enough.

"I thought so."

"You could have Emmett do it."

Webb's lips suddenly felt dry. He had hoped Fuller's name wouldn't come up. "Yeah, I've been meaning to talk to you about that. I had to get rid of him."

"What do you mean, like fire him?"

"No ... more than that."

Eaton's eyes slowly widened as the implication sank in. "You killed him? You killed my sister's kid?"

"He gave me no choice, Mitch. He was planning to kill me. He came into my bedroom with a gun."

"That can't be."

"I've got him planning it on tape." Webb hoped Eaton wouldn't ask who Fuller was planning it with.

"Where is he now?"

"I buried him out in the cedar."

Eaton fell silent, but his face simmered with anger.

"You once told me yourself he was a screwup," said Webb.

"That didn't give you the right to kill him."

"It's not a question of rights. It's a question of necessity."

The ticking of a wall clock marked time in the awkward silence that followed. Each tick sounded louder to Webb than the last.

Eaton said, "I'm gonna need more money."

Not this again. "You said the last time you wouldn't need any more."

"I told you I *probably* wouldn't need more. I was wrong."

"Forget it. It's too risky with that deputy snooping around."

"Do you want me to be sheriff or not?"

Webb chewed his lip. Yes, he wanted Eaton to be sheriff. He could then live his life without fear of local law enforcement. He stood up. "I'll be right back."

Webb went to his bedroom and opened the safe in his closet. He plucked a Gold Britannia coin from one of the neat stacks lining the shelves. Back in the den, he handed it to Eaton.

"Take this straight to a coin shop. No more flashing it at the Firewheel."

"Got it."

Eaton rose to leave.

"And Mitch?"

"Yeah?"

"Forget about your nephew."

"How do you expect me to do that?"

Webb added some menace. "You'll find a way. If you can't, there's room for two bodies in those woods."

31

Webb reached out a hand and felt nothing but bedsheets. Right. Bonnie was locked in the other bedroom. It felt strange waking up without her beside him. He wondered how long that would be necessary.

He had gotten little sleep. Eaton's warning about the nosy deputy had shaken him. Would God really allow his life to blow up just as he was preparing to launch another YouTube ministry? He had already constructed an altar in the barn. A second coat of varnish and it would be ready. He'd preach against a green screen backdrop and use his video-editing skills to make it appear as if he was in a real church. He'd even written his first three sermons. Why would God disrupt those plans?

"He knows your real name." Webb couldn't get Eaton's words out of his mind. He had taken great care to erase all evidence of Maurice Trahan's existence. Why couldn't the name stay dead and buried?

Eaton was right. The deputy had to go. God was merely testing him. Did he possess the fortitude to persist in his journey along the path laid out by the Lord? Could he do whatever was necessary to put himself in position to spread the holy word?

Of course he could. He always had, hadn't he? The thought gave him renewed confidence, and an idea came to him. He turned it over and over in his mind until a plan came into focus. A plan that would solve two problems: getting rid of the deputy and giving Bonnie a chance to redeem herself.

He reached for his phone and called Eaton.

"Yeah?"

"I've been thinking about what you said. How well do you know that deputy?"

"Cash? We're not close if that's what you're thinking."

"Is he married?"

"No, he has a girlfriend but they've only been together a few weeks."

"What about family in town?"

"None that I—wait a minute. He has a kid. Had a one-night stand a year or so ago."

"I forgot about that. Bonnie met her."

"Why do you want to know?"

"The less you know, the better."

***

Bonnie hadn't slept much either. When she did manage to nod off, she was tortured by terrifying nightmares. Dennis would say it was God's punishment, but she didn't believe God troubled himself with such matters. She saw it as her guilty conscience.

What had she been thinking? Run off with Emmett Fuller? How long would that have lasted? The man was a lion in bed but had the brains of a squirrel. He would have pissed the money away, and then what would she have done? Who would take care of her? Not Emmett Fuller. He'd blame her for their poverty and find somebody else.

She needed Maurice. She still liked that name better than Dennis. It rolled sensuously off the tongue, like a hot breath. Dennis sounded like somebody's goofy little brother.

But Dennis had been good to her. He had plucked her from a drab existence and given her more luxury than she could ever have imagined. A nice car. Fancy restaurants. Trips to the Caribbean. That idiot Tammy had all that, too, but didn't want to share. She deserved what she got. Stupid bitch. Now everything was on hold.

She had betrayed him. She had been blinded by the promises of a fool—the devil, really—and betrayed the man she loved. And he had been merciful. Instead of killing her, like she deserved, he had spared her. Forced himself on her, sure, but that beat being dead. And last night had been like old times. The two of them nuzzling each other in post-coital bliss. Maybe next time he'd sleep with her all night.

As Bonnie stared at the ceiling she realized the one and only truth: she had to make this right. She had to redeem herself in Maurice's eyes. She had to regain his trust, his affection, his protection. No matter what.

***

Webb opened the safe and took stock of the weapons available for what he had in mind. He had locked up all of his guns after Bonnie's transgression. Of the three pistols in the safe, one of them had belonged to Emmett Fuller. His shotgun and deer rifle were in a locked gun cabinet.

He picked up Fuller's Kimber and smiled. Perfect. The gun Fuller had tried to kill him with would be used for Bonnie's redemption.

No sound came from Bonnie's room. Webb unlocked the door and stepped inside. Bonnie lay asleep in bed wearing only the T-shirt she had donned after the previous night's intimacy.

He sat on the edge of the bed and she opened her eyes. "You said you still love me," he said.

"That's right, I do." She pulled herself upright and kissed him. "More than anything."

"You went to see that deputy's baby mama, right?"

Her touch became more uncertain.

"Yes."

"How well do they get along."

"Pretty good, from what I could tell."

"Does he care about her?"

She was starting to see where this was going. "I'm not sure. I can tell you he's crazy about that baby, though."

Webb removed the Kimber from his belt and put it in Bonnie's hand. "Here's your chance to prove yourself."

***

"How do I get a picture of him?" Hodge asked.

Cash laughed. "Just grab one of his campaign posters. They're plastered all over town."

Hodge flipped open the box on the conference room table. She eyed the last donut, a maple cream with sprinkles. Yet the dough underneath looked wrinkled. "How long has this been here?"

"I don't know. Two, three days."

She plucked the donut from the box. "Fresh enough. I'm starving." She took a bite. "Just the one shop, right? Or did you want me to check any others?"

"Just that one we visited before. We know for sure that Bonnie has gone there. If Webb is feeding Eaton gold coins, there's a good chance Eaton uses it, too."

"What are you going to do?"

"I'm going to go see Alissa Collins' children. The girl is probably too young to be of much help, but the boy might be useful." He picked a sizeable crumb out of the donut box and gulped it down.

Hodge handed him the last bite of her donut. As Cash gobbled it, she said, "We should have thought of this before."

Cash stood up. "Yep."

***

Jordan Uhler was waiting for Cash when he pulled into her driveway. She greeted him as he got out of the car. "The kids are in the house."

He followed her inside to the den, and she invited him to sit on a green upholstered sofa. The intoxicating odor of freshly baked bread wafted into his nose.

"Your house smells delicious," Cash said.

"I just took some bread out of the oven. Would you like some?'

He started to say no, but the yeasty scent was too tempting. "I wouldn't turn it down."

She disappeared into the kitchen, emerging with a plate of bread, a knife, and a stick of butter. "It's sourdough. My husband's favorite."

Cash spread a generous portion of butter on a bread slice and bit into it. "I can see why."

She dropped onto the far end of the couch. "As good as my bread may be, you didn't come all the way out here to eat. What do you have to tell me?"

"We believe Alissa Collins is dead."

Cash thought a look of excitement sparked on her face, but it quickly gave way to a more somber expression.

"That's terrible. I don't know how we'll tell Ginny and Isaiah."

"You could have the social worker do that."

"No. They've gotten to know me. I think I should do it."

Cash produced a photograph of Fuller and Spencer each holding a fish. He had gotten it from Alissa's house. "I'm chasing a lead on who might have done it. I'd like to show the photo to them to see if they recognize the man their mother left with." He handed the photograph to her. "You don't know him, do you?"

She gave the photo a close look. "I don't know either one of them. But didn't the kids tell you they didn't see the man that day?"

Cash nodded. "Yes, but maybe a picture will jog their memories. They were pretty distraught when I talked to them."

After handing the photo back, she hollered, "Ginny, Isaiah, would you come here, please?"

The two children bounded into the den. They froze at the sight of Cash.

Jordan said, "You remember Deputy Cash, don't you? He'd like to ask you something."

Neither one said anything. Cash beckoned them over. He held out the photo and pointed at Fuller. "Is this the man your mother left the house with?"

Ginny said, "No," and ran back down the hall. Isaiah scrunched his nose. "I think so." He spoke barely above a whisper.

Cash waited for him to say more, but he kept mum. Cash said, "How sure are you, Isaiah? This is important."

This time when the child spoke, his voice was louder. "I'm sure. I saw him through the window. Then I ran back to the bedroom to watch TV with Ginny."

"Thank you. You can go back to your room if you'd like."

The boy left.

Jordan said, "It looks like you've got your man."

Cash stood up. "I'll keep you posted."

***

Cash drove back to the department to brief Santos on his findings. "The kid recognized Fuller in the picture I showed him. He ID'd him as the man his mother left the house with."

"That's helpful, but I know what Lars will say," Santos said, referring to the Noble County district attorney. "We don't even have a body."

"I think we can sweat the location out of Fuller."

"I doubt it. What leverage do we have over him? And a good defense lawyer would destroy the boy's testimony."

"Why do you say that? He said he was certain."

"But it contradicts what he told you the day it happened. Which statement do you think a jury would give more credence to? And he's a kid. No telling how he'd react on the stand."

Cash let out an exasperated sigh.

Santos said, "If it's any consolation, I'm as frustrated as you. I didn't believe you at first when you started this obsession with Dennis Webb and Bonnie Hart. But I do now. Keep at it."

"Will do."

Cash stood up to leave. As he reached the office door, Santos said, "Cash?"

"Yes?"

"Good work."

32

Bonnie drove the SUV with her hands wrapped tightly around the steering wheel. What was she thinking? So far she had kept herself clean. She knew of the crimes committed by Dennis, Ralph Spencer, and Emmett Fuller, but she had taken an active part in none of them. No one could prosecute her for anything. But if she followed through on Dennis' instructions, she could be sent away for a long time.

But would prison be much worse than life without Dennis? He had given her so much, and that tap wasn't running dry anytime soon. She could never be happy returning to the life she had lived before meeting him. Getting up at six-thirty every morning, Monday through Friday, and schlepping off to work eight-hour days shuffling papers in the St. Tammany Parish tax assessor's office. Coming home exhausted to watch TV and smoke weed or drink herself into a stupor before crawling off to bed. Weekends were better, but their joy was dampened by the knowledge that Monday morning loomed like a flock of turkey buzzards. Most Saturdays, she'd head to the nearest casino to play blackjack, winning more often than not. Winning eased the financial strain of scraping by on her miserly salary but once she paid her monthly bills and bought gas and groceries, she never had enough left to enjoy life. Dennis was worth the risk of going to prison if it meant avoiding a return to life as an office drone.

Dennis told her that no one would get hurt if she followed instructions. No one, that is, but the handsome deputy who had been dogging them so relentlessly. She had asked Dennis to promise that the woman and her baby would remain unharmed and he had done so. He even told her she probably wouldn't need the gun, but should keep it handy as a last resort. She glanced at it tucked into the console. The thought of shooting someone sent a chill down her spine. She had fired a gun many times with Dennis at the shooting range, but had never pointed one at another person.

Bonnie entered Pinyon and followed the Terrain's GPS to Bernadette's single-wide trailer on the edge of town. A blue Hyundai Elantra was parked in the crushed shell driveway. Judging by the rust spots around the wheel wells and hail damage to the roof, it looked twenty years old. Its presence meant that Bernadette was home.

She braked to a stop in front of the driveway, blocking the Elantra in. Dennis had told her to do that to prevent Bernadette from escaping. Steeling herself, she grabbed the gun and stuck it in her purse. She glanced at herself in the mirror, opened the door, and got out of the car. Despite the Kimber's light weight, Bonnie felt like she was carrying a bowling ball in her purse as she approached the house. She thought about showing the gun to Bernadette and decided against it. A final step and her nose was nearly touching the door. She took a deep breath and knocked.

***

Bernadette almost didn't answer the knock at her door. She had just put Emma down for a nap and was planning on one for herself. Then she remembered an Amazon order she was waiting on. She got up from the couch and opened the door.

"Bonnie!" she squeaked. "Hi."

"Hi, Bernadette. I was in the neighborhood and thought I'd drop by."

"Come in."

As Bonnie found a seat on the sofa, Bernadette said, "Would you like something to drink?"

"No, thanks. Where's Emma?"

"She's taking a nap." She sat tightly in the rocker. "How are you?"

"Actually, this isn't a social visit. The sheriff's department sent me. Emma's father was injured today while trying to make an arrest."

Bernadette gasped. "Is he okay?"

"It's too early to tell. They asked me to bring you to the hospital in Junction."

"Why would they want me there?"

"They have some permission forms for you to sign. They can't operate without them. He has no other relatives in town."

"He needs an operation?"

"I'm afraid so. It's serious."

Any doubts she had seemed to dwindle away. "I'll get Emma."

She rushed to the child's room and checked the contents of her diaper bag. She realized she might be gone for quite some time so she stuffed in a few more diapers and a fresh box of wipes. After adding a change of clothes, she woke Emma up. The child looked puzzled at first, then began crying in ear-splitting wails that reverberated against the walls of the small room. "Hush, now. You can sleep in the car."

Bernadette hurried back into the den and snatched her keys from a hook by the front door. "I'll follow you."

"No," said Bonnie. "You can ride with me."

"How will I get home?"

That seemed to stump Bonnie. Finally, she said, "Don't worry about that. The sheriff will send a patrol car for you."

"But why can't I just take my car?"

Before Bonnie could respond, Bernadette's mother entered the room. "Bernie, have you seen my cigarettes?"

"They're in the kitchen by the toaster."

Mrs. Fenster noticed Bonnie. "Who's this?"

"This is Bonnie. She's come from the sheriff's department. Emma's daddy has been hurt. He's in a hospital in Junction. I need to go there to sign some papers so they can operate."

Mrs. Fenster's eyes narrowed to slits. "That don't sound right. You're not kin."

"He's Emma's daddy."

"That doesn't make him related to you. They'd need a blood relative to give permission for an operation."

Bonnie said, "Ordinarily that would be true. But this is an emergency."

"You don't say." She cocked her head. "What if I say I don't believe you? Let me grab my cigarettes. Then I have some questions."

While she disappeared into the kitchen, Bonnie pulled the gun from her purse. "I'm sorry, but you need to come with me."

Bernadette gasped. Mrs. Fenster reappeared with a phone in one hand—and a shotgun in the other. An unlit cigarette dangled from her lips. She pointed the barrel of the shotgun at Bonnie. "Gal, you'd best let go of that gun."

Bonnie hesitated. When Mrs. Fenster said, "I'll blow your head clean off," she dropped the gun.

"Bernie," Mrs. Fenster said. "Pick up that phone and call the sheriff's office."

Before Bernadette could react, they all heard a loud thump outside the door as someone dropped a package on the porch. Bonnie used the distraction to bolt for the door, fling it open, and sprint toward her car. Mrs. Fenster appeared in the doorway. "Don't you ever come back here."

Without a word Bonnie leapt into her car, fired the engine, and sped away.

Mrs. Fenster watched the car until it disappeared around a corner. Looking down, she spotted a shoebox-sized Amazon package. "Hey, Bernie, looks like them baby toys are here."

33

"How sure was he?" Cash asked.

Hodge said, "As sure as he could be. I showed him Eaton's picture and right away he said, 'Yeah, he's been here.'"

They sat at a table in the Packsaddle. Frustrated by his conversation with Santos, Cash had come here hoping to find Steve. His friend was always willing to listen to him gripe, no matter how big or small the topic. But upon learning from the server that Steve had gone to the brewery on the other side of town, Cash texted Hodge and asked her to meet him to provide an update.

"Did you ask him if Eaton's been cashing out gold coins?"

"I did. He has."

"So he *is* involved."

Hodge flagged down the server and asked for an iced tea. When he was gone, she said, "Do you think he killed Alissa Collins?"

Cash shook his head. "No, I'm thinking that was Emmett Fuller. Probably with Dennis Webb's help."

"Lay it out for me."

"Here's how I see it. Webb and Bonnie Hart are really Maurice Trahan and Jessica Patrice from Slidell, Louisiana. Trahan was milking money from people who watched his YouTube ministry. Maybe by selling them Bibles like the one I saw at Webb's house. Maurice Trahan was married to a woman named Tammy. Trahan and Tammy supposedly died when their car flipped into a swamp. But they never found the bodies. The sheriff over there wonders if Trahan didn't murder Tammy."

"What about Trahan? You said he and Webb are the same person."

"The best explanation I can think of is that Trahan killed Tammy and staged the accident. He would have needed help, so maybe that came from Jessica Patrice or Ralph Spencer. By the way, Spencer's real name was Landry Fontenot. My bet is that Trahan and Patrice were having an affair and Tammy got in the way."

"How do the gold coins fit in?"

"I'm getting to that. Trahan needed a fresh start. He was an ex-con and I'm sure he rightly figured he'd be high on the suspect list if his wife went missing. He and Patrice changed their names and moved to Texas. But not before Trahan bought a boatload of Gold Britannia coins."

"Why would he do that?"

"Keep in mind he wants Maurice Trahan to disappear. But he has to transport his money to Texas somehow, and he can't do that with a bank transfer. So he buys the coins, figuring he could sell them for cash as needed. He tried to pay his mortgage here with them, so he's likely got a stash of them at his house."

"If he has so much money, why not pay outright for the house?"

"The value of his property is worth well north of two million dollars. Maybe it's not possible to move that many coins."

The server returned with Hodge's tea. She took a sip of it and asked, "Why kill Ralph Spencer?"

"That I'm not sure of. Maybe that was the plan all along. A 'dead men tell no tales' sort of thing. Or maybe he was paying Spencer to keep quiet and Spencer got greedy."

"And Alissa Collins?"

"Yeah, why go after her? She's a lifelong Texan who lived in Noble County for at least twenty years before she disappeared. I wonder if Webb saw her as a loose end. After all, Spencer could have told her a lot in the time he was with her."

"Your reasoning makes sense."

"The more I think about it, the more convinced I am that it's true. Why else would Trahan never leave his property?"

Hodge finished crunching an ice cube in her mouth. "Here's the problem. Even if all of this is true and Webb—or Maurice Trahan—killed his wife and Alissa Collins, there are no bodies. So we have no proof there has even been a murder."

"Murder?" a new voice exclaimed. "Who got murdered?"

It was Steve, who had slipped up behind Cash without him noticing.

Cash said, "Sorry, police business."

Steve grabbed a seat. "Okay, Mr. Big Shot Deputy, don't tell your best friend. I'm just the guy who let you stay in his basement when you were hiding from the law. I'm just the guy who saved your ass."

"All right, already," Cash said with a sigh. "I suppose there's no harm in telling you we're spitballing about Alissa Collins."

"The missing woman? She was murdered?"

"Maybe. We're not sure. That's what we were discussing when you butted in."

Hodge said, "Do you mind if I head out? I promised my grandmother I'd go to a church potluck with her tonight."

"No problem," said Cash. "We'll regroup in the morning."

As Hodge headed for the door, Steve waved the server over and told him to bring a sausage and mushroom pizza to the table.

Cash's phone buzzed. He glanced at the screen. "I should answer this. "Hey, Bernadette," he said into the phone.

"Cash?"

"What's up?"

"You're okay?"

"Yeah, why shouldn't I be?"

"Do you remember that woman you made leave my house?"

His jaw tightened. "Bonnie."

"She was here. She said she was at the sheriff's and heard that you were in a bad car accident. She wanted me to go with her to Junction to sign papers so you could have an operation."

"That doesn't make any sense."

"That's what Momma said. She told her she didn't believe her and Bonnie took a gun out of her purse to make us go. But you know Momma has a shotgun and she made her drop it. Then she ran to her car and drove away."

Cash did not know that Bernadette's mother had a shotgun but it didn't surprise him. "Are you still at home?"

"Yes."

"Is Emma with you?"

"Yes. Momma too."

"I want all three of you to go to the Firewheel. I'll let Edie know you're coming. When she gets off work, she'll take you to her house. Stay there until you hear from me."

"Are we in danger?" Bernadette asked in a shaky voice.

"I don't think so, but it doesn't hurt to be careful."

"Where are you going?"

"To have a chat with Bonnie."

Cash ended the call. He opened his mouth to speak, but no words came out.

"What's going on, man? You look like your dog just died," said Steve.

He relayed what Bernadette had just told him.

"That woman sounds like a real psycho. Why would she kidnap Bernadette?"

"I think she wants leverage over me."

"Why?"

"Because I'm getting close to the truth."

***

Cash called Edie to explain the situation.

"Is her mother coming, too?" Edie asked.

"Yes, and that's a good thing," he said, knowing that Edie wasn't fond of Mrs. Fenster's abrasive personality. "She's mighty handy with a shotgun."

Next, Cash called Santos. After bringing the sheriff up to speed, he said, "We need to arrest her."

"Shit."

"What's wrong?"

"Deke and I are in San Antonio."

"What the hell are you doing in San Antonio? That's almost three hours away."

"I stopped a guy for speeding this morning who's wanted here for breaking and entering. We just dropped him off with local law enforcement."

Cash swore under his breath. "I don't think I should wait that long to pick her up."

"Agreed. But take Hodge with you."

Cash ended the call and stood up.

Steve popped to his feet as well. "Where are we going?"

"'We' aren't going anywhere. Me and Hodge will handle this."

"You're shorthanded. Take me with you."

"Forget it."

"You're not leaving me behind."

"Sit your butt down, Steve. You know I can't let you go."

Steve glared at his friend for an awkward moment before lowering himself into the chair. "Fine. But the next time you want to use my truck, the answer is no."

***

"What do you mean she got the drop on you? Didn't you show them the gun?" Webb was pacing back and forth. Bonnie was perched on the sofa cowering below him.

"Yes. I mean, no, not at first. I had it in my purse."

"I told you to go in there with it already out."

"I know, but I thought I could talk her into coming without it. It would have worked except for her mother butting in."

"Where's the gun now?"

"I dropped it at the house when she pulled that shotgun."

Webb stopped before Bonnie, his massive frame looming over her like a mountain. She dropped her gaze, afraid to look him in the eye. Webb said, "You know what happens now, don't you? She'll call the sheriff. Soon this place will be crawling with cops."

"What are we going to do?"

"You ..." His voice trailed off as he thought. "They'll be coming here. I'll do the talking. You are going to sit there and say nothing. Do you understand?" When she didn't respond right away, he shouted, "Do you understand!"

"Yes," she said. "What if you didn't let them through the gate."

The slap came out of nowhere, slamming into Bonnie's cheek. She reeled backward.

"Not let them through the gate?" Webb said. "Don't be an idiot. That wouldn't make this go away." He stroked his beard. "It's your word against those two women, right? Here's what you say. You and that old lady got into an argument and she threatened you with a shotgun. You only pulled your gun to protect yourself."

"What were we arguing about?"

Webb threw up his hands. "I don't know. What does it matter? Just make something up."

"What if they don't believe it?"

He opened an end table to check that his Ruger LCP was there. "They'll wish they did."

Bonnie stared at her feet. "I'm sorry, Maurice."

"Shut up." He raised his hand to strike her again but stopped when she shrank back like a whipped dog. If he showed her mercy, perhaps the Lord would extend the same to him. "I told you. Don't call me that."

34

Cash eased the squad car to a stop in front of the station. Hodge emerged from the building and hopped in.

"Sorry to ruin your potluck supper," Cash said.

"You should be. They were just about to set out the desserts when you called."

Cash cocked his head, unsure whether she was serious.

"Relax," she said. "This is what we live for."

On the way to Webb's, Cash filled Hodge in on what had happened.

"Are we going out there to arrest them or to question them?" Hodge said.

"Both."

At the gate, Cash pushed the intercom button. He didn't have to wait long before he heard Webb's voice. "What can I do for you, Deputy?"

"I think you know."

"That answer won't get you onto my property."

"Don't play games, Webb. You know damn well why I'm here."

With a loud click, the gate swung open.

The sun had dipped below the hills and darkness would soon overtake the landscape. Cash clicked on the headlights and drove toward the house. Hodge pointed at the stock pond. "Is there really an alligator in there?"

"Yep. I saw it."

Cash reached the house and killed the engine. "I don't expect this to be easy. Be ready for anything."

They got out and strode to the house. Cash knocked, then stepped to the side to get out of the line of fire. He motioned for Hodge to do the same.

The door opened. Webb glowered at them before stepping aside and heading for the den. Cash and Hodge followed.

"Have a seat, deputies," Webb said, motioning to the couch.

Cash ignored him. "Where's your wife?"

Webb stared at them without speaking.

"I said, where's your wife?" Cash repeated.

The big man strolled to the hallway and said, "Bonnie, can you come here a minute? We have visitors."

An unseen door opened and Bonnie stepped into the den. Cash said, "Turn around, please." He took out his handcuffs.

"What are you doing?" Webb said roughly.

"Bonnie Hart, you're under arrest for attempted kidnapping."

Bonnie's eyes grew wide. "Dennis ..."

Webb started toward Cash but stopped when Cash put his hand on his sidearm. "You're crazy," Webb said. "She did no such thing."

"She pulled a gun and tried to kidnap two women and a baby. The only thing that stopped her was Mrs. Fenster's shotgun."

"That's not how she remembers it."

Cash cut his eyes toward Bonnie. "Let's hear it."

Her words came out in a flood. "I was just visiting Bernadette. She was going to let me hold her baby when her mother charged in with a shotgun and pointed it at me. Told me to get the hell out of her house. Yes, I took out a gun but only to defend myself."

"Come down to the station with me and we'll sort it out."

Webb stepped between Cash and Bonnie. "She's not going anywhere."

"Let's cut the bullshit, Webb" Cash said. "Or should I say Trahan." He looked past him at Bonnie. "And her name isn't Bonnie Hart, it's Jessica Patrice. You're a two-bit huckster from Slidell, Louisiana who murdered his wife and fled to Texas. She came with you but not before breaking up your marriage."

"That's a nice fairy tale," Webb said with a laugh.

"Ralph Spencer came with you as well. I don't know why, but I suspect it's because he helped you kill your wife. Then you two had a falling-out and you killed him."

Webb sighed, strolled to the sofa, and took a seat. He draped his arm on the end table and fiddled with the drawer handle. Cash took notice and tensed.

"I don't know where you got your information," Webb said, "but it's dead wrong."

Cash said, "The only thing dead is poor Tammy. And Ralph. And Landry Fontenot, as he was known in Slidell." He paused. The ticking of a wall clock reminded Cash of a time bomb counting down. "Where's Alissa Collins?"

"I don't know."

"Is she dead, too?"

Silence.

"You bought the gold coins at Blair Precious Metals in Covington. Bonnie sells them at Frederick Family Coins. Pretty slick of you, converting the money you bilked from people to gold. Makes it untraceable, doesn't it?"

Hodge said, "Ask him about Mitch Eaton's coin."

"Oh, yeah," said Cash. "What about it, Webb? Why does Eaton have a Gold Britannia coin?"

In the next few seconds the room exploded with action. Webb jerked the drawer open and snatched the Ruger. Cash drew his gun. Bonnie took off down the hall with Hodge giving chase. Sensing that he had been too slow with his draw, Cash dove into the kitchen just as Webb got off a wild shot. Without showing himself, Cash stuck his hand above the kitchen counter and fired two quick shots into the ceiling as a distraction. Just as he was about to charge into the den the front door of the house slammed shut. He risked a peek over the counter to see that Webb had fled.

Hodge chased Bonnie into the main bedroom in time to see Bonnie opening a dresser drawer. She aimed her pistol and said, "I don't want to shoot you, but I will."

Bonnie dropped her arms to her side and turned around. Keeping the gun trained on her, Hodge cuffed one of her hands and dragged her to the bed. She snapped the other cuff around an iron bedpost and said, "Stay here." She opened the drawer Bonnie had been going for, found a pistol, and shoved it in her belt.

Suspecting an ambush, Cash jerked the door open and leapt back. Shots sounded and bullets snapped through the open doorway. He picked up a lamp and hurled it through the adjacent plate glass window. As broken glass dropped from the frame he bolted through the doorway, flung himself to the ground, and drew a bead on Webb at the end of the driveway. "Drop the gun, Webb," he shouted.

Webb turned and ran. "The son of a bitch," Cash muttered as he gave chase. When Webb reached the stock pond fence, he turned and raised his arm to fire. Rushing his two-handed stance, Cash put a bullet into his shoulder. The force of the bullet's impact flipped Webb backward over the fence.

By now it was completely dark outside. Cash could hear Webb thrashing through the waist-high grass but he couldn't see him. He came closer and could just make out Webb hauling himself to his feet.

"Put the gun down," Cash shouted, spreading his legs once again.

Webb lifted his eyes skyward. "Help me, Lord Jesus." He jerked his hand up to fire but Cash shot him a second time. He couldn't see where, but Webb staggered backward through the weeds, tripped, and splashed into the water.

Keeping his gun raised, Cash hustled to the fence and vaulted over it. He couldn't see Webb in the dark, but he could hear him floundering in the water. Then a shriek pierced the night, followed by more shrieks and loud splashing. Stepping cautiously through the weeds, Cash pulled a small Maglite from his pocket and clicked it on. He pointed it at the water in time to see the alligator dragging Webb's lifeless body toward the middle of the pond. It repositioned its huge jaws on one of Webb's legs and performed a death roll. The limb snapped free and, in a flash, disappeared down the gator's throat.

Cash turned away and fought down an urge to vomit. He left the enclosure—this time through the gate—and holstered his weapon.

Gun drawn, Hodge appeared in the open doorway of the house. Spotting Cash, she said, "I heard shots."

"Where's Bonnie?"

"Handcuffed to a bed."

"Go watch her. It's clear out here."

She backed into the house and shut the door. For the first time Cash noticed a black Tesla parked behind the squad car. All but invisible in the shadows next to it was Mitch Eaton. He pointed a handgun at Cash.

"Why am I not surprised?" said Cash.

"Where's Webb?"

"Over in that stock pond. I imagine most of him is in that gator's belly by now."

"You're lying."

"Why don't you swim out there and see for yourself?"

"Toss your gun toward me."

He didn't figure Eaton for a hard guy. "Are you sure you want to do this? So far, the only thing you're guilty of is being a dumbass."

"Toss your fucking gun!"

Cash complied. "You gonna shoot me, Mitch?"

A loud crack sounded and the Tesla's rear window exploded in a shower of glass. Another crack split the night and pebbles flew into the air five feet from Eaton.

"That's Santos and Deke Conrad," Cash said. "They're not aiming at me."

Frightened, Eaton hesitated. To make him more sure, a third shot thudded into one of the Tesla's tires.

Cash said, "I'm going to pick up my gun, Mitch. I suggest you give yours to me."

Keeping a wary eye on Eaton, Cash retrieved his weapon. Eaton gripped his by the barrel and held it out. Cash took it and stuck it in his belt.

The dark silhouette of a man rose in the field fifty yards from the house and began making his way toward them. "How'd you get here so fast?" Cash hollered.

"I drove like a bat out of hell," the man shouted back.

The voice belonged to Steve. Cash trained his Maglite on the man and saw his friend's face. "Pretty good shooting, wasn't it?" Steve said.

"You missed him three times."

"I wasn't trying to hit him," he said, pleased to be part of a police operation. "I figured you'd want him alive."

Cash had to smile. "What the hell are you doing here?"

Steve grinned even harder. "Saving your ass."

35

C ash adjusted the volume of the recorder. "Miss Patrice, are you answering these questions voluntarily?"

"I am."

Marshall Snyder, Jessica Patrice's attorney, a no-nonsense fortyish man dressed in a navy blue jacket, gray slacks, and open-collar white shirt, said, "I wish to add this is being conducted against her attorney's advice."

"Noted," said Cash. He directed his attention at Patrice. "Your name isn't Bonnie Hart, is it?"

"No, it's Jessica Patrice."

"And the man you were living with, what is his real name?"

"Maurice Trahan."

"The two of you moved to Noble County from Slidell, Louisiana?"

"That is correct."

"Why?"

"Maurice and I were having an affair. His wife found out and told him to break it off. Instead, he ..." She hung her head and stared at her hands.

"He what?"

"He killed her. Then he and Landry made it look like she and Maurice were killed when their car went into the swamp."

"What happened to his wife's body?"

She wrung her hands and gulped. "I didn't take part in it. I want to make that clear. I didn't even know about it until after it was done."

"Understood. Go on."

"Landry drove the body here, to Noble County. Maurice fed it to Jeremiah."

"Who is Jeremiah?"

"Maurice's alligator."

"Who is Landry?"

"Landry Fontenot. Here he went by Ralph Spencer."

Santos, seated next to Cash, drew in a sharp breath. When he noticed everyone looking at him, he said, "Sorry. Please continue."

Cash said, "How did Maurice earn a living in Slidell?"

"He recorded sermons for his YouTube channel. He sold Bibles through the channel, a lot of Bibles. People also sent money."

"Why?"

"Donations to his ministry."

"What happened to that money?"

"Some of it went to charity." She paused. "Maurice kept most of it. Before he killed Tammy, he converted it to gold coins. He said he wanted it readily accessible."

"Why did he come to Noble County?"

"Because of Mitch."

"Mitch Eaton?"

"Yes. Maurice knew him from when Mitch lived in New Orleans. I think he went to school there. He had a job there for a while, too. He was in Maurice's motorcycle club."

"Whose idea was it for Mitch to run for sheriff?"

"Maurice's. He said, what better place to hide than a county where the sheriff was his friend?"

"Did Maurice kill Landry Fontenot?"

"No. He paid Emmett Fuller to blow up his truck. Landry got greedy. He wanted more than what Maurice was giving him to keep quiet. The explosion was just supposed to scare him, but he fell and hit his head." Her eyes flitted between Cash and Santos. "I guess you know that."

"What happened to Alissa Collins?"

"Maurice paid Emmett to bring her to him. He wanted to see if she knew anything about Maurice from Louisiana. She didn't."

"But he killed her anyway."

"Yes. He fed the body to Jeremiah."

"Was Terry Moreno involved?"

"No."

"How did the hammer end up at the poker club?"

She hesitated. "I put it there. Maurice forced me to do it."

"Did you try to kidnap Bernadette, Darlene, and Emma Fenster?"

"Yes. After Maurice killed Emmett—"

"Wait," said Cash. "Emmett Fuller is dead?"

She paused, raising her eyebrows in surprise. "Yes. Maurice shot him. I don't know why. Mitch said he was worried that you were close to figuring things out, so Maurice told me to bring Bernadette to you. He meant to kill you too."

"And Emma. My daughter."

Her eyes widened. "He promised he wasn't going to hurt her."

"Did you believe his promise?"

Before Patrice could answer, Snyder raised a finger. "I want to make it clear that my client acted under duress. Trahan threatened her with physical harm if she didn't do what he said."

"So she told me at her arrest." Cash returned his attention to Patrice. "One last thing. Who put the bomb under my truck?"

"Emmett." When Cash didn't react, she added, "Maurice told him to."

Cash turned off the recorder. "That will be all. For now."

He motioned to Santos and the two of them stepped into the hall. Santos closed the door. "What do you think? Is she telling the truth?"

"Most of it," said Cash. "Although she's blaming it all on Trahan and Fuller. And I think she's holding back on Fuller's death. That was the first I'd heard of it."

"See if she knows where the body is."

"All right." Cash put his hand on the door handle.

Santos said, "Before we go back in ..."

"Yes?"

"You were right all along. I'm sorry I wasn't much help."

Cash pushed the door open. "I was just trying to make sure you got reelected."

***

"All right, turn it off," Cash said. He stood next to the stock pond that, until recently, had been Jeremiah the alligator's home. It had shrunk to a muck-filled hole, after the water was drained by a pump. With the assistance of an animal control officer from coastal Matagorda County named Jed Warren, Noble County game warden Phil Somers had maneuvered Jeremiah into a tube for transport, which the two men were now straining to lift onto Warren's truck. County medical examiner Frida Simmons stood by.

Cash caught Frida's eye. "Do you see what I see?"

"Yep."

Cash was glad to be wearing muck boots as he followed Frida to the center of the pond. She bent over and tugged a long bone from the mud. "This is human." She pointed at other bones protruding from the muck. "I'll bet those are, too."

"Alissa Collins?"

"Or Tammy Trahan. Could be some from Maurice, too. We'll sort it out with DNA testing. That just leaves Emmett Fuller."

"Santos and Conrad are digging him up right now. Bonnie told them where to look."

"You mean Jessica."

Cash spat. "Whatever."

36

Cash handed Steve a bottle of Bud Light and took the seat next to him.

Steve made a face. "What is this?"

"Sorry, that's all they had. Conrad bought the beer."

"Conrad is a cretin." He took a long pull from the bottle. "But I'm thirsty."

"I want to thank you."

"You should."

They clinked bottles. Cash said, "Here's to good friends."

Steve feigned annoyance. "Would a good friend refuse the help of his best friend?"

"I didn't want you to get hurt," Cash pointed out. "Or end up in prison."

"Justifiable risks. A good friend has his buddy's back."

Edie came in. She and Cash had decorated the department conference room with balloons and a large banner that said, "Congratulations, Sheriff." "He's coming," she said.

In walked Gabe Santos, winner of yesterday's race for sheriff. Cash clapped and everyone joined in. Santos raised a hand. "Thank you."

"Landslide Santos," Cash said in a loud voice. "Ninety-two percent of the vote."

"Who got the other eight percent?" Conrad asked.

Edie said, "Believe it or not, soon-to-be convicted felon Mitch Eaton got six percent. The other two percent was split between Mickey Mouse, Luke Skywalker, Clint Eastwood, and Bevo, the UT mascot."

"Bevo for sheriff!" shouted Steve, raising his beer.

Santos raised his hand in a "Hook 'em Horns" sign, with the index and pinky fingers raised and the middle two fingers folded down under the thumb. "Hook 'em."

Everyone began speaking at once, with the voices of the thirty celebrants merging into a loud buzz. Cash spotted Terry Moreno across the room deep in conversation with Hodge. Watching them, he wondered how Clete Borden would describe his false accusation of Moreno in his report to the Texas Rangers.

Beer in hand, Santos sauntered up to Cash. "I have some bad news."

"Let's hear it."

"I can't keep paying you the same salary."

Cash gritted his teeth but said nothing. His salary already was barely enough to live on.

"I talked to Fred Uecker. He gave me the okay to bump my deputies by two thousand a year."

"I can't afford a cut like that."

Santos grinned. "I'm bumping you up, you idiot. You'll also get a bonus for solving the Collins case."

Cash stared open-mouthed. He could pay off his truck repairs.

"You're welcome."

Recovering, Cash said, "Thank you."

Edie waved for Cash's attention. He thanked Santos again and followed her into the hall. He leaned in for a quick kiss but she pulled back, frowning. "You almost got killed. Again."

Cash didn't speak. What could he say?

"You are damn lucky that I love you."

He smiled. "I can't help being irresistible."

She pushed him against the wall. "Don't get cocky."

"I love you, too."

Cash put his arms around her. They leaned toward each other, their lips drawing close. Cash closed his eyes.

"Cash, I was wondering—oh, sorry."

They pulled apart. It was Bernadette.

"It's okay," Edie said. "What do you need?"

"I just wondered if you'd like to hold Emma for a while."

Cash held out his arms. "I'd love to."

She handed Emma to him. Cash stroked the infant's fine hair and said, "Hello there, sweetie pie." Emma babbled something unintelligible and buried her head under his chin.

"I think she likes you," said Bernadette.

Cash said, "I just wish your mother did."

"She's coming around."

Bernadette excused herself and ducked back into the conference room. Edie raised an eyebrow. "You never call me 'sweetie pie.'"

Cash pressed his lips together. "Busted."

She planted a quick kiss on him. "And if you ever do, I'll kick your ass."

***

Hodge tossed the ball to Cash. "Nine all," she said. "Game point."

Cash gripped the ball and dropped into a crouch. He feinted left and drove right. Hodge attempted to block his way, but he slid past her, dribbled to the basket, and laid the ball against the backboard.

The shot hit the glass, bounced off the front rim, and into Hodge's hands. Before Cash could react, she dribbled to the top of the key and launched a shot. Swish. She raised her arms in triumph. "Oh, yeah!"

Cash grabbed the ball, bounced it hard off the floor, and tossed it to Hodge. "Let's go again."

Thank you ...

... for reading *Second Death*. Want to keep up to date on my upcoming books and giveaways? Sign up for my newsletter by **clicking on this link** or by visiting my website **www.jeffreykerrauthor.com** and I'll send you a free copy of *Cash: The Prequels,* a collection of three exciting short stories that introduce The Adam Cash series.

Got a moment?

The best way to help an independent author like me is to post an honest review on Amazon or any other reading platform you use. Reviews are critical to a book's success. And success is what allows any author to continue writing the books you want to read.

To leave an Amazon review, **click here**.

If you're reading the paperback or pdf version, please visit the book's Amazon page and scroll down to the customer reviews. Then click on "Write a customer review."

Word of mouth and posting on social media also help. I appreciate anything you can do to spread the word!

If you enjoyed
Second Death ...

... you'll love *Murder Creek*, book three in The Adam Cash series, in which Cash investigates an old man's shooting and the theft of over a million dollars in cash from his ranch. As he digs deeper, Cash encounters not only long-buried secrets but one dead body after another. After fighting off an armed intruder at his house, he knows he must catch the killer or become the next victim.

Watching closely for footprints, Cash started up the path. A sharp bend led through an open area before the woods started up again. He made his way across the opening and pushed aside a large cedar branch blocking the trail. He froze. A man's body sprawled before him, face down, arms extending outward, ski mask pulled over his head. An irregular patch of blood stained the man's shirt, in the middle of which was a small dark hole. Breathing hard, Cash knelt and felt unsuccessfully for a radial pulse. He tugged off the ski mask. "I'll be damned," he said. "What the hell are you doing here?"

Buy *Murder Creek*

https://geni.us/MurderCreek

About Jeff Kerr

Jeff Kerr wasn't born in Texas but says "y'all" like a native. He wrote a poem in the third grade that earned him a school prize, a book about the American flag. You'd think that would have inspired him to become a writer but that came later.

Jeff wrote and published his first book twenty years ago. He hadn't planned on doing so until one night at supper his son interrupted a discourse about local history by saying, "Enough, Dad. Write a book!" Choosing to interpret a teenager's flip remark as sage advice, he did. Seven books later, he calls himself an author. So there.

When Jeff isn't writing you can find him floating a Texas river or battling cedar on his small slice of Hill Country land. When he *is* writing, he stays busy by creating pulse-pounding crime thrillers that, according to one reader, "move along like a runaway locomotive." Thank you, son.

Learn more about Jeff and his work at **www.jeffreykerrauthor. com**.

Drop him a line at **jeffkerr@jeffreykerrauthor.com**. He'll write back!

Twitter: https://twitter.com/jkerr50

Instagram: https://www.instagram.com/jkerr50

Facebook: https://www.facebook.com/JeffKerrAuthor

Bookbub: https://www.bookbub.com/authors/jeffrey-kerr

Also By Jeff Kerr

FICTION

Stand-alone novels

Refuge

Lamar's Folly

The Republic of Jack

The Adam Cash series

Blunt Force Trauma

Murder Creek

NONFICTION

Austin, Texas: Then and Now

The Republic of Austin

Seat of Empire: The Embattled Birth of Austin, Texas

www.ingramcontent.com/pod-product-compliance
Lightning Source LLC
Chambersburg PA
CBHW020345120726
47904CB00002B/459